Agonal Whispers

A Collection

by

B. D. Yates

This book is for my children, Jameson and Ruby. I hope you two will be proud of me someday, and maybe even think of me as one of those "cool guy" dads I keep hearing about. I love you both, so very much, and I promise I'm not crazy. I just love a good scary story.

Contents

Foreword……………………………………………………1

The Visitor……………………………………………..….4

Pecos Charlie…………………………………………….6

The Box at the Front of the Room……………………88

Abaddon………………………………………………….89

Karma: The Confession of David Lee Redfield………107

Bugs………………………………………………………174

The Avid Reader……………………………………….184

Crazy Sadie……………………………………………..186

Friends Like These……………………………………..189

Foreword

Well, what do you know? I'm sitting in our office typing something I never thought I'd ever type— a foreword to my second book. I'm not a famous author yet; I'm working in a football factory to make ends meet. Money isn't why I write anyway. You should never write solely for money, not if you want it to be any good. Writing should be an impulse. In a way, the writer's brain does most of the work for him. All I do is serve as a conduit for the stories my brain seems hellbent on telling. It can be very intrusive, sometimes making it impossible to read a book or listen to an audiobook. Then, once you find the "hole in the page", as the great Stephen King once put it, the story usually writes itself and it can be hard to discern where the hell the material is even coming from. If you enjoyed my first book, and if you enjoy this one, then that's all the payment I really need (although the profits from my last collection *definitely* helped to pay my bills). I wanted to include a foreword to this book because there are some things that I felt needed to be said, and then I promise we'll get to the killing and the blood.

    The first tale in this collection is a flash fiction story called *The Visitor*. It began as a novella entitled *The Quiet Ones* and is loosely based on an actual event. I used to drive past a little house on my way to college, and I always noticed it because it shared a property line with a cemetery. One day was a little different, however. I drove past and the place was swarming with cops. As it turned out, the man who lived there had committed suicide that same morning. Although I pitied him, my brain did what it does, and a story idea was born. What if there was a man who could see ghosts and just happened to live beside a cemetery? The constant barrage of ghostly visitors would eventually drive him insane until he could stand it no more and eventually decided to take his own life. I know, not a very happy story. That's why I ended up scrapping it. Writing that miserable story was so depressing that it became very mentally trying to go back into that world, and so it was abandoned.

    Until I discovered Wattpad, that is. Wattpad is a wonderful little reading/writing app I use so I can work on my books anywhere.

They were hosting a contest promoting an Amazon original movie called *Welcome to the Blumhouse* and I immediately got excited. If you're a horror movie fan like me, you'll recognize the name Blumhouse. They brought us incredible films like *Get Out*, *The Purge*, and *Paranormal Activity* just to name a few. I thought it sounded like a fun challenge; they wanted a psychological horror story, 500 words or less, that ended in a cliffhanger. *The Quiet Ones* became *The Visitor* and I submitted it, not actually expecting to win anything—but I *did* win, the *Grand Prize* even, and to this very moment I'm still stunned. I hadn't won an award for writing since High School, and one of the prizes was an autographed poster from Jason Blum himself (which is proudly hung on the wall behind me). That contest reignited my love for writing and made me feel like maybe I'm not such a bad writer after all, and now here we are. I might never get famous, but that made me feel like a million bucks. Oh, and I've included several of my submissions to that contest; they're scattered throughout this book. They weren't contest winners, so I've taken the liberty of changing them as I see fit.

    There is another story in this collection called *Pecos Charlie*, which is a work of fiction, but it draws a lot from reality. In a way, it's my love letter to storm chasers and tornadoes. The title character, "Pecos" Charlie Dillon, is based on myself— he's a weather nerd, to put it bluntly. I mention several notable tornadoes in the story, such as Tuscaloosa, Moore, and of course, the infamous El Reno tornado. I also mention Gary England and the TWISTEX storm chasing team. For those of you who don't know (and aren't weather nerds like Charlie and me) TWISTEX (Tactical Weather-Instrumented Sampling in/near Tornadoes Experiment) was founded by Tim Samaras, a personal hero of mine. Tim was tragically killed, along with his son Paul and meteorologist Carl Young, while chasing the El Reno tornado on May 31st, 2013. I use these key disasters and these brave men in my story because they were important to me, and so I felt they would be important to someone like Charlie Dillon as well. I use their names with the utmost respect.

    Alright, I think that's enough from me. Time to get to the real reason you bought this book. Before I go, though, I just want to thank you for reading, supporting my passion and helping me pay my bills. I also want to say a special thank you to my friend Stasi Snyder, who takes the time to read my rough drafts (even though I never have the time to return the favor) and gives me honest feedback. I really do appreciate it, Stasi. Until next time.

    --B. D. Yates

The Visitor

Frank Gardener sat alone in his kitchen, staring at his old checkerboard and listening to the rain on the kitchen window. With tears in his eyes, he moved a piece with one oversized hand. Then, he selected a piece from the opposite side of the board and moved it toward himself.

Kinda funny, he thought humorlessly. *I always win and I always lose.*

Checkers had always been Frank's favorite game, ever since he was young. Throughout his life he had played with his best friend Bill Brayton, meeting every Sunday for a beer and a game. But Bill was sick with brain cancer; the kind you didn't get better from. He hadn't seen him in nearly a year.

Cancer had also taken the life of his wife, Jenny, just six months past. The bedroom they had shared sat empty, just the way she left it, and Frank snoozed on the couch. Going in there reminded him of her too much, and really made his loneliness more concrete. Sometimes, he wished he could be dead too. If only to see his loved ones again. But death terrified him.

Frank kinged himself as, following a deep rumble of thunder, there came a quiet knock at the front door. He looked at the kitchen clock; it was nearly 11:00 pm. Who would visit at this late hour?

He shuffled to the front door, lightning flashing blue through the windows and casting long melancholy pools across the floor. Frank clawed at his hair to try to bring some order to it, then opened the door.

Standing in the rain was Bill, a skinnier and sicker version of himself. He looked weary and lost. His face was a gaunt mask of confusion and terror.

"*Bill!*" Frank cried. "My God, what are you doing here?!" Frank scooped Bill into his arms, hugging his skeletal form tightly.

"I just came to see an old friend," Bill said quietly.

"But aren't you sick?" Frank asked, hugging him again. "Sick with the cancer?"

"Not anymore," Bill said with a frail smile.

Then Frank heard a sound he hadn't heard in what felt like a century: the phone ringing. This late at night, it could be important. It could be someone looking for Bill, too. He seemed awfully out of place as he sat down at the checkerboard and began to survey it.

"I'm sorry Bill, relax and get warm. I'll make it quick."

Bill began to bring his pieces back to his side of the board.

"This is Frank," he said into the phone nervously. The voice on the other end was thick with tears.

"Frank, it's Jameson Brayton. Bill's son. Sorry to call so late, but... I wanted to let you know that dad passed away tonight."

Frank's body went numb. The phone fell from his fingers, swinging like a hung corpse.

From the checkerboard, Bill said softly:

"I come with bad news, old buddy. When was the last time you went to the doctor?"

Pecos Charlie

    I swear, these storms always take their sweet time getting around to throwing a fit. It's like they spend all day preparing to explode, building up their strength and biding their time while outside it feels like everything is holding its breath. Waiting. Then, right around sunset, one big chunk of the sky starts to turn blue, then purple-gray, then the kind of ominous black that makes you feel like you need to shit no matter how many storms you've lived through. That's how today went, anyway. The tornado watches started around noon, and about ten minutes ago the TV made that god awful shrieking noise it makes when a weather alert goes out, and the National Weather Service issued a tornado warning for all of Hancock County.

    So now I'm down in the basement, writing this longhand by the light of my emergency candles. It seems like I spend more and more time down here each tornado season; some say it's because of climate change, a warmer planet fueling stronger storms. I'm starting to believe it is. Anyway, my hand-crank emergency radio is still putting out music, so I guess that means the new radio station is still standing. It must not be too crazy out there yet.

    You know, I'm not entirely sure *why* I'm writing this. I guess to keep me occupied while the storm blows over, and I could always turn it into an eBook or something later on. I've always been a pretty solid writer. And, I suppose, I'm writing it because sometimes you get an idea in your head that stays around like a bad itch, and a bad itch needs to be scratched— just like some stories *need* to be told. That story, for me, is the legend of Pecos Charlie.

    I did what Charlie would have done as soon as I heard the tornado warning come across the TV. I went out on the porch to see what it looked like outside, and there wasn't a breath of air. I've always heard that when it gets unnaturally still, that's when you need to start worrying. I could smell the rain coming, and there were so many forks of bright blue lightning flickering across the horizon that the sky looked permanently cracked. This one's gonna pack a punch.

The thunder doesn't ever stop when the lightning is that frequent; it's a hell of a thing. It's just one continuous rumble that will rattle the dishes in your cupboard, kinda like the sound of a big freight train ripping down the tracks. The tornadoes (and living here in Bent Knee, Oklahoma, I've seen my share) sound like that too, as I'm sure you've heard. Tornadoes sound meaner though, like if maybe you mixed that train sound with a jet engine and a hungry lion. They *hiss*, too. Just like snakes. They have a pants-shitting roar that makes them sound not just alive, but extremely pissed off for having been born in the first place. Sometimes they scream, whistling banshee shrieks that chill you right to your core. I lived through the big EF-5 that hit Bent Knee on May 16th, 2018, and you could actually *feel* that noise under your feet. I'll write about that nightmare later, when it's time. Right now, I want to write about how I met Pecos Charlie. Nights like these always make me think of him, and where he might be now.

Now, Pecos Charlie obviously wasn't the name he was born with. It wasn't even his nickname while he was still alive; no, he had to die to earn it. At least we *think* he died. Truth be told, none of us really knows just what the hell happened to him. That's why a nerdy little weather geek like him is a local legend now, and why his name often comes up whenever the sky turns green.

I guess I'll start by telling you how I came to know him. My name is Maxwell Bailey, and I worked with Charles "Charlie" Dillon and a few other wiseass knuckleheads at the old DashMart in the business district of Bent Knee. I say "old" because the big one of '18 leveled it and left a clean foundation; it was damn near in the center of the damage path, which, if memory serves, ended up being about a mile and a half wide. Anyway, I didn't take the offer to work at the new one. Too many memories, you see, and the place feels as soulless and sterile as a hospital. All the essence of myself and my friends was blown to kingdom come, and that's not something the insurance company can replace.

DashMart was like the kid brother of Kmart for the Bent Knee locals, a little department store that was just big enough to warrant a garage for a handful of semi-trucks in the rear. We sold a little bit of everything there. You could make one quick stop and get your groceries, your dog food, a new pair of pants, and maybe even a new Blu Ray to watch when you got home. It was a minimum wage job and God knows I wasn't rich, but I loved working there. The manager at the time was... well, she was a demonic bitch, to be honest, and I'm not gonna write her name because I don't want sued (and she would do it, too). But she always scheduled me in the entertainment department (the "department" consisted of a counter and cash register with a handful of shelves behind it) which was my favorite place to work. I think she knew that if she kept me there, I was more willing to stay late if one of the other guys called in.

    I always like to say that Charlie came in with a storm, because on his first day it was storming like a *motherfucker* outside. I could look all the way up through the front of the store from my counter. The trees that lined the street beyond the parking lot were bent almost to the breaking point, their whipping leaves hanging on to the branches for dear life. The whole front of the DashMart was plate glass, and the driving rain from that storm made them look like solid walls once the wind really started raging. I can't recall if we were under a tornado warning or not; this is Oklahoma, so I'm gonna say probably. We were all used to the severe weather and uneventful warnings, so I was relaxed and leaning on the counter, sipping a pop while I thumbed through a comic book I hadn't paid for.

    One of the stock boys I palled around with sometimes was a beefy country-boy type named James Klingler. He always tried to get us to refer to him as "Diesel", because he had a love affair with his oversized monster of a truck. I promise you, if we *ever* called him that, it was only on a day when the big bastard broke down in the parking lot. Sometimes I called him "truck fucker". Most of the time, we just called him plain old Jim.

    Jim was the one who told me we had a new guy, and although I liked him, he did it out of pure meanness. Jim had seen Charlie run in and ask for the manager and thought maybe I would join him in mocking the poor kid before I had even had the chance to meet him.

    Jim jogged out of the swinging doors that led to our small loading dock and made a beeline for my counter, his smock covered with dirt and cardboard dust and his sleeves rolled up to his shoulders so he could treat us all with his considerable muscles and bad tattoos. He wore a shit-eating grin that wrapped all the way around his head. I had just started a new page when he slapped the comic book out of my hands.

"I was reading that, prick—" I started to say, but Jim cut me off.

"Dude. *Dude.* Have you seen the new guy?"

He cocked a thumb over his shoulder, gesturing to the checkout lanes up front. I glanced up there and didn't see anyone but Elias, the lovable old door greeter.

Elias Vermillion was easily one of my favorite human beings of all time. He was a scrawny old black man who always sported a small gray-white afro and a bushy mustache that draped down and covered his mouth, which was always turned up in a toothless smile. We loved that old man to death; he was like our community grandpa. On slow days (like the one I'm writing about now) he liked to pull a battered harmonica out of his smock and puff away at it, singing songs he made up on the spot about whatever he felt like singing about. He was doing that on that stormy day, resting his thin body on a padded stool and tapping his foot as he curled his long fingers around the harmonica. I can see him there now as I write about him, tooting a few notes and closing his eyes as he sang the words to himself.

"Elias?" I said sarcastically. "Elias was working here when the place had dirt floors, Jim."

"No, *dumbass.* He's starting today, he came in for his final interview a little while ago. This dude *walked* here. Walked through that shit, man. And he was wearing a bike helmet— I shit you not, Max— with a fucking camera mounted on the side of it."

I must admit, I chuckled at that image. I mean if the guy was walking, why was he wearing a bike helmet? And why the *camera?*

"Is he... you know..." I asked, twirling a finger beside my temple. I know, I know. It was a shitty assumption to make. But he *was* wearing a helmet, can you blame me?

Jim threw his head back and laughed hysterically.

"Dude he's *gotta* be a retard. No way he isn't. How am I supposed to work with a 'tard? What do I feed it?"

I felt a little stab of pity for the mysterious new guy and I smirked at Jim, my subtle way of letting him know he was getting a little too liberal with his insults. When he realized he was the only one laughing, he trailed off awkwardly.

"Anyway... yeah. Dude looks like a nut, you two should get along just fine. You're on diaper duty."

I shrugged and checked my phone. I hadn't done much anyone would call "work", but it was time for lunch.

"Maybe we will," I said to Jim, meaning it. "Will you keep an eye on the counter so I can go to break?"

Jim waved me off, already balls-deep in his phone as I plodded into the little oversized closet that we used as a break room. The first thing I saw when I walked in was something shiny and black, sitting on the table in a little puddle of rainwater. It was a pummeled and dented bicycle helmet, and a kid with shaggy blonde hair was busy tinkering with a camera mount that had been crudely screwed to its side. It looked like he was using chewed gum to help stick the thing back together.

"Hi," I said, amiably enough, and scooted a chair out. I sat my grocery bag full of junk food on the table beside the weathered helmet. "New guy?"

"Oh, *shit*, I'm sorry man," the new guy said, hastily moving the helmet out of my way and swiping at the water with the side of his hand. "Damn thing is like a sponge. Yeah, I'm the new guy. Charles Dillon; call me Charlie."

He held out his hand, which was still shiny with rainwater, but I shook it anyway. It was a nice handshake. Most guys seem to want to break your hand, like that will somehow prove that their dicks are bigger than yours. In fact, "Diesel" did that pretty much every time he met someone new. But not Charlie. He never had anything to prove to anyone but himself.

"Max," I said, and he smiled at me. His eyes were huge and a bright baby blue; wide open, too, as if he wanted to take in absolutely everything and not miss a single detail. He looked like a twelve-year-old kid, but I knew if he was working at the DashMart he had to be at least eighteen. As it turned out, he *was* only eighteen. I was twenty-six, so to me, Charlie did sort of seem like a little kid.

"Take it to the *Max*," he growled in a goofy movie-narrator voice, seemingly more to himself than to me. I snorted laughter.

"So, Charlie," I said, tapping the bicycle helmet with my finger. The top of that thing looked like a goddamned golf ball with all the dents and divots in it. "I gotta ask, what's with the helmet?"

It was like I had lit a short fuse connected to a fat bundle of fireworks. Charlie's face lit up like a Christmas tree, and he was nearly hopping off his chair with boyish enthusiasm.

"Oh *man,* did you see that monster hail earlier?"

I furrowed my brow, shaking my head. I didn't notice, nor did I care, about hail.

"No, but... I've seen it before. Sometimes they get pretty big."

Charlie began talking with his hands, raising them above our heads and painting invisible pictures across the plain break room ceiling.

"Right, because this is tornado alley. That's why I wanted to move here, dude. My aunt and uncle live in the apartments over on Espy Street. So yeah, in your typical severe thunderstorm, hail is pretty common. But the hail we had on my way here, the hail that gave me *this*..."

He pointed to a dent near the front of the bike helmet, one that had been made by a hailstone that had hit hard enough to remove the paint. I chuckled again, amused by how well he seemed to know every nick and dash in his helmet.

"*That* hail was the size of a golf ball. You ever see hail that big, Max?"

I didn't know if I had or not. Truthfully, at that particular moment, I didn't really care about anything but my Doritos. Hail was hail to me. But Charlie had intrigued me, and surprisingly, I found myself wanting to hear what he had to say. I wanted to be kind to him, to be the white that countered Jim's black.

"I think so, yeah," I said stupidly. Charlie didn't need me to carry the conversation.

"Golf ball sized hail is actually pretty rare. See, what happens is, the updraft inside a supercell—"

"A super...?"

"Cell, yeah. A tornadic thunderstorm. A *supercell*. The updraft is so strong that it sort of lofts the ice up and down, over and over again, and it just keeps building layers of ice until it's heavy enough to fall to Earth as hail. Think about how strong the winds up there have to be to make a hailstone the size of a golf ball. Golf ball is rookie-size though. I've seen hail the size of a *baseball,* dude. Had one punch right through my Uncle Doug's windshield and shatter a coffee mug."

He slammed his fist into the palm of his hand.

"So, this is your hail helmet?" I asked, unable to keep the smile from my face. Luckily, he wasn't offended and grinned back at me.

"Sure is," he said, patting it like a middle-aged man might pat the hood of his prized project muscle car. "It's saved me more times than I can count. I need to get some pads for my arms though. Maybe like... hockey pads or something. I don't know."

I couldn't stop beaming at this strange new kid, and I knew immediately that I liked him. That's a special feeling, and it only happens a handful of times throughout our lives.

"So you like to take pictures of the storms?" I asked, cracking open a Monster and nodding towards the camera lying in front of him. Again, he nearly leapt off his seat, and couldn't wrestle his phone out of his jeans pocket fast enough.

"Oh, *man!* I can't even tell you how much I love it. I mostly just use my phone, but my helmet cam records everywhere I look so my hands are free to take stills and collect samples. I keep hailstones in the freezer, but they never seem to last."

He scooted closer to me, holding his phone out and tapping in the passcode with no concern about me learning it. When the main screen appeared, I saw a colorful plethora of weather app icons, more than I could count. The wallpaper of his phone was— of course— a still photograph of a tornado, looming over some dark, abandoned-looking buildings. It was bigger than any I'd ever seen myself, an ugly gray-green funnel that looked like it was almost as wide as it was tall. The tornado looked like it had tentacles wrapping around and flailing out from it, and as I leaned in to look closer, I realized that the photographer had been pretty damned close to it when he took the picture. Talk about balls.

"Holy *fuck* Charles, you got that close to that thing on *foot?"* I asked incredulously. He shook his head, but the look on his face was unmistakable; he looked disappointed that he hadn't been.

"It's Charlie. And no, that's the Tuscaloosa Alabama tornado, back in 2011. That thing was a *monster.* Rated EF-4. It lasted about an hour and a half and killed nearly 70 people."

Living in tornado alley, I was familiar with the rating system for tornadoes, but I could never remember the name. Even now I can't, but I know it sounds like "fajita". Still, it felt good to get what he was talking about for once, because I suspected that probably wouldn't happen very often.

"I remember seeing that on TV," I said. "It was sad, man. We had an EF-5 here, not too long ago. Ever hear of the Moore tornado?"

Charlie was nodding enthusiastically as he tapped his phone, opening his photo app.

"Absolutely. Wind speeds reached 210 miles per hour in that storm, that's insane. 2013 was a bad year for tornadoes. I lost some heroes of mine in El Reno."

I had *definitely* heard of the El Reno tornado. *Everyone* in Bent Knee had. The town talked about it fairly often because it was a frightening example of what could happen to our own town. In case you've never heard of it, that tornado is famous because of how many records it broke. It was *two and a half miles wide.* No matter how comfortable you are with bad storms and tornado warnings, the pictures and videos of that thing will pucker up your asshole. It looked like something that should have been on Jupiter; not here on planet Earth where people and animals live.

Charlie was showing me a picture of what appeared to be the remnants of a white vehicle sitting crookedly on the side of a dirt road, but it was basically a wadded-up piece of metal with one lonely tire clinging to the rear axle.

"That's what it did to their car," Charlie said solemnly, and for a moment I thought he might cry right there in front of me. "First storm chasers to be killed by a tornado in history. Tim Samaras was like a *god* to people like me. He died with his son Paul, and a meteorologist named Carl Young. The Twistex team. *Heroes*, man."

"That's crazy," I said, my go-to response when I have no idea how to respond to something. "You really love weather, don't you Charlie?"

He was now swiping through his own photos, and I'm telling you, even at his young age he could have been a professional. He showed me incredible shots of lightning bolts mid-strike, one of which he had managed to capture just as it struck a tree. You could even see burning wood and smoke flying through the air like confetti. There were shots of massive hailstones that looked like mace heads, held in his hand for size comparison. He seemed to have hundreds of landscape shots, waving corn and wheat fields frozen in time with imposing cloud formations of all shapes and colors encroaching from the horizon. The final picture he showed me was of a small funnel, dangling from a swirling cloud base like a green bob tail.

"See how there's no dust kicking up from the ground?" he said, in a teacherly tone. I looked at the empty grass under the funnel cloud and nodded like a good student. "That means a condensation funnel hasn't made contact with the ground yet, so *technically* it's not a tornado."

I pretended to be insulted.

"You're a weather nerd, living in tornado alley, and you don't have a single picture of a full-fledged tornado?" I scolded, but Charlie could see the humor in my eyes. He wagged his finger at me.

"Not *yet*," he said, and then rubbed his hands together like a supervillain. "But it's tornado season, Max."

We had overstayed our break by nearly thirty minutes. *Thirty minutes.* I had never given a single solitary ounce of dog shit about science or weather, not in my whole life. But Charlie's enthusiasm was contagious and seeing how excited he got when he talked about it with that childlike wonder in those blue eyes, you just kinda wanted to listen to him.

The bitch manager never mentioned us taking an extra-long break that day, and after Jim had given up on my returning, Elias had shuffled back and was watching the counter for me. He grinned mischievously, his mustache morphing ever so slightly.

"Nice nap, boys?" he said in his high, scratchy voice.

"Nah, he kept trying to spoon me," I said, and lightly punched Charlie in the arm.

"He's handsome," Charlie joked, shrugging. We all laughed together. Man, that felt good. Charlie was a part of the family almost immediately, and in a town like Bent Knee, where being different can mean social suicide, that's no mean feat.

There was a loud crack of thunder, one of those artillery shell blasts that you can feel shaking the ground under your feet. Outside, the rain really started to show its true colors. There wouldn't be any new customers for a while, and the few we had would be camping out. It happened like that all the time.

"Starting to get some marble hail out there," Elias said, gesturing outside. Sure enough, amongst the sheets of pounding rain, we could see them bouncing across the pavement. "'Diesel' ain't gonna be too happy if his truck gets dented up."

I sniggered, turning to Charlie so I could let my new friend in on the joke. I was facing empty space. As soon as he had heard the word "hail" he had slapped his helmet down over his blonde head and sprinted for the door, his shoes slapping as he fidgeted with the mounted camera. He shouldered the front door open and fought the onslaught of wind to close it behind him. Elias and I watched as he fished his phone out and began taking a video of the sky above him, even as tiny pellets of ice were ricocheting off his head and shoulders. We laughed at him as he staggered through the vicious precipitation, the wind nearly sweeping him off his feet several times. We weren't laughing because we were mocking him, I gotta make that clear. He was just a funny guy, an instant mood lightener. Elias once said that Charlie was like the cream in a cup of coffee so black that you could "stand a spoon up in it".

Oh yeah, you could say I liked Charlie immediately— I just wish the rest of Bent Knee had felt the same. He wasn't mistreated or beaten up, nothing bad like that. The most he got in the way of bullying was some roasting on our breaks at work and Jim pushing him around when he was in a shit mood. For the most part, the townspeople tolerated him. From a distance, that is. They treated him like a leper, at least until he got his fifteen minutes of fame on the local news. *Then* he was worthy of their adoration.

He often drew confused stares from the customers when the skies would blacken outside and he would rush out, right in the middle of his shift, to document it. He even took it upon himself to page any and all updates he got from his weather apps over our staticky PA system. Usually, his announcements were a little drawn out and full of scientific facts that no one paid much attention to, but the bitch boss actually encouraged him to do it. She told us it helped keep the customers safe, and I guess she was right about that.

It took some time, as it always does, but Charlie eventually found his place in Bent Knee. He was our resident weatherman, and if I say so myself, much more likable than Bill Travers, the clown on channel 5 that looks like a pedo with a bad tie.

This next part you might find strange when you read it, because I've spent all this time telling you how much I liked Charlie— but the truth is, one stormy May morning back in '17, right in the crotch of tornado season, he almost got us *both* killed. I could have declined his invitation; I could have told him to go fuck himself and blow me while he was at it. But he'd been working on me, making me interested, making me care. I suddenly wanted to see a tornado, out in the wild, roaring across the Oklahoma plains like the finger of God Himself. No more peeking between houses and stores to watch a weak one spinning outside of town. No more hiding in the break room at work, hugging my knees with a bunch of funky-smelling strangers. No more funnel clouds that hung quietly for two or three minutes and then disappeared.

Charlie talked me into going on a storm chase with him, and Christ almighty, I got exactly what I wanted.

* * *

I woke up for work on the morning of May 10th, 2017, and I already knew we were in for it that day.

I always sleep with my bedroom window open at night; I like the night air and the burring of the crickets and tree frogs, and Bent Knee isn't the kind of town where you have to worry about burglars and murderers all that often. I think it was the oppressive stillness outside that woke me, because I still had five minutes or so before my alarm went off.

There was no breeze. The curtains were hanging stock-still, and the morning light was an infected olive color. I could smell the rain already, that damp and earthy smell everyone seems to love so much. To me, that smell meant shoving trains of interlocked shopping carts while being beaten to death by fat drops of cold rain. Not my idea of a good time, but if it came down to me and Elias, I always jumped on that grenade. Charlie wasn't always there on stormy days, and when he was, he was too busy filming to be wrangling carts. We let him get away with it, although it earned him the title of "pussy lips" from Jim.

Stretching and trying to rub the sleep from my eyes, I snatched up my phone to silence the alarm and had to do a double take. *Ten* missed calls from Charlie. *Ten.* My first instinct was to panic a little; people don't usually call you like that unless someone is hurt or dead. Then I saw the texts.

He'd bombarded my phone with a whole book's worth of texts, more than I could ever hope to read. I scrolled through the stack, glossing over them. I glimpsed a few screenshots of weather maps, a diagram of a cartoon tornado with a big red circle around it (Charlie had edited the picture and scribbled the words BEAR CAGE above the circle with his finger). There were a few snapshots of what the sky currently looked like, a text about something called "mammatus" and about a thousand messages asking me if I was awake yet. The most recent text said, "Let's ditch work today, call me ASAP". Attached was a picture of a voluptuous woman in a raincoat that was much too small for her, her comically large breasts spilling out and her nipples at full attention. She held a toy umbrella, curling her freakishly long (and pierced) tongue around the curved handle. Across the bottom of the picture, in glowing pink cursive, were the words "gettin' wet".

Once I was able to stop laughing, I shuffled into the kitchen for an energy drink and finally called the crazy asshole, turning speakerphone on so my hands would be free to dig for my clothes. The tinny ringing sound barely had time to repeat before Charlie answered.

"*Max*!" He shouted, maxing out my phone's speaker. I swear, he made it vibrate on the table. "Where the hell have you been, dude?"

I wrestled out a pair of clean boxer shorts with minimal taint holes and called over my shoulder, "Asleep, dingus. Why did you send me a picture of your sister?"

"Well, nothing else was working, so I figured titties might do it. And what do you know?"

I couldn't help but snicker at how annoyed he sounded. To you, reading these pages, he probably sounds like someone you'd want to avoid. We've all known people that love to insert themselves into your life, butting in on conversations and inviting themselves to dinner when you can barely even remember their names. I can't stress enough; Charlie wasn't one of those people. He was a little odd, and I was almost always on the receiving end of his eccentricities. He didn't have anyone else, and I'd be lying if I said I didn't enjoy it. Most of the time.

"Yep, I took the big perky bait. What's this shit about skipping work?"

Charlie was so excited that he invented a new foreign language. I waited patiently for him to finish, tunneling deep into the clean clothes basket for an elusive work shirt.

"—and there was a DOW filling up at the gas station, so they know today is going to be big," he finished, audibly out of breath.

I picked the phone up and held it with my shoulder, chugging the fizzy energy drink down as fast as I could. I was going to need it.

"Alright Charlie, repeat that in English, and slow it down for me. I'm still half asleep."

Charlie made an angry grunting sound and began again.

"Okay. We should call in today, because the conditions are perfect for strong tornadoes. The TORCON index is at *eight out of ten*. We've been under a tornado watch since 6am, and a stovepipe already touched down outside of Fentonville that stayed on the ground for *a half hour*. I've been watching my weather apps, and right now, there is a massive squall line moving right toward Bent Knee. I started calling you when I saw a hook on the radar. It's a supercell, Max. When I walked to the gas station, I saw mammatus clouds over the fire department, which means this storm is going to be mega violent. Then, I saw a DOW pulling in for gas. Storm chasers are all over town, Max. I want to join them."

"What the hell is a DOW?"

"Don't worry about it. Are we going or not?"

It had taken me a few minutes and a couple more swigs of my ultra-caffeinated beverage to realize that he wasn't joking. He actually wanted to use my car, and together, try to chase a fucking tornado. I didn't know the first thing about storm chasing; to this day, I don't even think I'm a particularly good driver. It sounded like the plot of a bad buddy comedy.

"You want to use my car to chase a tornado."

"More than anything," he said without hesitation.

"Like that Helen Hunt movie."

"Just like that."

Outside, thunder growled in the distance as if the storm was encouraging me to go along with Charlie's crazy idea.

Yeah, come on out, Max. Come and chase me. See what I can do.

I could hear the susurrus of the wind as it rose through the trees outside, carrying the monolithic storm steadily toward us. I can't explain why, but a surge of high-voltage excitement shot through me when I saw the first flickers of lightning. It felt like a party was starting, a big and important event, and you didn't even need an invite to attend. All you had to do was nut up and show up.

Think of my options for a second. Was it dangerous and stupid? Of course it was. In one hand, I had another long, boring shift laid out in front of me. We would have no customers because of the weather, and I'd probably end up playing on my phone in the break room, listening to the howling wind and the inevitable rise and fall of the tornado sirens. The big ones never came through Bent Knee anyway— or so we thought back then.

In the other hand, I got to satisfy the steadily growing curiosity that Charlie had been sowing in my brain. I got to be a part of the action, out there in the shit, seeing raw power and fury that no YouTube video (Charlie sent me plenty of those) could ever convey. I could look death itself right in its black face on an adventure with my friend, maybe even live out a story I could proudly tell my grandkids. If I ever had any.

Hindsight is 20/20, and I can tell you now that I was deluding myself into thinking I had the stones to chase tornadoes that day; but my budding curiosity and the mysterious allure that seems to radiate from twisters won out, and I stopped searching for a work shirt. I was going to live a little. It was time to get some of the action.

"Max, I'm starting to decompose over here," Charlie moaned.

"We'll tell them we're not getting out in the weather, it's too risky." Nothing could have been further from the truth. "How many points do you have?"

DashMart had a point system to keep track of who showed up to work or not. Each day you didn't clock in earned you two points, and if you didn't call in to report your absence, you got three. Ten points, and you got shitcanned. I rarely ever missed work, so I had been sitting at a nice comfortable balance of zero that day. Plenty of breathing room to play hooky.

"Four points. I'm fine," he said, his voice tight and rising in pitch, keeping pace with his exponential excitement. "I'm calling in now. Come to my place as soon as humanly possible. Make sure you have a full tank."

"Anything else, boss?" I asked sarcastically, but I had been asking an empty line. The thunder rolled and thudded across our rustic little town and the miles of fields around it, vibrating the charged air and filling me with tingling adrenaline. The Monster I'd chugged had nothing on that kind of boost; there's nothing like it. I wondered if the other chasers in town, the professionals, felt the same way I did before they packed up their cars and trucks and sped *toward* the direction everyone else was fleeing *from*.

I dialed the number of the bitch boss's office with one hand while stuffing my feet into my stained mowing shoes with the other, and by the time her disapproving rant was burrowing into my ear canal, I was already jabbing my keys into the ignition. Scattered drops of rain were pattering on my windshield, and the sky above me looked like boiling, filthy water. I knew that it was my decision and that I was in control, but at the same time, I *wasn't* in control. It was like I was on autopilot, not allowing myself even one second of apprehension.

The wind was noticeably stronger as I drove down the overgrown country road into town, slamming into the side of my car in blitzkrieg bursts and threatening to push me over the faded lines. It felt like a ghost was sitting in the passenger seat, waiting until I was zoned out or busy looking up at the fomenting clouds and then snatching the wheel from my sweaty hands. My car kept lurching towards the drainage ditch that ran along the shoulder of the road.

It made me think of a story Jim had tagged me in on Facebook once, an article about a haunted road somewhere in Kentucky where the ghost of some dead kid would appear in your car and make you crash if you were brave enough to drive down it at high speeds. There weren't any ghosts in the car with me, other than maybe the spirit of my better judgment chastising me for what I was about to do. The wind alone was strong enough to do the job of crashing me, no dead kids required, and the storm hadn't even arrived yet.

When I pulled into Skinny's, our local gas station and greasy spoon, the fact that I had been sleeping while everything in the outside world was going to shit started to make me feel uneasy. The streetlights were beginning to switch on as the sun was overcome by suffocating black thunderheads, fooling them into thinking twilight had come early. Bent Knee had become an old western ghost town.

The sidewalks were empty and deserted, nothing traversing their lengths except for trash. Small pieces of paper, empty coffee cups and rotten leaves swept to and fro and sometimes whirled up into little dust devils that rotated furiously, as if trying to impress their bigger brothers. I stood under the metal awning that shielded the gas pumps, funneling my money into the tank as the wind tore at my shirt and pants. It made them feel too tight against my body. The metal structure over my head creaked and groaned, almost like it was in pain, and the sudden rushes of air over my face and hair forced me to gasp to get a full breath.

Skinny (real name Dallas Stayman, the scarecrow-like redneck who owned the establishment) hadn't even bothered to open that day. There was a hand-written sign taped in the big front window that said "Closed for STORM. Pumps still work with card. Be safe". It was spooky to peek inside and see the empty counter, abandoned under the dimmed lights that hung from the grease-spotted ceiling. The window glass flexed with the force of the wind, morphing and changing my reflection from fat to skinny.

Earlier, I told you that I've seen my share of tornadoes, and that's true. But up to that point, I'd never seen it like that outside. I didn't know it then, but we were about to endure one of the worst severe storms in the town's history and Charlie and I were headed to the front lines. There's a difference between a baby funnel cloud and the beast that threatened our little town that day. Until the EF-5, I had never seen a twister that had any real size or power. Not until Pecos Charlie led me into one.

I was starting to sweat, and a panicky little fluttering feeling was irritating my bowels. When the wind changed direction, which it seemed to be doing frequently and randomly, the next gust had switched from warm and humid to cold and dry. A long stripe of goosebumps traveled up my spine and I shivered. I felt alone, vulnerable, and very very small.

The pump stopped at $25.38, and I goosed the lever until I made an even $25.50. There were no more tasks to be done now. All that was left was to go get Charlie, who was probably doing somersaults in his front yard, and venture out to see what Mother Nature had in store for us.

I pulled up to the intersection of Main and Greely, barely registering the need to obey the traffic light because in my mind, there would be no one coming. I cursed and slammed on my brakes at the last minute when I saw what was approaching from my left, plowing through the blowing dirt clouds and clusters of leaves like a battleship.

It was a huge vehicle that looked like a crimson army tank. I couldn't tell what it *used* to be, but now it was an armor-plated machine, steel walls extending down to cover all but the smallest sliver of tires. I could be crazy, but it looked like the thing had spikes mounted on the sides of it, like… anchor stakes or something. I stared in awe as the tank glided down the street in front of me, lurching left before the yellow light could change to red.

That guy has the right idea, I thought, suddenly feeling naked and outmatched in my little car. That thing looked like it was designed to be *inside* a tornado. I had only been hoping to get within eyeshot of one, and that helped to steel my nerves a little. Surely any action we saw would be from a safe distance away, and the tank driver could handle the up close and personal stuff.

It'll be fine, I reassured myself, following the same path the tank had gone. *Charlie knows what he's doing, or we wouldn't be going.*

Charlie came galloping down the stairs of his apartment complex before my car had stopped moving, hail helmet strapped on tight and mounted camera secured, eager face illuminated by the glow of his phone. He was stabbing and swiping at it with his finger even as he ran to my car; I have no earthly idea how he didn't trip on those stairs and break his ass.

Before he could even get the door closed, he demanded, "Do you know where 90 is?"

I wracked my brain, trying to remember the tangled web of country roads around Bent Knee that only locals dared to travel. 90 was a road most people called "triangle", because it cut right through the wide square of bean fields between 95 and 305. It was a relatively dangerous road, scarcely maintained and usually crowded with lumbering farm equipment that took up both lanes. The only landmark on 90 was a dilapidated barn, one that was so old and neglected that no one was even sure who owned it anymore.

"Yeah, I've been down it a few times. Is that where we're headed?"

Charlie nodded his head so fast that it seemed to vibrate, jostling his headgear around. He held his phone out to me, presenting swirling blobs of red and green as if I could understand what the hell I was looking at. I smirked at him, arching my eyebrows and nodding.

"I'm not real sure what I'm supposed to be seeing, Charlie. It just looks like a storm to me."

He placed his fingertip on a deep red section of the weather map and it zoomed in, and I noticed that it sort of looked like the red and purple blobs were swirling down a drain. They formed a hook shape, and even I, a layman, knew what that meant.

"That's a hook echo," Charlie said, grinning wide.

"It's rotating," I deduced, feeling nauseas. I didn't bother to hide the nervous farts that were brewing in my gut like the storm outside.

"What's happening is rain and hail, maybe even some debris, are wrapping around the storm. This isn't just any old thunderstorm, Max. This is a *supercell*. And if they haven't called a tornado warning yet, they're about to."

He tapped the tiny play button and the colors began to swirl and move like oil in a rain puddle, then the image froze and played again. The supercell was traveling from the southwest corner of the "pan" of Oklahoma to the northeast, the worst of it slowly inching into Hancock County and Bent Knee's border like a line of stalking bears. County Road 90, where Charlie wanted me to take him, was directly in the path of the hook signature. That evil eye would cross the road with us on it.

Somehow, against the adrenaline tightening my chest and the constant gnawing of mortal fear in my guts, I shifted my car into reverse and backed out onto the deserted road. In the passenger seat Charlie was grinning like a mental patient, looking like a Space Trooper with his dented helmet and mounted camera blinking on the side. Lightning flashed through the windows, illuminating the right side of his face with an icy blue glow.

"Scared?" He said, holding out his fist for me to bump it. I rapped my knuckles against his and lied to his face.

"Not scared at all, my dude."

"You gotta die somehow, right?" He added, perhaps testing my resolve. I gave him an awkward thumbs up and stepped on the gas before I could stop myself.

It was raining steadily then, and I pulled the windshield wiper lever down from moderate to high. As soon as they swiped away the cascades of water, more were waiting to take their places. I hunched over the wheel, refusing to blink as I scanned the shoulder of the road for the little green CR 90 sign. The wind pushed and shoved my car like a belligerent drunk.

"Make a right up here," Charlie said distractedly. "Once we get a few miles down the road, the precip should stop and we'll have a clear view. A strong updraft means the rain can't even fall."

I nodded, trying to watch the road and the sky at the same time. The very second my wheels touched the surface of 90, I hit a massive pothole that knocked my teeth together and sent a geyser of brown water spraying up over my headlights. We were lucky I didn't pop my fucking tire. 90 wasn't a road you wanted to be on if you needed to move in a hurry; I didn't use it often, but I knew several lower lying parts of it tended to flood with the slightest bit of rain, and it had more holes in it than a shooting range target. In hindsight, I realize that's probably why we never saw any of the professional storm chasers speeding down it ahead of us. They probably attempted it, realized the danger, and moved on to a better option. A *safer* option. Only two idiots tried to chase down 90 that day.

As we rolled and bounced down the haggard county road, the sky ahead of us dried all the spit in my mouth and turned my tongue to sandpaper. It was the color of a gangrenous wound, ugly shades of black and green and even a noxious brown. Lightning stabbed all the way down to the ground, cutting meandering cracks of burning light across the poisoned sky that left hovering afterimages dancing across my windshield. The thunder that followed each strike made my ass leave the seat, every single time, the car surging forward as my foot accidentally crushed the gas pedal.

Charlie didn't seem to notice the dark bib of sweat collecting around the collar of my prized Fear Factory shirt. He casually cocked a thumb toward his window and said "Look up there Max. See those weird clouds that look like bumps?"

I leaned over, as stiff as a corpse, and stole a quick glance up. There was a small patch of rounded lobes clustered together on the shifting underside of the storm, strange looking clouds that were unnaturally smooth and hung like overripe fruit. I had never seen anything like that before. I slowed the car and leaned over again, amazed by their delicate shape, as if they had been shaped and smoothed by the hands of angry angels.

"Mammatus," Charlie said, grinning proudly at my gaping mouth as he snapped a few photos. "It means 'breast cloud.'"

A strong wind gust butted against my car, jolting me out of hypnosis. I realized then that the rain had stopped except for a light drizzle, and my wipers were squealing across the windshield like it hurt. Charlie reached over and snapped them off so that my white-knuckle grip on the wheel could hold steady. Ahead of us, falling in on itself and decaying on the right side of the road, was the abandoned barn that marked the near-halfway point of 90. It exuded horror movie vibes, standing alone like that in the middle of nowhere with a black sky for a backdrop. It looked haunted.

"Man," I said, fighting the stubborn wheel like a ship captain guiding a liner through rough seas. "You just have titties on the brain today, don't you?" I was resorting to playful teasing to distract myself from my fear.

"Better than what—"

Charlie's words cut off suddenly, as if invisible hands had pinched his windpipe shut. He was staring at something outside my window. I turned to ask if he was enjoying my nervous gas, and then I froze as well. Charlie looked like he had seen a ghost, his blue eyes bugging out of their lids and his mouth hanging open like a broken drawbridge. He reminded me of that slasher movie, the one where the two psychos wore a ghost mask and terrorized people over the phone before they killed them. That mask; picture it in your mind, if you've seen the movie. That was Charlie's face.

I turned my head to match his gaze and survival instinct hijacked my muscular control, forcing my foot onto the brake pedal. My tires screeched angrily at me as we skidded to a sideways stop on the wet road, now within a stone's throw of the creepy old barn. I kept swallowing, my throat clicking as I fought vomit. Jesus *Christ*, I was so scared.

A small conical dust cloud was whirling up out of the field, spinning furiously and drawing in puffs of black soil like a colossal vacuum cleaner. As we watched, it tripled in size in a matter of seconds, elongating and widening out at the top until I had to practically lay in the driver's seat to see the top of it. It began to darken, taking on the color of the dirt it was eating. Pebbles and dirt clods began to tap and bounce across my hood. To my untrained eye, that dust cloud was the whole tornado. I was blind to the danger we were really in.

Charlie was out of the car in a flash, filming from his helmet and his phone simultaneously. I was confused; the tornado was forming to my left, but Charlie was sweeping his camera up above the car. I was left out of the loop, and it was pissing me off. Charlie was alone in the universe as he watched that tornado be born, his face bright and alive and countering my terrified grimace.

"The tornado is over here!" I yelled at him, rolling the window down and hearing the true volume of the twister's roar for the first time. It sounded like I had parked at the edge of Niagara Falls. I could feel my car rocking on its shocks, tilting towards the tornado as it tried to suck us into it even from a good distance away.

"No it's not!" He screamed back, jabbing his finger up above us. I hesitated, cursing under my breath as my heart began to pump overtime. I forced my hand to the door handle and willed my fingers to close around it. I stepped timidly out into the ceaseless wind and looked up.

The dust whirl I had *thought* was the fully formed tornado was nothing more than the bottom tip of the funnel. The twister had actually begun to form right over the roof of my car, extending down from the slowly rotating storm clouds and curving like a huge, elongated letter S. The funnel snaked across the sky like an elephant's trunk, spinning so fast that it almost appeared to be composed of greenish-gray velvet. It resembled a questing tongue, extending and retracting as if tasting the earth to see if it was suitable for pairing. The funnel morphed into a violently rotating arch over the road, widening out at the top and fading out to invisibility just before it reached the wisps of dust and black dirt at its base. Lightning flashed somewhere behind it, periodically giving the funnel an otherworldly glow. It was terrifyingly beautiful. Back in Bent Knee, the tornado siren began its long, mournful warning cry. That sound is terrifying even when they're just testing it—

coupled with a twister being born right in front of me, it was enough to freeze the blood in my veins.

Charlie was going ballistic as I stood with my hands braced against the car door and the roof, rocking from foot to foot as I fought my sense of self-preservation. He was holding his phone out in front of him, panning up to film the full length of the tornado, then slowly tracing the funnel back down to where the dust cloud had found a couple of lonely trees. The spinning dust washed over them, splintering the branches and trunks and yanking the leaves off in a chaotic flurry. I could see all the little pieces as they were carried up into the sky, lofted high and orbiting the funnel like small moons.

For a while the tornado was lazily drifting away from us, leaving a long scar of tossed earth and stripped weeds behind it. It was moving away, but it was still throwing things at us. I could hear gravel and branches pelting the car and bouncing off the pavement like bullets. I ducked behind the door, using it as a shield.

"Charlie!" I bellowed, struggling to be heard over the onslaught of hissing wind feeding into the twister. *"I think maybe we should get the hell out of here!"*

"Are you fucking crazy?!" He shouted over his shoulder, pumping his legs into a blur as he continued the chase on foot. He held his phone over his head like a lightning rod— fortunately, it didn't prove to be a very effective one. He looked very small running after the churning tornado, which, when compared to the human body, resembled a tall and narrow cloud tower that leaned to one side as it was dragged across the earth.

"I'm not the one running after a fucking tornado in a bicycle helmet!" I snapped back, my anxiety working me up into an irate frenzy. I slapped the roof of my car, leaving a smeared handprint in the fresh blanket of dirt.

I watched in awe as the vortex stopped moving away from us and began to drift to the right, threatening to cross the road right in front of where I stood paralyzed. Charlie was getting farther and farther away from the safety of the car, and I realized then why they say most people who die in tornadoes are caught driving; not only do they change direction and speed without any rhyme or reason, but it can be dangerously difficult to gauge their path, their momentum, and their distance away from you. Even a small tornado is so huge that it's like normal perspective gets thrown out of whack. Something so big should not be able to move with such fluidity.

I have to admit, I was so terrified in that moment that I was almost angry at Charlie for convincing me to follow him, but I was also mesmerized. The funnel spun dizzyingly fast, but the lowering mass of cloud it descended from (which I now know is called the "wall cloud") spun slowly and gracefully. It was like a sluggish, hypnotic whirlpool. I could smell the strong stench of wet dirt, shredded wood, and sap mixing with the scent of rain on the air. Somehow, Charlie had guided us to the perfect vantage point. *How?* How could Charlie have known that there wouldn't be any heavy precipitation where we were heading? Science, I suppose you'd say, but it was a little terrifying to a dope like me who was strung along for the ride like a flea in a vacuum cleaner. His intimate knowledge of storms almost made him psychic.

As the funnel left the field and spun across the road ahead of us, the billowing dust whirl enveloping it began to scatter and I saw several *baby* tornadoes, four of five of them, dancing around each other in a tight circle. They formed, spun ferociously, dissipated, and formed again. They reminded me of the blades inside a hand-crank pencil sharpener; when I was a kid, we used to take the guards off to see how they worked. If you've ever had to use one without the guard around it, you'll know what I mean. It was like a blender made of nothing but air and water.

I leapt into the driver's seat and began to crawl down the road to catch up with my crazed friend, wary of the branches and rocks the twister had thrown around like parade candy. Luckily there had been no power lines for it to knock over; a road that was already in shit condition with live wires draped across it would have made our eventual escape even harder. No, that particular twister was right where it needed to be: out in the middle of nowhere, away from houses and the people who lived in them.

Charlie had stopped running after the tornado and was again standing with his phone held above his head, his arms extended as if he were trying to signal a UFO to swoop down and beam him up. Behind him, the twister had taken on a sinister black hue as the sun began to show through the cloud cover, searing the sky behind it into a burnt and hazy shade of orange. The whirling mass of cloud and dirt began to widen, slowly but steadily, growing into a monster. I didn't realize that I had to crane my neck to see the top of it until the muscles began to ache. We were closer than we ever should have been, and even now I'm hanging my head in shame. We could have *died*.

  Charlie abruptly spun on his heels and began running for his life, pumping his arms and legs and quickly closing the distance between himself and my car. I gave it a little gas and met him halfway. He tore the door open and collapsed inside, reeking of mud and sweat. He was shivering like he'd just skinny dipped in a frozen pond and might be suffering a heart attack.

  "Look at that thing *grow*," I marveled, wanting to hide my fear and maybe even impress him.

  "*Shut the fuck up and get us out of here!*" Charlie exploded, gesturing wildly for me to back the car up.

  "What—"

  "*It's not growing, it's fucking coming right at us!*"

  Charlie told me later on that I screamed then, high and shrill, right in his face. He said I sounded like a cat with its balls snagged on a steel fence, but for the life of me I don't remember doing it. All I remember is slamming the car into reverse and rocketing backwards down the unforgiving surface of 90, leaving a trail of white smoke that was instantly sucked into the approaching funnel. I remember my ears popping from the immense change in pressure. Suddenly they were both full of cotton, and yet I could still hear that menacing roar.

  Charlie's head flipped back and forth like a weathervane, trying to monitor the twister and the road behind us at the same time. His helmet hung slightly sideways, a single blade of grass embedded in the cracked plastic and hanging down like a green rabbit ear. Beneath the car, I could feel the ground shaking like a slow, constant earthquake. Somewhere, muffled but persistent, the siren wailed on. I had time to wonder if the people back in town might be out on their porches, perhaps snapping photos of the tornado that was about to shred us alive and turn my little car into a coffin.

"It's gonna take the barn!" He screamed, cackling like a madman as he raised his phone to film it. He'd forgotten, I guess, that the fucking tornado was going to take us too. Shit on that barn. It was going to kill us, and he was hooting about it.

"You're a goddamned maniac!" I shouted back, and I don't know if it was the blind panic making me twitchy or the Swiss cheese road under us, but I lost total control of the car and put us ass first into the drainage ditch. My back bumper slammed into the muddy embankment, knocking the wind out of both of us and knocking my teeth together with a loud *clack*. The nose of the car was pointed slightly up, giving me a front row seat to the approaching storm. A chunk of the doomed barn snapped off and fired through the air like an arrow, slammed into the windshield, and turned it into a glistening spiderweb. Charlie had rolled his window down and was hanging half out of the car, totally ignoring the bullets of debris flying around us. If not for the tenacious little strap holding his hail helmet on, it would have been blown to Tulsa.

Even at such an awkward angle, I didn't have to move much to see the death of that old barn (other than leaning over to squint through my ruined windshield). I can't explain why I didn't tuck my head down and kiss my ass goodbye, God knows that's what I wanted to do. I think it's the same for a lot of people. You see their videos online all the time; you can hear the terror in their voices, often times you can hear their wives or kids in the background, begging them to stop filming and get down to the basement. And yet they go on recording, muttering to themselves, not wanting to miss their rare glimpse of pure, uncontrolled power tearing its way through their lives. In some cases, *ending* their lives.

That was me, channeling my inner Charlie Dillon. I was scared like I had never been scared before, feeling like my car seat had become an electric chair and I was just waiting for the man behind the curtain to throw the hot switch. You can bet your ass I watched every solitary second, and it was a sight I'll not soon forget.

You ever see test footage from the army, when they detonate one of their bombs? That's what it looked like. As the funnel got close to the barn—

not even touching it yet, just close— it began to disintegrate. It was just like an explosive shockwave, except traveling in a blazingly fast circle instead of spreading out in all directions. The barn appeared to have smoke pouring out of it, just from the sheer force of the wind pushing through it. The roof, which was barely on there to begin with, went first. It peeled back like the top of a soup can, twisting and deforming as shingles and massive, ragged hunks of crumbling wood fragmented from it. It floated off the barn and tumbled through the cluttered air like a propeller, sucked up and up and then carried out of sight. As far as I know, whatever was left of it never touched the ground again.

The walls went next. It was like a gigantic invisible foot was kicking them over, as easily as you might kick weeds away from your mailbox. I couldn't tell you what all had been stored inside that thing over the years, but I *can* tell you that all of it got sucked out into that black tower. I even saw a rust-eaten tractor get pulled out and thrown through the air like an unwanted toy, one of its thick rear tires wrenched off and sent rolling down 90 like a bowling ball.

As the shrieking funnel moved over the barn, the one wall that had been left standing simply exploded; it looked like a hundred thousand toothpicks revolving around the undulating dirt cloud like a swarm of gnats. All that wooden debris churning and grinding sounded like a million sets of deer antler wind chimes, all clanging together at once as they dangled from the engine of a freight train.

Once the debris really began to fly and the base of the twister had become a woodchipper, even Charlie hunkered down inside the car with me. His face was the color of cottage cheese, and a bright red trail of blood was trickling from a fresh cut under his left eye. I know he could feel what I was feeling— the wheels of my car leaving the walls of the ditch and slamming back down again, as if a team of angry men were trying in vain to flip it like a coin. We had both seen it take that tractor like it was nothing. We were done for.

"*We're gonna be okay, Max!*" Charlie screamed, even as his blood reached the upturned side of his mouth and he licked it away. He leaned over and wrapped his dirt-grimed arms around me, and I buried my face between his neck and his shoulder. I knew he was lying, but I loved him for it anyway. He was trying to keep me calm in the face of my death, with no thought spared for his own.

My car kept lurching and pulling beneath us, struggling against the deafening roar and relentless force of that insane wind. I hugged Charlie so tight that I thought I might break his narrow back, and he was patting my shoulder, shouting something into my ear that I couldn't hear. The tornado was so close, the noise so absolute, that even screaming was useless.

The vicious growling of the hateful vortex swelled and then finally began to quiet down to a saner sound, the typical whoosh and sigh of cool storm winds that promised more heavy rain to come. Debris was still falling from the turbulent sky like alien rain; when I dared to look up, peering through what was left of my windshield, I saw an oily adjustable wrench laid carefully between my windshield wipers like a parting gift from the tornado.

County Road 90 really *did* look like the landscape of an alien planet after the twister had finished with it. I had never considered what it might look like when the old barn finally gave it up and fell over, and seeing it was strange. There was nothing but a big structureless field now, full of jutting slats of wood, glittering glass shards, tractor parts, various tools, scattered fluffs of old insulation. I didn't know then what *real* devastation was like. A leaky old barn doesn't really compare to the sudden absence of a town you'd grown up in. I'll be writing about that, and Charlie's death, next. Once I have some alcohol in me.

Anyhow, we stayed that way, holding on to each other like a couple of lovers until the roar was all but gone and the car stopped trying to leap into the air. The tornado continued out through the fields, eating more dirt and growing ever blacker. It had long invisible arms, reaching out and lifting mammoth handfuls of thick earth into itself. Charlie and I finally climbed out of my car, toeing broken boards out of our way, and watched it leave in stunned silence.

As it gouged its way across the muddy fields, it grew. And grew. And *grew*. It seemed like the dirt it was sucking up was feeding it, and in a matter of minutes that thing had quadrupled in thickness. It no longer resembled a funnel; it had ballooned out into a bowl, a fat, squat thing wedged in between the clouds and the ground. It was wider than it was tall. Seeing it move was like watching a stalking dinosaur or something; things that huge just weren't supposed to move the way it did. It didn't feel possible.

"Wedge," Charlie crooned in a dreamy, fascinated mumble. I snuck a peek over his dirt-blasted shoulder and watched as he filmed. He had the tornado framed perfectly, and with the early afternoon sunlight sneaking peeks from behind the blockade of storm clouds, the sky behind it was a work of art. It was streaked with shades of orange, blue, and murky green. Small pieces of debris soared and hovered around it like drunken birds.

"Good name for it," I managed, suddenly feeling very tired as I came down from my adrenaline high. I wanted to go back to bed and think of nothing other than what we had just survived; perhaps try to wrap my mind around how close we'd come to death. That was enough adventure for the week, thank you very much.

I was finally able to breathe a little easier watching the monster twister moving out into the nothingness of rural Oklahoma. I knew there were scarcely any houses or farms out that way and no lives were in danger, except for maybe some grazing cattle. I've never been big on praying, but I can tell you I prayed right then and there, standing in the middle of C.R. 90 with a mixture of mud and nervous sweat beading on my forehead. I thanked God that the tornado had shifted its path (even though that meant it had turned back on us) and chose to eat dirt instead of Bent Knee. If it had grown to that size just before it struck town... well, I imagine it would have been about like what happened a year later. Total devastation, scattered bodies... and then days later, the subtle sweet-sour odor of the bodies yet to be pulled from the wreckage. Hell on earth.

We watched the twister until it weakened, shedding girth like a cancer patient until it was nothing more than a looping, writhing snake that barely maintained contact with the ground. Charlie told me it was "roping out", which I took to be a good thing if it meant it was dying. When the funnel disappeared, there was still a little ball of dust and wreckage left behind, levitating and swirling like a multitude of flies. It was the only thing that kept me believing I had just seen what I had seen. As soon as a tornado is gone, it becomes mythical again. You start questioning if it was even there at all. That is, until you walk through the carnage it left behind.

Warbling sirens began to mix and overlap with the air raid screaming of the tornado alarm. Charlie and I glanced back to see the purple flashes of red and blue police lights, coming fast but late to the party. I could hear the screech of rubber and the crunch of gravel as they cut onto 90.

Little late to the movie, fellas, I thought to myself as my teeth began to chatter.

Charlie nudged my arm, and when I turned back, he was holding an ancient screwdriver in his scratched and bloodied hand. The metal shaft of the tool had been bent onto a check mark shape, the faded plastic handle shattered and barely hanging on.

"Souvenir for ya, Max," he said with a proud grin, slapping it into my sweaty palm. He tapped the mounted camera on the side of his helmet, knocking a tiny clot of dirt from it. "I got mine right here. We're going to be famous."

* * *

You know, it's amazing how much shit can happen once you get started reading something. Or in my case, writing something. My wrist feels hot and a little bit broken from all that scribbling, and I need a new pen to even attempt to finish this. More than a fresh pen, though, I need a drink.

The power is still out, and the wind is rushing around my little place like white water rapids around an unimpressive rock. I filled a tall glass with peach flavored Ol' Smokey, no ice to dilute it, and shuffled out onto my little porch. Sipping on some cheap 'shine, even as the wind threatened to yank it out of my mouth, I gazed out over the fields with a sense of calm that is still relatively new to me. You wouldn't believe what I saw.

There's a tornado on the ground out there as I'm writing this, what Charlie once called a "night devil" in one of our million conversations about severe weather. It's pitch-black outside if not for the lightning, and that's the only way anyone would be able to see it coming. It reminds me of the strobe lights in the half-assed haunted house they put up at the fair every fall. Every few seconds or so the whole sky lights up blue-white and you can spot it, only for a breath or two; a long black vine growing down out of the clouds, reaching to tear up the Oklahoma dirt that is already so weary of twisters. I just stood there and watched it, slurping the burning alcohol down and thumbing tears from my eyes. I don't think it will hit town, and I monitored it long enough to know that it's not heading my way. It's just a mindless force of nature, going about its temper tantrum with no regard to the lives it could change so easily. Then again, I've seen a tornado make a U turn and come right at me. If it comes my way, at least I'll be down here in the basement where it's safe. Maybe I should call it in after all, just to make sure the cops know it's out there.

 So. I mentioned earlier that Charlie made the local news, remember? The footage he shot during our storm chase turned out to be better, closer, and more visceral than *anything* the pros had sent in. I should hope so, seeing as how it nearly took my car with both of us in it. He came out to my place to watch the newscast the night it was set to air, only a day or two after our little cuddle session on county road 90. He showed up with a 24 pack of beer (that he had convinced his uncle to buy for him, I might add) and a grease-spotted brown bag of double cheeseburgers from Skinny's. As I welcomed him in, he fished a crumpled piece of paper from his jeans pocket and tossed it at me. I unfolded it and saw that it was a shittily drawn I.O.U card, complete with a cartoon tornado hurtling trees at two frowning stick figures. The letters I, O and U were being thrown through the air above the stick people's lopsided heads.

 "The hell is this, your homework?" I chuckled, helping myself to a lukewarm beer.

 "For your windshield, asshole," he said, chugging from his own can and then burping like a bullfrog. "They *bought* my video, Max. I didn't donate it to them."

 "No *shit!*" I hollered, slapping him a brisk high five that echoed off the walls of my cramped living room. "How much?"

 Charlie's face turned a muted shade of red, and it wasn't from the beer raising his temperature.

"Five hundred," he said, with a humble shrug. "It's not much, but it'll at least help pay for a new one. Least I can do for the experience of a lifetime."

He held his can out to me, and I tapped it gently with mine. I hated to take his money. Every fiber of my being was screaming at me to refuse it, but I honestly had no choice. I only had one car, and I barely had enough money in the bank to cover my mortgage for the month. That's not counting groceries and utilities, either. Had I been pulled over and ticketed for driving with my windshield looking like a dropped jigsaw puzzle, I would have been deep in the red.

We each had a decent buzz on even before the news started; I was never big on drinking, and when I did (as I do now) I never bothered to pace myself. Charlie was still a young kid who really hadn't had time to do much partying. As you may have guessed, he wasn't exactly the partying type anyway. We both had the tolerance of toddlers.

I was kicked back in the recliner with a loopy grin on my face that wouldn't seem to go away, and Charlie was stretched out on my couch. We had begun to build a short, flimsy tower of dented beer cans on my wobbly antique coffee table. It served as a fort to help defend against the noxious farts we kept firing at each other.

"I wonder..." Charlie said, pausing to think as he tapped one finger on his forehead. "I wonder if they'll see this news report in Kalida."

"Where the fuck is Kalida?" I asked, stuffing my face with a soggy burger I was too full to eat.

"Where my dad lives," he replied distantly, his eyes shimmering and unfocused. "Where I moved here from. It's in Ohio."

"Well, it's a local station," I slurred. "It's WBLO. I think Owenton is the farthest town away that can pick it up. It's a great video though dude. It might go viral."

"Bummer," he said, and his usual bright and alert expression was replaced with one that looked more like a lonely old man. His whole body seemed to slump down into the couch.

"Maybe we can record it somehow," I said. "Mail it to him or put it on YouTube or something. We'll find a way to show your dad, man."

Charlie waved me off.

"He probably wouldn't give a shit anyway. He's pretty much always told me that my obsession with storms and science and anything *not* football is stupid, and that I'll end up on the street if I don't learn a 'real trade'. He's a mechanic. I always told my mom that if I had a broken engine, he'd care about me more. Probably understand me a little more, too."

Charlie stared at my floor, his pointer fingers picking ceaselessly at the skin around his thumbnails. Then, he went back to stroking his forehead.

"I told him once that I would rather die in a tornado, with a two-by-four through my head, than end up a grease monkey like him. That was *not* a smart thing to say to him, Max. He punched me for it. Right here." He flipped his bangs out of his face and tapped the center of his forehead, the spot he had been habitually massaging. Even through my beer goggles I could make out a tiny arrow-shaped scar just under his hairline that I had never noticed before. I assumed it was because his hair or his helmet hid it most of the time, but even so; how had I never noticed it? "Knocked me out cold, right there in the garage. Bastard had a ring on too, a stupid skull with wrenches instead of crossbones."

Charlie became lost in a tide of painful memories, his eyes twitching in their sockets and his lips moving to form silent words. He seemed to be praying, though I never knew him to be religious at all. Religion and sciency-type people don't mix, and it's a rare case when they do.

"You know, I don't even remember what it *felt* like when he decked me. All I remember is waking up in the hospital, and of course he was there. Sitting beside the bed, rubbing his eyes like he was so worried about me. He was talking to all the doctors and nurses like nothing was wrong, nothing had happened between us, like he wasn't the one that..."

He disappeared again, reliving it. He flinched, a hardly noticeable twitch of facial muscles, like that ringed fist was striking him again. *No,* I thought sternly to myself. *I will not let his big night be ruined. Charlie Dillon* will *be happy tonight.*

I downed the rest of my beer and chucked the empty can at him. It bounced from his temple with a hollow ringing sound and clattered to the floor. His head snapped up, and I guffawed at the stunned look on his face.

"Why?" He stammered, and I lost my shit all over again. It may seem cruel, but it snapped him out of those nightmare memories, didn't it?

"Listen," I finally gasped out, once my laughing fit had subsided. I dumped myself out of the chair and tottered over to him. I slapped my palm against his, hooking our thumbs together and yanking him up from the couch and into a tight bear hug. "Fuck your dad and fuck grease monkeys. *I'm* proud of you. The whole town is. You made the news, dude, that's something a legit storm chaser would do. If it hadn't been for you, how brave you were staring that thing down, I would have hauled ass out of there as soon as I saw the dirt whirl. Shit, pretty soon everyone in town is gonna want to meet you, and then you'll have to fight the women off with both hands. Guys like me won't be able to get laid around you. Unless we crawl up a chicken's ass and wait, that's the fastest way. Or so my grandpa said."

He blushed, the welling redness of his skin making his hair look startlingly blonde. That contagious grin found its way back again and he finally allowed himself to laugh. He didn't want to. He wanted to do as he had been trained to do. Beat himself up. Question his sanity because of the things he had come to love about life. That kind of self-hatred was rare for Charlie, but when it reared its ugly head, it came on… well, it came on like a tornado. I wouldn't allow it.

"Thanks, Max," he said quietly. "I had a good partner."

The opening melody of trumpet blasts blared from the TV speakers as the WBLO nightly news started, and our mouths stayed sealed all the way up until the newscast ended. I half watched the segment and half watched him. I wish I had a picture of that, especially now that he's gone. It was pure happiness, and the tiny hint of sadness that always haunted Charlie's eyes and cast a worried shadow over his face was nowhere to be seen. I don't know which part he liked more; seeing his footage used on the news, or just seeing CLOSE CALL WITH MONSTER TORNADO (VIDEO BY CHARLIE DILLON) superimposed on a dangerous looking red banner beneath it. One thing I *do* know for certain is that Charlie's father, whoever he is, threw away a fortune when he drove Charlie away. I hope he ended up miserable and alone, with nothing but junk cars and stuck bolts to keep him company.

    I was right, you know. Bent Knee fell in love with Charlie after seeing his tornado video, and that's when his legend really began. You know how small towns are. The stories get told and retold, this person adds a bit on to make it more exciting. It's all a giant game of "telephone". I think the craziest thing I heard about that day was that Charlie had been impaled by a flying piece of timber and kept on filming, holding the camera with one hand and keeping his guts in with the other. We laughed our asses off at that one. Some of the stories mentioned my name; my car had been flipped or picked up and carried a few miles before being sat down, unharmed on its wheels. Or I was sucked out the windshield and thrown, wrapped in a barbed wire fence and found, unharmed, in the branches of a tree. Crazy stories that could have been disproven simply by looking at us and our lack of scars, but they spread through town like a wildfire. I never got as popular as Charlie though, and I'm glad for it. *He* deserved all that fame, not the guy who tagged along with him down a road that scared the pros away. I was just glad you couldn't hear me screaming in the video.

* * *

    Five months before he died, Charlie finally got himself a pretty little girlfriend. We were at work the day they met, and at first, I thought she was there to see me. I saw this gorgeous little thing glide in the front door of the DashMart, the summer sun glowing in her strawberry blonde hair as a gentle breeze blew it from her shoulders. She pulled it back into a ponytail as she approached my counter, her upraised arms pulling a faded Van Halen T-shirt tight across her breasts and exposing the smooth ridges of her swaying hips. Her jean shorts were so high on those tanned thighs that at first, I thought she was wearing a bikini. I was eyeing the tattered white strings that trailed across her skin as she finally stood in front of me, carrying with her the scent of some wonderful perfume.

"You're Max, right?" She said, batting her honey brown eyes and tossing gum around with her tongue. She smiled, and I noticed that she had a smattering of freckles across the bridge of her nose. That smile stopped my heart and erased the English language from my brain.

"Uh... yeah, that's uh… that's what they named me," I managed, struggling against the horny nervousness thrashing around in my lower stomach like an alligator caught in a snare. I'll admit here in these pages that it was a struggle to keep my eyes locked on hers. They wanted to wander up and down, document every curve and detail, but I had made up my mind not to be crude. It's not impossible for a man to behave himself. I had never seen the beautiful girl before, and if she had come in specifically to meet me, I didn't want her first impression of me to be that I was a creep. "Can I uh... can I help you?"

"I hope so," she said confidently. "You know Charlie Dillon, right? The guy that filmed the tornado video, out on 90?"

My heart sank into the pit of ice water that had replaced my stomach. I relaxed my chest, which I hadn't even realized I'd been puffing out at her like a horned-up bird.

"Charlie, yeah. He's one of my best friends. My best friend, actually." I hesitated, then shamelessly added, "I was driving when we chased the tornado." What a loser.

"I heard that. You guys are *wild.* So... is he here?"

She stared at me expectantly, eyes shining like a cat's. She had given me all the time she was willing to, which I imagine was ten seconds longer than most guys got.

Wow, I thought with a proud little smirk. *You know who I am?* I freely admit, I was a little jealous of Charlie. That jealousy intensified when I paged him back to my desk and she walked away to meet him, and my eyes started to wander again. I never let that jealously interfere with my happiness for him.

When he came out of the warehouse, covered in a coat of sweat and dust and his hair an absolute rat's nest, I feared for his chances with that stunning gal. But he surprised me again, as he always did; he was totally cool and calm, and she seemed to find every word he said to be hilarious or stupefyingly interesting. I tried to busy myself with reading another borrowed comic, but I couldn't help but steal glances at them. I smiled to myself as I saw him hand her his phone, and she began typing her number into his contacts with one slender finger.

Atta boy, Charles. If only your bastard dad could see you now.

That pretty girl was named Cassie Beltzer, and I know what you must be thinking of her— she was a slut who wanted to get with Charlie because he was getting popular. I thought that too at first, when I'd had a little time to consider it all. I was shocked to find out later that she was kind of a closeted weather nerd herself. She kept it hidden because it clashed with the image the people of Bent Knee demanded her to maintain (lest she become a social pariah like Charlie was). She had been forced into cheerleading in junior high and then every sport she was eligible for. She was a slave to her mother, the head coach of girls' basketball, volleyball, and softball, and her heart had been promised without her consent to the most celebrated football player in town. That curse had followed her even after she had graduated and started college hunting, and so she was trapped in a limbo of young adulthood.

Charlie was like her savior, a modern-day Romeo Montague who wore a busted hail helmet and a mounted camera instead of a dagger on his hip. It took some time, but he taught her to love herself, to embrace who she was regardless of what other people might say about it. Her mom and his dad would have made a nice couple, don't you think? That gift was a treasure not many other guys in town could have offered her, and she knew it. Her devotion to him was absolute.

I watched their relationship grow over the last months of Charlie's life, like watching a stubborn rosebush finally bloom in a barren flower bed. It all started with one light touch on his bicep, right after she had given him her coveted phone number. In no time at all they were leaving the store with their arms locked around each other, walking slowly, enjoying every second of it. I never bothered to spy on anything else they did. Like I said, I'm not a creep.

You could tell by the way Cassie stared at Charlie that she loved him. He'd be miles away, focused on some cloud formation or analyzing some new development on his radar apps, and she'd just be fixated on him. Grinning all the while. As stunning as Cassie was to look at, no matter what outfit she chose to wear on any given day, I would have chosen death over even *considering* pursuing her myself. It would have been a lost cause anyway. Cassie and Charlie were inseparable.

She liked to spend most of her free time hanging around the DashMart once she and Charlie had dared to make it official. Nobody minded having her around. To Elias and me, she had become the female version of Charlie himself, which automatically earned her a place in our hearts. You could say we loved her too, but in a way that transcended her physical beauty and cut to the good stuff, the *important* stuff, under her skin. To Jim... well, "Diesel" was never interested in speaking to her. He chose to speak *about* her, but he learned fast to watch what he said around us. I know Charlie saw him drooling over his girl; Jim was about as stealthy as an army tank. I'm happy to write that Cassie was about as impressed by his muscles and his truck as the rest of us, and he began to pull away from our little clan. We didn't force him out, we weren't that kind of people, but there was no denying that he was a square peg and we were a round hole. People grow, people change, and sometimes good friends become total strangers. It's a hard fact of life, but one you can bet on.

Cassie was there on the last day we saw Charlie alive. Looking back, it's just like watching a movie; I remember every detail down to the smudges in the dust on my counter and Jim brooding outside, leaning against a cart corral with a cigarette in his mouth. Elias was at his usual post by the door, beaming at the customers and locking them into the occasional chat. He had made a pot of coffee that morning that had somehow left the break room smelling like burnt skunk, and I never got used to that smell. Not for my entire shift. I can smell it like he's upstairs in the kitchen brewing it right now, a phantom scent from the scarred part of my memory bank. I'd give anything to smell it for real.

Jim had bathed in cheap cologne that day and had suddenly wanted to spend more time crowding my counter than he did stocking shelves. He reeked of cigarette smoke and kept his eyes on Cassie's body even as he described to me (in painful detail) what type of giant tires he was saving up to buy. Trying his best to fit in, you know? I never did make it through the Spawn comic I had borrowed from the magazine rack.

"Attention DashMart shoppers," came Charlie's voice over the PA. He'd really refined his voice by then, he sounded every bit as professional as someone you'd see on the Weather Channel. "This is just an update on today's weather conditions. There's a small line of storms developing west of Bent Knee that is intensifying as it approaches, and one cell in particular is showing signs of rotation. Hancock county is currently under a tornado watch, and I expect things to get rocky within the next few hours. I suggest you finish your shopping and head home immediately, and make sure your tornado safety plan is in order."

Writing this now, I can't help but wonder how many lives Charlie might have saved with that page. People listened to him. He was like a local celebrity at that point, on his way to becoming the next Gary England (another hero of his) and anyone who could get as close as we got to a tornado and survived *had* to know what he was talking about. It makes me nauseous to think that he was analyzing and tracking the very same storm that would kill him a handful of hours later. He had no idea that his time on Earth was counting down with each mile that supercell traveled closer to our town. Then again, not many people who bite the big one wake up planning to die. No one gets into their car and expects the fatal accident that closes out the final chapter of their lives. Fuck, I might not even survive *tonight*. But that's the essence of living in tornado alley. Every tornado season could be your last.

I started to get that hot nervous ache in my guts when everything outside went green. It was ugly out there. Fun fact: the sky turning green doesn't *always* mean a tornado is going to happen, it has something to do with the sun setting behind a particularly big thunderhead that causes that ugly shade to happen. But you bet your ass it was green that day, as green as a martini olive. The few customers that had trickled in after Charlie's announcement were milling around the aisles, not shopping, but waiting. They knew better than to try to make it home. Once it looks like that outside, it's too late. You're fucked. And most people killed by twisters are caught in their cars, trying to outrun them.

    Cassie was sitting on my counter with her arms wrapped around Charlie's narrow frame, periodically kissing his hairless cheek and watching him thoughtfully. She didn't have the option to kiss his mouth. His gaze stayed locked to the front of the store, as if he were some sort of meteorological security guard that could somehow prevent a tornado if he just kept his eye on the storm. I could see his cheek flexing as he ground his teeth together, his Adam's apple bobbing as he swallowed.

    "It looks like tornado weather," Cassie said, punctuating the thought with another kiss.

    I reached my arm out and flicked the lobe of Charlie's ear, harder than I meant to, and he didn't even blink.

    "Dude. You alright?" I asked, waving my hand and snapping my fingers to get his attention. He nodded slowly, like a toddler absorbed in cartoons. "You got a pretty girl smooching on you, you know. You might want to enjoy it a little."

    "Max," he said, his voice gravelly. I was instantly struck by that fatal, doomy tone. "This is *bad.* I've been tracking this system, watching it form and eat smaller systems, watching it build, and... I think we're in deep shit, man."

    Cassie's face drained of blood, turning her cheeks into sheets of wax paper. Her face was an odd mixture of fear and excitement; she was thrilled at the possibility of seeing a tornado, but she knew Charlie as well as I did. His expression carried the same punch as a terminal cancer diagnosis, and it terrified both of us.

    "What do you mean, babe?" She asked, her eyes shining wetly. He lifted her hand from his waist and kissed her knuckles, keeping her fingers pressed against his lips for a few moments before he spoke again.

"I think… I *know* this storm is going to produce a whole family of tornadoes. The wind shear, the humidity today... it's hard to explain, but we are directly in the path of one of the worst lines of storms I've ever seen. You couldn't ask for better conditions to see a strong tornado. I'm talking EF-4, EF-5 type shit."

Elias slowly plodded over to us, coming from the direction of the bitch boss's office as thunder began to vibrate the hot, thick air outside. It sounded like a giant bowling ball rolling down the street and stood my hair on end.

"Darke county got a tornado warning," Elias said, his ever-present smile lingering under his mustache but his eyes alert and serious. "It's headin' right our way, boys. Boss lady thinks we might oughtta start bringing customers back to the warehouse, but I think all that's gonna do is scare 'em half to death."

He fished his harmonica out of his breast pocket and tooted it a few times, as if confirming that the ancient instrument still worked.

"I think I might join 'em up front for a while, see if I can't lighten it up in here. Shit, we're gonna be just fine. Just fine."

Charlie patted the old man's back.

"It's been too long since I've heard you play anyway," he said, and Elias glowed like a brand-new light bulb. Charlie was acting more like a supervisor than the bitch boss was, and we were all more than willing to listen to him. He was a born leader, and you can't convince me that he wouldn't have gone on to be the lead scientist of his own storm chasing caravan if he had survived. He was worried sick; no man can every *truly* hide that. But he was getting shit done.

"Max, I think you should head back to the warehouse and make sure we have everything we need for an emergency. Bottled water, pillar candles, blankets. Stuff like that. If bitch boss says anything to you, tell her I'll pay for it. If we're lucky, we won't need it and there will still be shelves to put it all back on."

I didn't say a word— I nodded once and followed my orders. I zig zagged up and down the aisles, grabbing an armful of scented pillar candles and a package of Bic lighters. Next, I grabbed three or four quilts, smashing their plastic packaging against my chest and scampering through the double doors to drop them off. Finally, I lugged two packs of bottled water back, adding them to my little emergency stockpile and swiping one for myself. My mouth was dry and sandy.

Elias was doing his job and doing it well. It had begun to rain outside as the storm front moved in, and the strengthening winds were pushing sheets of it across the cracked pavement like miniature tidal waves. The customers in the store were shifty and tense, but they were all smiling through it. They stood clustered around Elias as he cupped his hands around the harmonica and made up another song. His long right leg bounced up and down rhythmically as he tapped his loafer against the floor.

"Well, we're stuck here at the DashMart," he sang, pausing between each line to blow a few tinny notes. *"Nowhere else to go. That wind is gettin' nasty boy, but we're gonna let it blow. The sun, it ain't a shinin'. But I know it will again. Ain't scared of no tornadoes boy, they only make me grin!"*

Jim skulked out of the break room, a sickened look on his face and a dead cigarette jutting from his teeth like a toothpick.

"You guys might want to come in here," he murmured. We exchanged worried glances and turned to follow him, leaving Elias and his small audience behind.

The TV caught my attention immediately. The blood red banner across the bottom of the video feed read TORNADO EMERGENCY in bold, white letters. Someone in a helicopter was circling just outside the storm's reach, drifting in slow circles. I could hear the muffled *chuppa chuppa chuppa* of the rotor blades and the insectile whine of the engine. At that moment they were flying over a field, indistinguishable from the hundred thousand other fields just like it. There were no landmarks that we could spot. Slashing through the field was a young twister, looping and curving its way down from the smoky clouds like a wayward shoestring. It was blue green, a color that reminded me of rotten Robin's eggs. The little whirl of dirt rapidly orbiting its base looked like the haggard bristles on the end of an old broom.

"Right now, we're calling tornado warnings in Darke and Hancock counties," came the dry and analytic voice of the WBLO weatherman, Bill Travers. "If you live in those counties, you need to seek shelter immediately. This line of storms is nothing to scoff at, this is the kind of storm we always tell you folks to prepare for."

"That's going to grow," Charlie said, fixated on the TV screen. Cassie pulled him in close to her, and he began to brush through her long hair with his fingers. "You can tell just by looking at the way the storm moves, the inflow is insane." His face was a maniacal mixture of terror and fascination, like his brain couldn't decipher which emotion was the dominant one.

"Well, maybe *you* can tell," I said, feeling like I was back in the car again with yet another tornado hunting me down. My stomach ached and I thought I might need to listen for weather updates from the crapper, and soon. "All I see is a big ugly spaghetti noodle."

My bad sense of humor wasn't working any miracles, and the grim silence that followed my piss-poor attempt at a joke was embarrassing. The break room felt more like a funeral parlor than our place for eating and swapping dirty jokes.

As if in response to Charlie, Bill Travers said, "Those of you watching at home, I cannot stress this enough: do not be fooled by the appearance of this tornado, this is an intense, *strong* tornado. Storm chasers on the ground are reporting wind speeds approaching 138 miles per hour and *climbing*. I wouldn't be surprised to see this thing balloon out."

"Do we have a rating on this tornado, Bill?" Came the shaky voice of a female newscaster; I can't recall her name.

"We won't have a definitive rating until damage is assessed, but the wind speed already has this storm in the EF-3 range; this has the potential to be a deadly, *deadly* tornado. Conway, Buck, Bent Knee, Salisbury— all these cities are directly in the damage path, if you're living in those cities you need to seek shelter *immediately*. I'm gonna go ahead and say it, you need to be underground for this storm. I'm gonna repeat that. You need to be *beneath ground level* for this tornado."

As the helicopter completed another circle, a thin ribbon of country road came into view. I could see a line of three or four chase vehicles tearing down it, leaving wispy clouds of dirt and mist in their paths. One of them, a decent-sized truck, had a big rotating radar dish mounted on the back of it. Compared to the funnel, they looked like nothing more than frightened ants trying to escape a bird. My heart skipped a beat as I registered just how close to the churning debris cloud they were. If the tornado shifted its path and headed for the road, as *our* tornado had done, they would all be killed.

The staticky voice of the helicopter pilot buzzed in and said, "Bill, the funnel is getting thicker, do you see that?"

It was. We watched it happen. At first, I thought the tornado was just wrapped in a veil of rain and dust, but then when the swirling vapor began to condense into cloud, I realized how wrong I was. It only took a minute or two and then I was totally slack jawed, watching yet *another* tornado morph into a bulbous cone, a beast that was as wide as it was tall. Then, *wider* than it was tall. I was thrown back to my storm chase with Charlie; there was a name for a tornado like that. What had he called it?

Wedge.

"That's a wedge, right Charlie?" I asked, timid but proud.

"Oh yeah, that's a wedge alright. We need to get our shit together here."

On the TV, I watched as the spinning cylinder of cloud lurched toward a farm. A grain silo was blown backwards and crushed in like an old pop can, hundreds of thousands of microscopic kernels of corn spraying out and swarming into the funnel like fireflies. The barn and farmhouse stood no chance. They were there and then they were rubble, huge sections of the buildings lifting off their foundations like ramshackle airplanes and immediately being devoured by the savage upward rotation. The cameraman in the helicopter zoomed in on the impossibly wide base of the twister, trying to focus on something white and glinting that was rolling around among the swirling chaos and merciless violence. It was a semi-truck, still clinging tenuously to its trailer. Barrel rolling and collapsing, it took clumsy flight and then crashed back down to the unforgiving earth to start the process over again. I still promise myself that no one was inside the cab. Somewhere deep inside the funnel, the bright blue flashes of shredding power lines popped and sparkled like cheap fireworks.

"Oh, Jesus I hope they're okay!" The pilot shouted, his voice breaking with undeniable panic. The tornado was now so gigantic that the video feed looked like nothing more than a black horizon, the picture tilting crazily as the chopper banked to flee the area.

"Ladies and gentlemen this is developing into a massive wedge tornado, uh... we're praying for the residents of that farmhouse, but you all just saw the destructive capability..." Travers began to sputter, but none of us were listening. We were listening to the wail of the tornado siren outside, its low mechanical groan rising steadily into another ear-piercing, pants-shitting scream.

The boss (I'll refrain from calling her the bitch boss this time, because she did end up handling herself bravely and compassionately that day) jogged into the break room with us. She was glistening with sweat, her usually neat and tidy hair frazzled and radiating a corona of rogue hairs that made her look like she'd been struck by lightning. I could smell her rapid breaths from across the room; she'd been chain smoking again, probably to cope with her nerves. Up until that day, we'd all thought she'd quit. Apparently beating cancer wasn't quite the motivator we all thought it would be.

"A shopping cart just hit someone's car and shattered the window," she said in a traumatized, robotic voice. "Elias is taking all of the customers back to the warehouse until this thing blows over. You guys too, come on."

"Not good enough," Charlie snapped at her, and she recoiled as if he had thrown a brick at her head.

"It's all we have, Charles. It'll have to be good enough."

Charlie shook his head, closing his eyes as he sifted through every possible option.

"This storm isn't going to 'blow over' any more than a lawn mower 'blows over' grass. It's going to tear right through us. If we're above ground when it gets here, we're as good as dead."

The power flickered off, and when it came back on the fluorescent lights had a sick, weak glow. The siren moaned on and on, reaching its highest note and holding it for what felt like hours before whooping back down again.

"Jim. The semi garage out back; does it have a pit? For oil changes and stuff?" Charlie demanded.

Jim looked out of breath, sheer terror sending his heart into rapid, epileptic spasms. He nodded his head as if his neck were a short, taught spring.

"Yeah. It's not very long, but it's about as deep as I am tall. There are wooden planks they use to cover it with, so nobody falls in. We could make a roof over our heads with those!"

Charlie slapped the idea away with a quick, decisive swipe of his hand.

"They won't stay in place, but if we're all down in the pit we might stand a chance. A lot of the debris should be carried right over us."

He turned to the boss lady, who shuddered like a frightened mouse awaiting the claws of an approaching cat. A *hungry* cat.

"*That's* where we need to go, ma'am. Trust me."

The power blinked again as if to reinforce his point. She considered it a moment, then gave him a shaky thumbs up and turned to run back out into the store, heels clacking against the linoleum.

"Max," he said, turning to face me. I glanced back and forth from his stony grimace to Cassie's pretty, agonized frown. "You'll help me bring the supplies?"

"Absolutely. But we gotta move, *now*."

"Agreed."

Despite the urgency that seemed to be stealing my ability to breathe, I hung behind for a few seconds and turned the TV back on. I was hypnotized by what the helicopter was filming. They had flown far enough away to bank around and show the entire tornado again, but by that point it didn't even *look* like a tornado anymore. You know how sometimes you can look out across the fields, right before a thunderstorm hits, and it looks like a huge patch of fog and dark clouds is coming all the way down to the ground? That's what it looked like, no clearly defined funnel shape. It was a monstrous blob of green and black and brown, rotating and eating.

I could see buildings in the shadow of the monster like doll houses about to be flattened by the unforgiving treads of a truck tire. I could also make out the Y shaped semicircles of the railroad tracks. From the height of the chopper, the stitch-like rail lines gave the fields the appearance of a crudely sewn quilt. That told me the twister was moving near the rail yard, which was across town and southwest from us; we had a little time, but not much. When I saw the boxy shapes of massive train cars pulling up from the station and hurtling into the chaotic debris cloud that tore around the base of the "funnel", I had seen enough. Train cars weigh about 130 tons, in case you didn't know.

When I finally got back to the warehouse, I saw Elias fighting to hold the back door open so a pair of sobbing Golden Girls could hobble through. His slender brown arms were quivering against the wind, beads of glistening sweat dotting his wrinkled forehead and the bridge of his button nose.

"Jim went on ahead to get the garage situated," Elias gasped in a husky voice, visibly shaken and already exhausted. He barely got clear of the door before the vicious winds slammed it shut like an angry spirit. "That thing ain't even to our side of town yet and it's already tearing stuff up, Max. I just saw a 'yield' sign fly over the store. I think it might be time to de-ass the area."

"Alright, me and Charlie will finish up in here. You go on and—"

My words snagged in my throat when I saw Elias fishing his jangling key ring from his pocket. A Jesus fish keychain glinted in the murky lights of the warehouse, alongside a crucifix and a homemade keychain made from tiny plastic letter beads. It read "GRAMPA".

"What the hell are you doing?" I asked, my voice trembling with anger that seemed to boil up in my chest from some demonic wellspring within me.

"Max, I ain't boxing myself in that little pit," Elias said matter-of-factly, his weathered face stoic and somehow free of any panic. "I'm gonna run my ass out of town. It can't be moving faster than my car can go. I offered a few customers the chance to go with me, but they wanted to hide out there. That's fine. That's their choice. But you can come if you want to."

Elias didn't seem to notice or care that all eyes were staring at him, our mouths agape.

"Are you fucking *crazy?!*" I shouted at him, and instantly regretted it. Elias just smirked, cocking his mustache to one side, and began to shuffle back towards the front of the store. I wasn't done yet. It felt like he was marching outside to kill himself, and if I let him do it, I would be just as responsible for his death as the incoming tornado. I snatched him by the arm, wincing at how thin and fragile his body felt beneath my digging fingers. I was terrified for his safety, and yet I wanted to pound him to the floor. Knock him out cold and drag him to our best chance at survival.

"Now, Max, you let me go," he said, with no trace of impatience or dread in his voice. His serenity was maddening. I hated him for making me worry about him. I hated him for making me love him. He was like a father to us guys, or at the very least, a favorite uncle. All I wanted was to keep him safe, to keep *everyone* safe. My head was a horror show of images I couldn't help but dream up. I kept imagining one of those train cars dropping from the sky and landing on Elias's car like a cruel boot heel dropping on a harmless insect.

"Elias," I barely managed, my voice trembling as I fought tears. "You could get killed out there man. You *know* that."

"I could get killed *here*," he said, extending a hand and squeezing my shoulder. "I lived through more tornadoes than you ever thought about, kid. Never seen one like this though. I think my best chance is to outrun it. I'm an old man, Max. My body can't handle what yours can. And you know every man's gotta go his own way."

He arched his eyebrows and cocked his head to one side, as if daring me to argue. I knew better, and every second I wasted trying to stop him was another second closer to annihilation we all got. I gave him a fast, tight hug, breathing in an aftershave that only an old man would have chosen for himself, and then lightly shoved him toward the door.

"We'll see you when it's over," I said, and forced a smile. Watching that lovable old man trot out the door and into the hostile wind was the last time any of us saw him alive. He didn't even wave. He was just gone.

Charlie and Cassie had busied themselves gathering up our emergency supplies, and as I began tucking packages under my elbows and chin, the tornado siren cut off so abruptly that it felt like the twister had slashed the town's throat. The power went out for good shortly after, plunging us all into near total darkness. All I could hear was my own fast, ragged breathing, and the howl and hiss of the wind outside. There was a hint of movement in front of me, and then sickly light slowly began to flood back in from outside. Charlie was fighting the door open, shoving with his legs and pushing with his back as papers and leaves and tiny pieces of pink fluff whirled around between his feet.

Insulation, I thought, eyeing the little pink tufts of cottony material. *It's taking houses.*

"We gotta move, Max!" Charlie bellowed, barely audible over the wind. He dug his shoes into the oily gravel and held the door open long enough for Cassie and me to dart through it. Then the three of us were making a panicked sprint to the garage. A middle-aged man I didn't know (though I recognized him as a DashMart regular) was fighting his own battle to keep the garage entrance open, beckoning to us frantically as the wind snatched the OU hat from his thinning scalp and carried it away into eternity. I'll never forget the flailing rope of drool that clung to his lips as he called out to us; the wind was literally sucking the spit from our mouths.

I nearly fell into the mechanics' pit. The sunlight we needed to navigate the cluttered workshop was already fading with the storm, not to mention the fact that the rays had to shine through dingy garage windows on the brightest of days. I could just make out a yawning blackness, cut into the floor like an open grave. Unseen tools clattered and clanked as we tripped over them. I prayed they wouldn't become bullets.

We dogpiled in, and the best way I can describe what it was like in that pit is a hot and sweaty mass of bodies, reeking of assorted perfumes and colognes and the acrid stench of terror. The first time I felt my hand crushed under someone's heavy work boot I remember thinking, *maybe Elias was on to something. Maybe we came down here to die like sardines.* I don't even know where most of our supplies ended up, we were all so damn scared for our lives. I could hear plastic crackling as the blankets were torn open, and then we were all clambering for them, unfolding them and draping them over our heads like children building a fort in the living room.

Nobody noticed that Charlie hadn't stayed in the pit until Cassie started screaming. I thought I had heard the heavy garage door open and slam shut again, but that could have been the suction of the wind for all I knew. Under that stifling blanket, claustrophobic and suffocating, it was hard to make heads or tails of *any* damn thing. Once she really got going though, I knew in my gut what had happened. I felt the blood in my veins chill over, and it didn't take long for the ice to reach my heart and shatter it like a frozen pipe.

Charlie couldn't resist seeing the tornado with his own eyes; couldn't allow himself to hide with the rest of us while the storm of a lifetime raged outside without him. I wish I knew when that thought had first infiltrated his rational thinking. He would have wanted to film it, further secure his reputation as a storm chaser who could hang with the big dogs. After a lifetime of watching other people's videos, gawking at other people's photos, he wanted to feel the power flowing around him for once in his life. I think he wanted that more than he wanted to live.

"He's gone!" Cassie was shrieking, hysterical, her voice no longer sounding like her own. *"He went outside, he said he loved me but he was going outside, why would he leave meeeeee..."*

There was an uproarious murmur as everyone in the pit lied to her in unison, trying to calm her down, trying to make her believe her boyfriend would survive outside as an EF-5 tornado charged towards him. They prayed at her, crooned to her, a woman sang to her. I heard a smattering of sentence fragments; "Nobody knows tornadoes better than Charlie does" and "God is with him, God will protect him" and "Maybe it won't even hit here, honey". But they all knew just like I knew. Just like Cassie knew. Charlie was a dead man.

I think I was in too much shock to really process everything that was happening. Elias and Charlie, two of the most beloved characters in the story of my life, were suddenly absent. It was agonizing to listen to the grizzly bear roar of that catastrophic storm approaching and to know that they were out in it, somewhere far from my reach. I felt like I needed to be in two places at once, to somehow have the ability to save my own skin and save theirs as well. In the end, all any of us could do was tuck our heads down and wait to live or die. None of us knew if we would ever see a blue sky or a white cloud again.

    I could feel the air change as the twister loomed. It carried with it a noise that I couldn't hope to describe here: the deep and angry bellowing of the wind, the crashes and bangs of large metal objects (most likely cars and dumpsters) being hoisted and slammed into the brick walls of the buildings, glass shattering, metal siding squealing and wrenching as it was twisted out of shape, wooden planks snapping and crunching, roofs peeling back like flakes of dead skin and disintegrating, millions of particles of debris colliding and knocking together like rocks in a juicer. I even heard an explosion. And screams. Jesus, the *screams*. Male and female alike; a chorus of overlapping, earsplitting shrieks and guttural cries that didn't sound like they always do in the movies. They were primal, uncontrollable. The body's strange response to certain death. A reflexive cry for help that wasn't coming.

    I closed my eyes tight, trying to focus on my own breathing as my left ear popped and then my right. I could feel the ache of my abdominal muscles straining as I curled into the tightest ball that I could manage, grabbing fistfuls of the blanket and wrapping it around myself. I couldn't draw a full breath. That was okay. The air smelled awful.

    Above us, the windows began to pop like glass balloons. I could feel the sharp pieces peppering the blanket like buckshot, and believe me, I was grateful to have something to cover my skin. The blanket that saved me from a thousand lacerations had been Charlie's idea. Thinking about him while I knew he was unprotected outside, while listening to Cassie mourn him at the top of her lungs, I began to cry. There aren't many feelings that are worse than seeing your loved ones face their deaths while you can't do one fucking thing about it.

    After an indeterminable period of agonized waiting, the tornado was finally on top of us. The roar was unbearable. I clapped my hands over my ears, not just to block out the constant barrage of thunderous sound but because the change in pressure made it feel like my brains were going to shoot out my ear holes.

"*Stop!*" I screamed, in blind, senseless panic-think. *"You have to stop!"* I don't even know who I was screaming at; the twister itself or God, who had apparently nodded off in his heavenly armchair and allowed his demented child to rampage through our town. I guess I thought I could wake him up, and he'd snap his all-powerful fingers and the monster storm would simply poof away.

It didn't stop, of course. Christ, does it ever? I went on screaming myself hoarse as the garage began to disintegrate around us. I could feel the rough and grating vibrations in my throat and I was grateful for the pain. It was something to focus on, a pitiful distraction but it was *something*. I was blind and deaf. The wind was so all-consuming that it swallowed up every sound except for its own: we were inside of a waterfall, and something was making a whipping noise like a massive piece of thick fabric ripping itself in half.

Through my clenched eyelids I could see the darkness lighten ever so slightly, and I knew that meant the roof was gone. Unseen objects began to slam into us like a barrage of baseballs, thudding off my limbs and leaving hot, throbbing bruises in their wake. The stink of the tornado washed over the collapsing garage, flooding it like a river of stagnant water that flowed down into our hiding place. It smelled like dirt. Gasoline. Smoke. Tree sap. Cut grass. There was the stinging ammonia scent of fertilizer or maybe pesticide, probably gobbled up from some obliterated farm equipment outside of town. I even remember the sour hint of cow shit carried in the stampede of air and cloud and debris.

A shrieking gust of damp wind swept beneath me and lofted me up from the floor, as if an invisible hand had scooped me up like an insect to be released outside. The blanket was snatched from my hooked fingers, taking my right pinky nail with it. My whole battered body went as limp as a well-loved dog toy, and I felt myself spiraling end over end like a dead eel caught in a strong current. My shirt was ripped violently up into my armpits, allowing the dust and grit carried by the twister to sandblast my exposed torso and leave it chafed and raw. I landed on the flailing body of someone else, the palm of my hand sinking into their soft midsection and forcing a pained cry out of them that I could hear even over the cacophony of an EF-5. Then I was airborne again, at the mercy of the storm.

You'd think in a moment like that I would have been terrified, I sure as hell was up until then. I wasn't scared anymore. When you know you're about to die, not *think* you are but *know* you are, it's very peaceful. All your worries and concerns from planet Earth are gone. No more bills, no more mortgage, no more work. No more filing taxes, no more heartbreak. You relinquish all control of yourself, and you wait for your heart to stop and your brain to switch off like an antique TV set. You bargain with God; you offer your life, give it freely, if he'll just make the end fast and painless. That was me as the tornado leveled the garage we had taken shelter in, and after a while I could barely even feel the pain anymore. I suppose it was right about then that something collided with my head, and I went out like a blown lightbulb. I wish I could give you more detail, but I wasn't even in my own body for at least a few hours after the tornado picked me up. How I survived after being carried and thrown, I'll never know. What I *do* know is that when I came to, groggy, bleeding and hurting from scalp to heel, I wasn't inside a building anymore. I was on a different planet altogether.

* * *

Not all the scars I have from that day are mental. Sitting down here in the dark, I can extend my arms to the tenacious little candle flames and watch the dark dimples in my flesh fill with shadows. They look like shallow bullet holes, which I guess they are, in a way. They're scars from gravel and glass and other bits of debris, sprayed into my body like buckshot. My skin looks like the surface of a golf ball, all up and down my arms and on my back too. I'm a freak. That twister made sure I'd never forget it in more ways than one.

I finally woke up to the shrill warbling of overlapping sirens. I jolted out of a coma-like sleep as heavy drops of rain plopped into my face and began to pool in my eye sockets. Shock had a firm grip on me, wrapping the fraying threads of my nerves around its electric fingers like a sadistic puppet master. All I could think to do was sit very still, take controlled breaths, and check myself out.

I looked myself over, making sure all my limbs were still attached and expecting to see the severed end of a traffic sign skewering my midsection or some other maiming war injury. I found myself questioning if I had actually survived or if I had become a spirit, sitting up out of my own dead body like something you'd see in an old *Casper* cartoon. Most of my bruised and bleeding body was buried under a heavy mound of pulverized brick and other unrecognizable detritus. I shoved at the junk with what little strength I had left in me, and that was when I started noticing all the little daggers jutting out of my skin. It looked like I was sprouting armor or something, like a human stegosaurus.

I didn't feel any pain as I yanked them out one by one, not even the ones that took some real effort and tore off thin ribbons of my skin as they came free. I stared stupidly at the rivulets of fresh blood that oozed from my wounds, and I couldn't bring myself to give a shit about the mud and mortar dust that was caked into the thousand other slices and chunks that were missing. My head felt like it was full of smoke, kinda like when your alarm goes off right in the deepest part of a dream. God, I wish it *had* been a dream.

When I became aware enough to try to take in my surroundings, the shock of it all dive-bombed back into my concussed brain like a kamikaze fighter. I was sitting in an ocean of devastation. The best way I can describe it is to tell you to hop on Google, open an image search tab, and type in the phrase "Hiroshima after the bomb". The similarities are striking.

Even sitting on my ass, I felt like I could see for miles. There was nothing to obstruct my view. No buildings, no stores, no power lines. There were only a few scattered tree trunks left standing upright, stripped of branches and bark and jutting into the glowering sky like pale, broken bones. Cars were piled on top of each other like wads of discarded aluminum foil. Foundations were swept clean. A faded yellow crop duster rested on its top, looking relatively undamaged save for the fact that it was upside down. It looked like the tornado had picked it up, inspected it, then gently sat it aside to look for some other more interesting object to shred. The windows weren't even broken. Strips of sheet metal had been twisted and warped into grotesque sculptures that jutted up out of the sea of wreckage like dirty icebergs. The air was thick with the earthy stench of dirt and fire.

Everywhere I looked, the ground was buried under a jagged carpet of multicolored debris, giving the Oklahoma countryside the look of some insane artist's paint palette. It hadn't registered yet, but Bent Knee was now a memory; erased from the canvas of the earth like a misspelled word and leaving only a smudged afterimage behind.

When I tried to stand, I noticed a waterlogged scrap of paper clinging to my palm. I peeled it off and squinted down at it. It was a piece of someone's personal check. Mud and water damage obscured most of the lettering on the half that remained, but I was able to make out "NK OF CONWAY". The tornado had carried that check scrap all the way from the next town over, easily fifteen or twenty miles. That was when I first learned that Bent Knee wasn't the only town that had been savaged. In a strange way, I sort of wish it *had* just been us. What did we do to earn that much suffering? Why us? Why us *again*?

I think it was my brain's natural defense mechanisms that kept all thoughts of Charlie out of my head. I couldn't think of him, Cassie, Elias, or Jim. I didn't even consider what might have happened to everyone else who had taken shelter with me. The only concern the stew in my skull could piece together was the fact that something had knocked me in the head hard enough to put me to sleep, and I needed to get some help. I wasn't going to get it by laying there like just another piece of wreckage. I grunted as I kicked a cracked hunk of faded gray siding away from me and pulled myself up on legs I couldn't feel, careful to avoid the bent and rusted screws that stabbed out from it like orange fangs.

Bent Knee, or rather what was left of it, looked like something out of an apocalypse movie. Forks of lighting were still streaking between the towering thunderheads above, flashing in the dim afternoon sunlight like little assurances that the storm was far from over (and it was, the same storm put down four more tornadoes that day, just as Charlie had predicted). Medical choppers were already thumping through the murky air, circling and looking for scarce safe places to put down. There were pillars of smoke that looked like miniature tornadoes themselves, billowing up from countless fires that had been caused by severed gas lines and sparking electricity. Fire hoses arced up into swaying white rooster tails as fire departments from the surrounding (surviving) cities arrived. Every now and then someone would scream for help, their frenzied cries muffled by the mounds of debris that had buried them alive. Paired with the ominous growls of thunder and the sickly green-brown sky, it was enough to make you lose your mind.

Paramedics, firefighters and cops were scampering around the devastation like panicked rabbits caught in a deadfall. I decided my best bet was to stagger in their general direction and hope one of them noticed me before I collapsed and disappeared into a pile of someone's shattered home. I walked in a daze, my brain on autopilot. I must have looked like a zombie; I certainly know I felt like one. I'm just glad the twister hadn't sucked my shoes off. I can still hear the brittle crunch and pop of every uncertain footstep, like walking across thin ice.

The two harried paramedics closest to me were standing at the base one of the naked tree trunks, struggling to tie a flapping white sheet to the ragged stump where a low-hanging branch had been. At first, I thought it was meant to be some sort of signal; maybe that they had searched the area and it was clear, or a rally point or something. I couldn't have been more wrong.

They had discovered the corpse of someone I recognized, but I won't mention his name here. All I'll say is that his tattoos were a dead giveaway, even with his body twisted and his flesh brutalized. He had been a short man in life, but in death, I bet he would have been eight or nine feet tall if he could have stood upright. His body had been stretched and wrapped around the tree like a ribbon, as if the tornado had tied him to it for decoration. Somehow, he had stayed in one piece. I'm guessing he had been dismembered internally, it's the only way the human body could elongate and twist up like that. Skin really is a miraculous organ.

As the two men struggled against the breeze, trying to grant the dead man a little dignity before he could be taken to a morgue (which ended up being a refrigerated truck that grumbled into town later that night) one of them clipped the dead man's chin with the heel of his rubber boot. I was close enough by then to see every gut-wrenching detail of his lifeless face. One eye was swollen closed in a shiny purple mound of traumatized flesh, the other wide open and rolled back to a solid, listless white. His mouth hung open in a silent, crooked scream. Seeing the way his head had lolled when the boot had connected, the loose and rubbery flop of his pulverized neck, the way he didn't flinch or react or feel anything at all— it was too much. I dropped to one knee and sprayed my lunch all over a dismembered car door, adding an orange flower of half-digested food chunks and stomach acid to the scratched yellow paint job.

One of the men, a fit-looking guy in a reflective orange vest and a neon yellow EMS hat, whipped his head in my direction at the sound of my retching and gagging.

"Hey!" He yelled through cupped hands. There was barely any echo at all; there was nothing left to reflect sound waves. *"Hey, you alright?!"*

He yanked on the white sheet hard enough to send a tremor all the way through the skinned tree trunk, securing the knot, and then the other paramedic began tucking the edges of it under the elongated corpse. I have so much respect for them for that, you know? The tattooed man was a goner. Nobody would have known any different if they had just left him there, broken and exposed, until he could be scraped up later. They had *still* taken the time to care for his body, even if covering it with a thin white sheet was all that could be done for him. EMS men and women are a different breed, let me tell you.

The fit-looking guy made his way to me, carefully scrabbling over and between the jackstraw mounds of debris. He grabbed my shoulders with strong hands sheathed in blue gloves, steadying me on my wobbly legs. I could smell strong menthol on him. There was a white smudge of stuff on his upper lip, just like one of those milk ads. I suppose that was to help cover up the bad odors he was bound to encounter soon enough.

"Hey," he said softly, grabbing my chin with his rubbery fingertips. "You doin' alright buddy?"

"My friend..." I attempted, my face feeling too numb to properly form words. I kept seeing flashes of the tattooed corpse, envisioning the way the twister had turned him into a Stretch Armstrong and tied him in a knot around the unforgiving trunk of a tree. What had it done to Charlie? "Charlie... he went outside... my friend..."

"Alright buddy, don't you worry. Your friend is fine, okay? We're gonna find him, alright? Right now, I need you to just look at me, focus on my face and don't turn your head."

I tried to nod in agreement like a drunken dope, and I felt his fingers clench my chin.

"Don't nod either, just stay still, okay?"

"Yeah," I grunted, and lowered myself down to sit on what I believe was a plastic laundry basket. My memory is a little fuzzy in places, but that's what I see when I look back. It was pink, or maybe purple.

"Can you tell me your name?"

"Max," I said. He held three fingers up in front of my face.

"How many fingers do you see, Max?"

"Three."

Next came a tiny flashlight from his breast pocket. He shined it into each of my eyes, then slowly moved it back and forth as if he were trying to hypnotize me.

"Don't turn your head, follow it with your eyes, okay, Max?"

"Okay," I said, and followed his instructions.

"Breathing okay, Max? Dizziness, nausea?"

"I can breathe, but... I'm dizzy as hell, and I feel like I could puke again."

The EMT kept a hand on my shoulder to steady me and turned to shout at his partner, who was still kneeling beside the dead man. The next thing I knew, they were slipping one of those uncomfortable neck braces under my chin and coaxing me to lay back onto an orange backboard. I stared up into that angry sky, squinting against the scattered drops of rain and clenching my jaw against the surge of vomit that threatened to make an encore appearance. The men were as careful as could be expected, given the terrain they had to lug my ass across. I felt like I was inside the tornado again; I let myself go, let the men carry my body wherever it was they were going to take me. I kept my eyes open as wide as I could, though. I knew you weren't supposed to go to sleep if you thought you might have a concussion.

They loaded me into the blinding white light of a waiting ambulance, and once the double doors swung shut, I was mercifully spared from seeing any more of the carnage the twister had left behind. I don't know how far they had to carry me or how they even managed to get rescue vehicles into Bent Knee, but they managed. They *always* manage when these things happen. What a thankless job.

I stared out the rear windows of the ambulance, watching the wavering streams of rain traverse the glass. They looked like they were melting out of the frames, stained red and blue and purple from the lights of the rescue vehicles that were still fighting their way into the city limits. I thought of the dead man, his body elongated and twisted, bones pulverized, the life beaten out of him by a random act of nature on a day that had begun just like every other day before. Had something like that happened to Charlie? Something worse? Was my friend dead, tied in a knot around a tree somewhere too? Was time running out for him as his heart pumped blood out of a dozen wounds, killing him with each panicked spurt?

I was sobbing breathlessly when the paramedics leapt into the back of the ambulance with me. I could hear things snapping and crunching under the wheels, the ambulance lurching from side to side as the driver carefully navigated through whatever narrow channel he'd managed to find or create. The swaying of the ambulance, the paramedics shushing me and rubbing my bleeding arms with cool disinfectant wipes, my tears that seemed to be springing from an endless well; all of it made me feel like I was a baby again. So I acted like one, and I cried until my facial muscles ached and my eyes were full of liquid fire.

* * *

The storm outside is finally starting to calm down and the tornado I saw has lifted back up into the clouds. What do you know;

I survived another one. This is when I love having a porch with a roof the most. I can sit out here, writing by the light of a candle and taking in the smell of recent rain and churned earth. The basement was starting to feel a little claustrophobic anyway. I wanted some fresh air to help me finish this. Even after everything I've told you, including the memory of the mutilated corpse I saw, this part will be the hardest to write.

First and foremost, I now realize how fortunate I am to live out in the middle of nowhere. The tornado that destroyed Bent Knee spared my house and a few isolated farms out here, unless you count some debris that landed in my yard and a drinking straw that got lodged in the trunk of one of Stu Winter's trees. Hell, I still find shit with the lawnmower that I *swear* isn't mine, and this is three years later. Having a house to come home to was a blessing to be sure, but that was about as far as my luck went. My car, which had been in the DashMart parking lot, was found in the vacant lot behind where the Good 'n' Tight bar had once stood. Needless to say, it was absolutely totaled.

It didn't take the NWS brains long to declare the twister an EF-5. A child could have told you that much. Any tornado that is strong enough to lift and carry train cars is a force of nature to be reckoned with. I've seen aerial photographs of the town, one of them taken as recently as January, and the scar on the earth is still there. It looks like someone carved a snake across the map. It's a miles-long faded patch that curves and drifts from side to side, like the tornado was drunk and staggering toward us in an alcoholic rage. You can still make out where it began to grow, the damage path widening out until it looks like the head of a gigantic golf tee. It was at its peak width, about 1.6 miles wide, just as it reached town. The maximum wind speed recorded was around 280 miles per hour.

In all, twenty-six people were killed by the storm. Seventeen died here in Bent Knee and nine were killed in Conway, the first town the tornado had struck. Charlie had managed to save everyone he'd sent to the DashMart's truck garage except for one much loved lady; again, I won't mention her name out of respect for her family. I can't begin to fathom what kind of forces were at play that allowed me to be picked up and carried with no fatal injuries while she was not so lucky. They found her, or at least most of her, seven blocks northeast of the DashMart ruins. She was hanging from a tree by the tangles of her long, black hair.

    Elias, my beloved old friend, was killed in his car as he tried to outrun the tornado. I don't know many details and I don't want to; I just know that the twister caught up with him somehow and he was recovered later that night, still strapped into the driver's seat. *God*, I wish he had listened to Charlie. I wish he had stayed behind with the rest of us where it was reasonably safe. Then again, I write that as if I didn't get picked up and thrown; maybe Elias had just as fair of a chance as we all did. Either way, his death turned my heart into a softening apple with a soggy brown spot marring the peel, and the grief that followed was like a burrowing, voracious little worm. Some people, once they're gone, can never truly be replaced. You never quite get used to their absence; you just learn to live with it. I once heard a saying about grief; that it's like a scar in the bark of a sapling. The sapling grows bigger and stronger until it's a towering tree, but the scar, permanent as it may be, stays the same size. I hope that's true for *my* grief. Three years isn't such a long time, and I think it's safe to say I still have a lot of growing to do.

    Cassie (who miraculously survived with only a handful of bruises and a welt across her lower back from a flying gas hose) was so hysterical as the paramedics pulled her from the remains of the garage that she had to be sedated. I'm glad I wasn't around to see that scene, but like I said, she was a popular girl. Everyone heard about it. She was escorted... well, *dragged,* to a waiting ambulance. They say her voice carried over the newly vacant landscape, screaming Charlie's name and even clawing at the paramedics because they were too busy taking care of her to go search for him.

    Poor girl. A face like hers should never do anything but smile. She deserved to become Cassie Dillon someday and grow old with him, sitting in matching rocking chairs and watching the incoming storms brooding over the Oklahoma fields. Charlie, old and hunched, would perhaps scoop up a young grandchild and plop him on his knee. He'd point a gnarled finger out at the stacking thunderheads and patiently explain to the child how the storm was made. "That there is a cumulonimbus," he might say. Jesus, why do

I imagine these things? It can never happen. Cassie doesn't even have a body to bury.

The week following May 16th passed like a nightmare that refused to end. The days were beautiful, almost mockingly so. The skies were the color of clean sea water with only the slightest wispy hints of cirrus clouds drifting slowly over our heads. It beat working in the rain, but the downside to all those gorgeous days was the heat that came with them. When there are dead bodies buried under wreckage that you have to locate *before* you can begin extraction, heat is not what you want. But heat is what we got. Medically it wasn't safe for me to be a part of the cleanup effort, especially when everyone was volunteering to work for twelve or more hours with very few breaks and an absolute absence of shade. I didn't let that stop me.

I had only spent one restless night of observation in the Salisbury General Hospital before I was cleared and released back into the wild. I had a small concussion, nothing that concerned the doctors too much. Only a few of my cuts required stitches, and the most I had to endure was six little threads along the back of my calf. The E.R. doctor ordered me to go home and get plenty of rest (once I let them know that I was one of the lucky few with a house to return to) but of course I didn't. Can you imagine the guilt I felt? The guilt I *still* feel? Go home and rest? Bullshit. What I *did* do was lean against the wall under a cold shower, grab some clean clothes, and head straight into the aftermath to volunteer with the cleanup crews. That was no mean feat since my car had been wadded up like a candy wrapper. I was given a free Uber ride the first day (thank you, Uber), then carpooled with the other volunteers every other day after that. We were all one giant team; sometimes we walked beside one another and sometimes we carried one another. We dressed each other's wounds and took turns distributing cold bottles of water. I did my fair share of crying on many a dirty shoulder, breathing in the smell of sweat and filth but somehow finding it comforting. If anything positive came from that godforsaken fucking storm, it was the companionship it bestowed upon even the bitterest of enemies.

I was taking the doctor's orders and essentially wiping my ass with them, but I did not care. I refused to hunker down in my unharmed house while the rest of the town began the long and arduous task of putting everything back together, and of course I had another motive. One that was more pressing to me than the cleanup, if I'm being honest with you. I wanted to find my friend. Alive or dead.

That's when things really started to get strange, and Charlie took his first steps into becoming an urban legend. With each passing day, we continued to find more bodies. I never had to *see* another one, thank God. All I ever saw was their lumpy, humanoid forms. They sagged in the middle as they were carried, their ice-white body bags crinkling and fluttering in the dry breeze.

After the first few days of work, we began to smell the ones that were still buried— I'll spare you the details of what a decomposing human smells like, but I can tell you it's nothing like passing a deer on the side of the highway. It was monstrous, and it drew in a hundred thousand flies to pester us as we panted through our mouths, not wanting to taste it but incapable of coping with the smell anymore. Cadaver dogs were eventually brought in to help with the recovery, their coppery fur shining in the sun and their tails wagging happily despite the grim task they had been trained to do. Thankfully those diligent hounds made short work of it, sniffing and pawing at rubble and then lying flat on their bellies when they found where the scent emanated from. They were good boys and girls. They earned every strip of doggy bacon they snatched out of their handler's hands, and when all was said and done, nobody's husband or grandpa or wife or baby was left behind.

Nobody except for Charlie. It was exhausting. Not just the physical work and the raw sting of deepening sunburn but hitching home every night and spending the ride thinking about how none of us had uncovered any clues. It was a strange, perverse sensation to find myself swelling with a tiny bit of excitement each time a volunteer would cup his dirty hands around his mouth and yell the word "body". When you hear that short but powerful word drifting across the wasteland, you start to think that maybe, just *maybe*, a firefighter lifted a section of wall or a tractor tire and found what was left of your loved one. Dead, which is devastating, but at least then you *know.* You can begin to mourn them and grieve for them, slowly willing your heart to accept that they didn't survive, and you will never see them again. We never got that with Charlie.

There was a mass funeral held for those killed by the storm three days or so after the body recovery efforts came to a close. I don't think I've ever dreaded anything more in my entire life. I can remember waking up that morning and rooting around for my best clothes, then deciding to leave them in a pile on the floor of my closet. Most of the people attending had lost everything they'd ever owned; who the fuck was I to show up in dress clothes? Call me disrespectful if you will, but I chose a pair of ancient blue jeans with tattered and mud-stained cuffs and one of my spare DashMart uniform shirts. It was almost like a tribute for the store I'd had a love/hate relationship with for so long. The store I had almost died in, and now, would never visit again. My brain tried to think of the day Charlie had blown my phone up, desperate to get me out of bed to go storm chasing with him, but I forced it out. It was the first battle of many, and God help me it took practice before I was able to drink Monster again.

The Bent Knee High School was set up like a college campus. We had the main building with K-12 classrooms and a "cafetorium" (a combination cafeteria and auditorium) connected by a short, covered walkway to the "field house". The field house was the newer of the two buildings and contained relatively high-tech equipment like retractable bleachers and basketball nets that could be raised and lowered on pneumatic arms. The high school's main building had taken the brunt of the twister's impact, and though none of the students hiding inside were killed, there wasn't much left of it but a haphazard outer shell. The field house, partially shielded by the main building, was mostly spared. It lost a section of roofing that had been curled back like the edge of an old scab, but someone had temporarily "repaired" the resulting hole with several layers of noisy tarps pinned down with a few hunks of cinder block. Otherwise, if you could handle the thick heat and the overpowering smell of apple candles, it served as a perfect makeshift funeral home.

To this day, I cannot stand the smell of apple anything. Every time I catch the scent, it throws me back to the day of the funeral. I can still see the gym's double doors propped open for some precious airflow, and I can still hear the hiss and snarl of construction equipment following me inside. Both my feet weighed about a thousand pounds each, and it took everything I had in me to make my legs scissor and carry me inside. It was set up like some kind of a morbid flea market with soft piano music twittering over the PA system and orchid wreaths hanging from the basketball nets.

 Some of the victims had opted for cremation, their pictures blown up to canvas size and resting on easels that were buried under heaps of flowers, windchimes, and decorative blankets. That was the first thing I saw as I walked in; those photographs of happy men and women, smiling pleasantly and unaware of the death that would come for them years before they expected it to. I glanced at each one out of the sides of my eyes, listening to the harsh rasp of my stubble as I rubbed my hand back and forth across my chin.

 There were seven caskets in all, spaced well apart and organized into an upside-down U shape. Between each casket was a small wooden coffee table adorned with a sweating vase of flowers, a box of tissues, and those shit sucking apple candles. Swarms of sobbing people milled around in the center of the U where rows of folding chairs had been set out like silent infantrymen, hugging and murmuring to each other. An empty podium stood at the front of the rows like an ominous figurehead. People were beginning to form a sloppy line off to my right, crowding around the first casket on display. I sighed, willing the uneasiness in my stomach down to a dull roar, and forced myself to join it. I knew right away that I would not be visiting every casket once the teddy bear caught my eye. I meant no disrespect, you understand. I just didn't have the strength to stand beside the casket that seemed to be the main attraction of the macabre market. It was much shorter than the others, the base painted neon pink and the bifurcated lid painted sparkling purple. Propped against the bier that held the kid's casket was an oversized teddy bear, flopped over to one side as if relaxing in an easy chair and holding a bright pile of flowers and toys. Its beady eyes were black and shiny, almost accusatory. *Why did a child die?* those eyes seemed to ask us all. *Children aren't supposed to die, only the very old or the very sick. This is wrong, don't you see that?*

My throat was in constant motion, my breaths hitching and pulling as I began the slow walk among the dead. I wasn't sure how to handle myself, and I was rubbing my cheek raw. The first casket I passed was closed, and I didn't recognize the old man that beamed at me from the Army picture that rested on the shiny wooden lid. I extended my hand and patted it gently, trying not to picture what was inside that was bad enough to warrant a closed casket.

Closed caskets are weird like that, know what I mean? They close them when someone gets so messed up that there's no fixing them. No amount of work or skill can make them appear to be sleeping peacefully rather than just looking dead. In a way, though, it's almost worse. Looking at that closed box is like looking at a ghastly Christmas gift, and the sick part of your brain where your most shameful and secret thoughts slither around begs you to open it and take a little peek. The images you come up with on your own are probably far worse than what's actually inside the casket, but I wouldn't want to see for myself. I traced my shaking fingers down the length of the lid and moved on to the next, which was open.

There was a kid inside, a local teenager. I didn't know him personally, but I recognized him just the same. He came into the DashMart every time a new sports or wrestling video game came out, on the day of release, without fail. I could have marked the calendar by him; whenever I sliced open a box of new releases, I knew he'd be coming soon enough. A small confession: we weren't supposed to, but if one of the games was selling particularly well and I thought we were going to run out, sometimes I'd stash one for him in the junk drawer under the counter. Just a small kindness for a loyal customer, and he was never an asshole to me. It was like an unspoken friendship that was beautiful and natural, like sunflowers growing out of spilled birdseed.

He had been dressed in a simple black button up shirt with an empty pocket on the left breast. It struck me as absurd. He had no use for pockets anymore. He had no use for *anything* anymore. The tornado had released him from all earthly needs or desires. He was simply a shell now; everything that made him who he was as a human being was gone with the wind, and everything that was left was laid out for all of us to file past and gawk at.

His hands, which would never hold a video game controller ever again, were gently laced together over his stomach. The morticians had done their best work for his family, but some of the scratches and bruises simply couldn't be hidden. They looked like squashed plums covered with a transparent white cloth. The gouges and cuts that would never heal were clotted with little crumbles of makeup.

I felt my breaths getting shorter and tighter as the line carried me past his head. Some repair work had been required in order to give his parents the open casket they had probably requested, desperate and pleading to see their son one last time. He looked like he had been sculpted out of clay. His skin was waxy and pallid, making him look more like a life-sized porcelain doll than the remains of a real person. His lips were a shade of bluish maroon, and they were pursed, as if he were blowing all his visitors a final kiss. His hair had been combed into a pompadour that an old man would wear, not a kid just beginning his life. No, his hair was always stiff and spiky. Messy but neat, if that makes sense. A cool kid hairdo.

I found myself staring at the motionless bulbs of his eyes. I held my breath, half expecting them to swivel behind the glossy lids. Of course I knew better; I knew that there were spiky, flesh-colored eye caps inserted under his eyelids to make sure they stayed closed, so he couldn't have blinked or looked around even if he had still been alive. But to see a human body that still, that motionless... it's unnerving. I left his casket behind with cold shivers dancing up and down my spine, but with them came closure. The consequences of the tornado were still becoming apparent, and acceptance they demanded of the town was agonizing but necessary.

The smell of cinnamon and apple was cloying. I felt like it was suffocating me, and the dried pit where my pinky nail had once been was throbbing with my quickening pulse. I wanted *out*. I wanted to run away from all the loss and death, shut my eyes and close my mind to it as I had done for my entire life up until then. But I also had that nagging, stern little whisper in the back of my mind that told me I had to stay the course. This funeral was for Elias too, and his casket, a gorgeous snowy white one that was mercifully closed, was near the end of the procession.

    I tried to shut my brain off as I passed the child's casket that marked the half-way point of the mourner procession. I kept my leaking eyes glued to the floor, fixating on the shaggy paws of the oversized teddy bear and examining every cowlick and curl of its faux fur in forensic detail. Everyone seemed to want to clot up and crowd around the poor kid; *why?* Why would you want to stand there and just stare at it, knowing full well what was inside? And Jesus *fuck* that scent of apples, it was everywhere. Permeating me. I felt like that stench would never come out of my clothes again, or the back of my throat for that matter.

    "I can't," I muttered to no one in particular, and shouldered my way through the outer layer of people. I meant no disrespect to those who didn't make it, I swear on my life, but I skipped the rest of the line and strode straight over to Elias's casket. I needed to escape that sweltering sickly-sweet smelling gymnasium, but I knew I'd never forgive myself if I didn't pay my respects to my old friend. To this day I still believe I was the last person he spoke to on earth.

    Elias's casket seemed to tower over me, even though I was able to look down and see my warped grimace staring back from the sleek metal lid. It was the only white one at the funeral, and it was beautiful despite what it was and what it held inside it. There was a metal plate bolted between the first and second handles that looked like it was made of polished brass. Etched into it in a fancy curled script were the words "Gone home". They had placed a giant bouquet of yellow roses on top of the lid, the heavy blooms jutting out from a haze of baby's breath and tufts of shiny greenery. At the base of the roses, resting on a small square of lacy cloth that looked like a napkin, was a harmonica. Elias smiled at me from his portrait atop the casket, his mustache slanting in that old familiar way, his eyes squinted nearly shut and yet still sparkling like polished jewels from somewhere in the past.

    Without warning, I no longer had bones in my legs. I dropped heavily to the floor, rapping my knees painfully against the wooden planks and struggling to suck in breaths before I sobbed them back out again. Another killer tornado formed, only *this* twister was tearing through my brain, and its pitiless brutality was absolute.

    A vortex of cruel images raged between the rounded walls of my skull. I unwillingly pictured what it might look like inside the tightly sealed casket; the darkest black you could ever imagine with no hope of sunlight ever penetrating the padded lining that held the body of my friend. I saw Elias staring into his rear-view mirror, his eyes wide and shining as the wall of swirling cloud steadily gained on him. I saw the brown skin of his knuckles give way to bloodless white as he clenched the steering wheel. I watched his car leave the road and soar through the air, slam callously into the ground and roll again and again, becoming a meat grinder with the friendly elderly door greeter trapped inside. Sense memories of his aftershave were interspersed like rotten Easter eggs, and with them came the words of countless songs he had written for me, goofy improvisations about me being a lady killer and the future CEO of DashMart. Then the realization that Elias was dead and gone, "gone home", gone forever, hammered down on me like the slamming of his coffin lid. I wailed, moaning and blubbering his name again and again, and the beveled white wall of the casket I was screaming at listened. It was silent and indifferent.

    The smell of apples and cinnamon became worse than the smell of the tornado had been. It was almost liquid, flooding into my nostrils and congealing inside my throat like thick mucus. I hated it. I was asphyxiated by it. I had to leave, find somewhere with oxygen that hadn't been tainted by noxious candles intended to comfort.

    I felt hands pressing into my armpits and rubbing gently across my shoulders, squeezing the tightened muscles and making them hurt worse. Someone was shushing me; some lady, I never bothered to look at her face or any of the faces around me. I could feel her lips brushing against my ear, and although she was trying to comfort me, it gave me the creeps. I waved my arms as if I could swim away, pushed myself to my feet and began to jog towards the double doors that led outside. They were like the sun, shining brilliantly down through the surface of a deep blue hole, one that I had been drowning in. All I had to do was pass through them.

When I saw what was posted to the right of the doors, I tried to stop myself so suddenly that my shoes screeched across the polished planks of the basketball court. I had been so focused on the display of death ahead of me that I hadn't even noticed it on the way in, not even with the vase full of red and white roses and drooping orchids that decorated a small table beneath it. There was a tiny white lamp behind the flowers, complete with a small box of tissues placed tactfully on its base. The faint cone of yellow light that shone out of the lampshade was like a spotlight, casting a feverish glow across a poster of Charlie Dillon.

Bold black letters dominated the top of the poster:

MISSING: CHARLES DILLON

It looked so ominous floating above his picture; I wonder if they do that on purpose? Seeing that one word felt the same to me as standing beside Elias's casket. MISSING. It was a threatening, hazardous word, and inspired anything but hope for him.

The picture they had used was black and white, and from a time when Charlie was much younger. Apparently, not even picture day at school had gotten that kid to tame his wild locks of blonde hair. His smile was awkward and strained, more like a sneer that had obviously been pushed on him by the photographer. He clearly hadn't wanted his picture taken; it looked like a driver's license or a mugshot. His eyes, on the other hand, made up for the lack of a toothy grin. Even without color they leapt from his face, and they seemed to follow my defeated trot outside. Wondering, perhaps, why I wasn't busy trying to find him instead of concerning myself with the known dead.

It was still hot and sticky-humid outside, but even the thick air laced with the stench of cigarette smoke and the sour tang of burning exhaust smelled sweeter than those fucking apple candles. I took in deep breaths, trying to center myself and slow the pounding of my heart. I think it would have been easier to walk on water, but I knew that if I didn't relax, I'd be the next one in a box. Death by heart failure, rather than natural disaster.

"You too, huh?" Came a familiar voice from beneath me. I started, shocked out of my breakdown. Jim Klingler was sitting with his back against the brick alcove just outside the double doors, pulling a fresh cigarette out of a crumpled pack even as one still smoldered between his lips. He touched the two ends together and puffed the new cig alight, flicking the spent butt carelessly into the grass. When he exhaled, his teeth chattered like he was somehow freezing while wearing a long-sleeved plaid work shirt in the relentless heat. The smoke came out in rapid little puffs, curling around his hand as he wiped absently at his nose. I didn't need to see his eyes, which were hidden behind massive aviator sunglasses, to know he was doing something he didn't think a burly man should ever do— he was crying.

"Yeah, me too," I said, swiping at my own nose and my spilling eyes. "I couldn't be in there anymore. It's too much."

He thumbed out a cigarette and held the pack out to me. I'm not a smoker; never have been and probably never will be, but in some situations you just take the damn cigarette and smoke it. I lowered myself down to sit beside him and parked it in my mouth, leaning to let him light it for me. I knew better than to inhale. Instead, I just sucked enough searing smoke into my mouth to taste the flavor and then exhaled it again. Jim seemed satisfied.

"Thanks, Diesel," I said, with real sincerity. For the first time since I'd met him, I called him by his preferred nickname without any sarcasm behind it. He smirked at me.

"You fuckers never call me that," he growled, but I could see a smile lurking on his face. I gestured toward his temple, where a small section of hair had been shorn off. He'd had his head cut open by flying debris as the tornado passed over the truck garage, and the cut had been *deep*. The missile had cleaved off a flap of scalp and exposed the skull beneath, and a nasty infection had already taken root when the paramedics had pulled him out. Now all that was left was a bruised frown of stitches.

"How's your head? It looks nasty, man. It'll be a cool scar though."

He shrugged, his lower lip quivering as he puffed out another cloud of blue smoke. One lonely tear emerged from behind the dark lenses and ambled down his cheek. He shouldered it away, furious at it.

"Didn't kill me. I'm alive." He turned to face me, and his entire face crumpled. His breaths came out in pitiful whines that I could barely hear over the snarl and whir of bulldozers and backhoes. "Because of Charlie."

That ripped my heart out and showed it to me. I couldn't help but recall the first time Jim had seen Charlie. He had been so eager to mock him, to label him a retard because of his hail helmet, and he'd wanted me to join him. He called him "pussy lips" for never taking his turn pushing the cart trains back inside. He flirted with his girlfriend right in front of him, daring him to defend her. Hearing Jim "Diesel" Klingler speak Charlie's name with such intense anguish and gratitude was like a kick to the stomach. That moment was the closest thing I ever had to an emotional connection with Jim; for a guy like him, you have to move mountains to get him to speak about his feelings. Talking about the mushy stuff, well, that's "faggy" to guys like him.

"He saved me too," I finally managed, sniffling snot and dabbing at my sore eyes with the collar of my shirt. My cigarette burned on, neglected, between my shaking fingers. "He managed to save almost everyone."

"Everybody but one, they said," he replied, and now his voice began to tremble as if fault lines were colliding in his chest. His eyebrows drew down in an expression of unfiltered hatred, his mouth warping into a hateful sneer. "And what does he get? Some fucking flowers and a god damned *poster*. That's his memorial?"

Now it was my turn to shrug. I had to yank my next words out of my mouth, and it felt a lot like digging the shrapnel out of my flesh had felt. Somehow, I could feel that it was going to piss him off.

"We don't know that he's dead, James."

He moved like lightning. With his cigarette crushed between his teeth and trailing crumbles of ash, he grabbed fistfuls of my shirt and yanked me forward with such ferocity that my neck cracked. I was staring at my own wide eyed reflected in those dark sunglasses, my legs hanging beneath me like they were broken.

"He's *dead*, Max. Don't you fucking kid yourself and don't you fucking put doubts in my head. He went outside and the tornado fucked him up just the way it fucked Elias up. Nobody could have survived that fucker. *Nobody*."

As he spat the word "nobody", he shoved me away from him and knocked me flat on my ass. I wasn't angry with him. I knew exactly how he felt; I had felt those same emotions stirring in my guts when I'd seen the MISSING poster with that ghoulish glow cast across Charlie's young face. The lamp, the flowers, the token box of tissues. None of it seemed worthy of the kid who had saved our lives. It felt like no thought had gone into it at all. But— it wasn't a memorial for Charlie. I still had that minuscule whisper in my ear, reminding me that no body had been found. *Nothing* had been found. Jim chose to take that as a death notice, while I found comfort in the fact that some small semblance of hope remained. It comforted me back *then*, I should say.

Jim also had another burden to carry. He had been unkind to Charlie more often than he'd been good to him, especially when he had first showed up at DashMart and the few weeks that followed. Childish bullying like hiding his helmet and cameras, stealing his lunch, calling him derogatory names like "tardo" and "re-re" and pronouncing his name in a slurred, impaired dialect. He had grown to care for Charlie long after the rest of the town had. Now he could never apologize to him, never make it right, never repay him. If Charlie was gone for good, he could focus on being free of that debt and learn to live with himself and the things he had done. If there was any chance that he was still alive, the wound would remain open. He'd have no closure, just like Cassie and me.

I stared out over the desolate plain that had once been my hometown and kept my mouth shut, letting things simmer down. My eyes were drawn to the partially collapsed wall of someone's home, jutting up into the azure sky like the sail of a windjammer. One wall was all that was left, and it was only upright because it had fallen onto a white wad that had once been an RV. A giant red X had been spray painted on the fractured drywall, and beneath it "1 DOA" had been added in spidery, runny letters. I knew what that meant and I looked away, shuddering.

"All we can do is wait, James," I finally said, bracing for his fist to fly at me this time. I was stunned to see him nod tiredly, flicking his cigarette butt away and leaning to fish a can of chew out of his back pocket. He pinched a tuft of tobacco out and stuffed it into his lip, making it bulge comically. James Klingler was (and still is) a country boy through and through.

"That's all we can ever do," he said, and spit into the grass. "At least we have that option. And we have it because of *him.*"

He shoved himself from the wall and stalked away, rubbing both hands irritably through the hair he had left. I didn't bother to stand. I didn't feel like I had regained the strength yet. The tenacious stench of apple candles was wafting out at me, so I picked up my wasted cigarette and held it under my nose, using the stink of burnt tobacco to block it out. I sat there in blissful solitude, watching the construction equipment trundle to and fro and staring at the crude red X that was someone's epitaph.

The voice of Gregory Caliander, Bent Knee's most popular and beloved pastor, echoed through the gym's PA system. His tone was light; almost cheery. It made my nausea worse.

"If everyone will make their way to their chairs, we'd like to begin the service." His words were punctuated by the scuffling of shoes and the whisper of clothes brushing together, then the ear-splitting squeak of chairs sliding across the gym floor. He cleared his throat into the microphone, triggering a jarring burst of feedback.

I went on sniffing the cigarette butt, my gaze locked enviously on the blades of grass Jim had crushed flat as he'd made his escape. They rose slowly but determinedly, twitching like the antennae of an insect as they rebounded. *Like Bent Knee,* I thought. *Knocked flat but rising, slowly, again.* I was back in limbo; I wanted to leave, wanted to follow the path Jim had left and put that awful place behind me. I also wanted to stay, out of respect for the victims. Respect for that poor gamer kid. Respect for the fallen baby. Respect for Elias.

I probably looked strange to the few stragglers who trickled in after the service had begun, squatting in the alcove and slowly passing a spent cigarette back and forth beneath my nose. I got a few confused stares and double takes, but nobody harassed me. I suppose they thought I was coping in my own strange way; they weren't exactly wrong, I suppose.

"The good book says, 'The wind blows where it wishes, and you hear its sound, but you do not know where it comes from or where it goes. So it is with everyone who is born of the Spirit.'"

That decided it for me. I don't know what I had expected the pastor to say, but I was *not* in the mood for a church service. I felt like I was betraying my fallen friend, but I stood and walked back towards the scattered corpse of Bent Knee. I swerved between the rows of parked cars glinting in the brilliant sunlight and stepped over pieces of wood and distorted metal that hadn't been picked up yet. The echo of Pastor Caliander's breathy voice followed, ethereal and ghostly as it was carried by the unobstructed wind that whistled around me. It felt wonderful combing through my sweaty hair and cooling my flushed face. I did not look back. I've tried *not* to look back ever since. Not until tonight.

* * *

My radar app is showing that this line of storms is speeding away, losing steam as it goes. There's a whole mess of storms coming behind it though; the tornado warning has been lifted but the tornado watch will continue until morning. So much for getting some restful sleep. The rainbow whirls of violent weather are washing over Oklahoma like waves of mixed dye, and those little lightning strike icons are beginning to overlap like curds of seawater foam.

Tomorrow morning is another big day for the new Bent Knee, and especially for those of us who knew Charlie the best. The fire department is holding another memorial ceremony, this one centered around the brand-new tornado siren they recently finished installing.

I saw it for myself this morning while I was out and about, straining my neck and shielding my eyes to peer all the way up to the top. It's like a skyscraper to us small town folk. It's painted a chilly white that blinds you when the sun hits it just right, and it's topped with an array of wide-mouthed amplifier dishes that almost make it look like a… I don't know, a robot mushroom? The rumor mill in town says that you'll be able to hear that baby go off in all the surrounding counties, and supposedly, it's wired directly into the National Weather Service's systems. If they issue a tornado warning for our area it goes off on its own, no phone calls or approval needed. I guess I could say it's comforting. Maximum warning time will help save lives, but if we get another twister like the big one of '18, we'll be installing a new town. *Again.*

There's a miniature park and a collection of flower boxes at the base of the siren. It's nothing big, just a cross-shaped intersection of concrete tiles and mulched gardens that are always swarming with butterflies and lazy bumblebees. In the center of the walkway is a rectangular plaque set into the stone. In raised golden letters that jut out from a black granite background, it reads:

IN MEMORY OF THE LOVED ONES LOST   DURING THE CONWAY/BENT KNEE TORNADO
5/16/18

Their names are listed as well— everyone except for Charlie. That's what's so peculiar about the ceremony tomorrow. It's the fortieth or fiftieth ribbon cutting ceremony Bent Knee has held (although everyone in town has seen the new siren by now) and it's also a dedication. They've decided to dedicate our new space age warning siren to Charlie Dillon. There's even a plaque for him bolted right onto the base of the tower that reads:

DEDICATED TO "PECOS" CHARLIE DILLON

They can't say "In loving memory of Charlie Dillon" because three years on, three *long* years on, no trace of my friend has ever been found. His body wasn't recovered under any of the wreckage. He wasn't found in any neighboring cities or even neighboring *counties* for that matter. He wasn't thrown into a field or a thicket of trees. Every lake, creek and river within a 50-mile radius has been dragged, dragged, and dragged again. Not a shoe, not a scrap of clothing, not his trademark hail helmet or his phone.

Nothing. How the fuck can that be? How does that *happen*? It's like Charlie was a ghost all along, haunting Bent Knee long enough to save a handful of lives and then disappearing back to the other side. He came in with a storm and went out with a storm.

We even had the fucking FBI cruising up and down the streets in big black SUVs, and those snobby pricks hung around long enough for us to get sick of seeing them. They had no emotion or sympathy for us. They moved and talked like robots in soul cancelling sunglasses and expensive suits, and they treated us all like we were criminals. We had kidnapped Charlie, or maybe lynched him from a tree in a secluded field somewhere and taken a citywide vow of silence. They somehow managed to act with urgency and bored indifference at the same damn time, as if Charlie's disappearance was about as pressing as a backlog of orders at a pizza joint. Still, even after those big shot detectives came in, circled with helicopters and mounted spotlights, grilled every man, woman, and child they met, *nothing* has been found. The last I heard, they were keeping the file on Charlie "open indefinitely". I think it's safe to call it a cold case now, and that file will be buried in some dusty and forgotten filing cabinet.

That kind of loss, a sudden death with no tangible closure to speak of, is almost elemental. It's like finding yourself lost in the frying pan of Death Valley and suddenly realizing you've misplaced your canteen. There is a vacuum left behind, a void not unlike the space left behind after a lightning bolt dissipates. But at least the lightning has thunder to fill it; what do we have? Unanswered questions. No release. I hope you won't be angry, having read this entire memoir only to reach the end and discover that no one really knows what happened to Charlie. You also have to understand that that is precisely what cemented him as a local legend, a good-natured ghost story that will mystify every bonfire for decades to come.

His story has now grown to the level of tall tale, hence the posthumous nickname. Pecos Bill, as you may or may not know, is right up there with the "big men" of American folklore, larger than life characters like John Henry and Paul Bunyan. In one of those stories, Pecos Bill managed to lasso a tornado and ride it like a bucking bronco all the way out of Texas. Seeing it written, it seems like kind of a sick nickname; Charlie certainly didn't "ride" a tornado anywhere. I'm sure it was violent, painful, and terrifying.

The nickname began with doodles on Charlie's MISSING posters, which still dot power poles and hang in almost every shop window. Talk about spooky; everywhere I go, I see his ageless face staring back at me. Some people, probably adventurous young preteens or drunken assholes, like to take permanent markers to them and add on scribbled funnels, flying stick cows, and crude lightning bolts. I saw one defaced poster in the new post office lobby that featured a crooked black cowboy hat scrawled onto Charlie's head and a bushy handlebar mustache masking most of his smile. I was tempted to grab it and rip it off the wall, but then I thought better of it. Charlie would have *loved* that nickname, even if some used it to mock him. He was used to mockery; it didn't faze him or distract him from his passion. Not even his own father had broken him, not completely. Most people use it in a warm and endearing way, usually with a sad smile before they wonder out loud where he might be now. That's why I started using it too.

Everyone in Bent Knee has their own theory. Some say Charlie faked his death and left to start over in a new town, but that doesn't make any sense to me. Why would he leave Cassie behind? How did he get there, and how did he afford it? How did he dodge the FBI? No, that one is just foolish.

Others say his body was accidentally scooped up and hauled away unceremoniously in the back of a dump truck, and his final resting place is a landfill or an incinerator somewhere. That one holds a little water, but I was a part of the cleanup crews. I *know* how surgical we were. We picked this town clean like buzzards on a carcass, and I, at least, was desperate to find any molecule of evidence that I could. If the tornado had left him here in town, he would have been found. *Something* would have been found.

I don't need to spend much time on the more outlandish theories, that he was struck by an especially powerful EF-5-sized lightning bolt and vaporized or that the twister was so powerful that it actually lobbed him into orbit. Personally, I think the storm carried

Charlie away just like it carried me and threw him into a river, and despite the best efforts of the BKPD and the FBI, his body was washed away. Maybe even all the way out to sea. Who can know for sure? If we haven't found him by now, we aren't going to. I don't like that thought, but doesn't it seem like the most logical? People don't just vanish into thin air.

I just wish the voices would stop. There's a tiny, tireless voice that seems to murmur from somewhere in the shadowy well of my chest, whispering to me from the moment I wake up to the moment I fall asleep. Sometimes, even *after* I'm asleep. It only ever says two words: *what if?* What if he is still alive somewhere, recovering, unable to contact his friends and family? What if I start accepting, this very second, that he's dead? Then, when I'm on my way to the construction site to clock in tomorrow morning, they tell me he's been found alive? How can I give up on my friend when I *know* he wouldn't have given up on me?

Every day, I think I'm finally ready. Every day I think about buying a *Storm Chasers* DVD or maybe a framed 8x10 poster from his favorite movie, *Twister*, and writing a little goodbye message to him on the back. Once he has a ceremonial grave, I'd leave it at the foot of the headstone and at long last begin to make my peace. But that voice always rasps at me, *what if, Max? What if you only have to wait one more day?*

I dream about him too. You could call them nightmares, I suppose, but they don't frighten me. I kinda look forward to them. Some would say it's his spirit, coming to visit me and let me know that he's safe and happy in a better place. Pardon me, but that's horse shit. I have the dreams because I think about that goofy bastard almost constantly, and after surviving the tornado that destroyed my town, I have them on my mind a lot too.

In my dreams, I find myself walking down a winding muddy road. I can hear my shoes squelching in the mud, and I always look down to see how dirty my shoes are getting. I begin stepping over debris, splintered two-by-fours and twisted road signs, flattened tires and twinkling lakes of broken glass. They jut out of the thick mud like tombstones. The wind is warm and wet, making my skin clammy, and then it shifts to a sudden cold dryness that shrivels my balls into walnuts. It changes direction as it blows around me, and I can actually *feel* it rotating. The leaves begin to lift off the ground and swirl around me like a cocoon, like a tornado is about to drop right on my fucking head. And yet I keep walking.

I look up ahead of me, and there's Bent Knee just after the twister. That same sea of carnage and destruction I woke up to behold, filled with broken homes and mangled bodies. The sky is like the belly of a rotten corpse, bloated and streaked layers of purple, blue, and green. Lightning licks down in savage stabbing forks and thunder roars, loud enough to make me clasp my dream hands over my ears. I see a tentacle of cloud drift down from the fomenting storm, followed by another. Then another. A writhing, screeching forest of tornadoes is rampaging on all sides of me, dancing around and among one another, filling the air with a haze of dirt and dust so thick that the lightning might set fire to the sky.

I turn, one full circle to try to count just how many twisters are on the ground at the same time. I can never reach a final count. They drop and dissipate too fast, as if I'm inside the body of some mad god's giant typewriter, and each keystroke sends another furious funnel crashing to the earth. When I face front again, Bent Knee is suddenly rebuilt. Not the new, sterile clone of the town but the town itself, as it was. Imperfect, but beloved by its inhabitants. Somewhere, a harmonica is playing softly. Standing on the path in front of me is Pecos Charlie.

His wild blonde hair is whipping into a twisted knot, his blue eyes shining excitedly and only slightly hidden by the rise of his cheekbones. He isn't wearing his hail helmet; he doesn't need it. He holds his arms out to either side of his body, as if presenting the psychotic show of weather to me. As if welcoming me into his palace of brooding cloud and snapping electricity and screaming wind.

That's when I wake up, reeling from the ache of relief and joy in my heart. There are always a few seconds where I forget that he's missing and most likely dead, and then it's like I get the news all over again. His number is still in my phone, all his texts still saved, and once or twice I've grabbed it and tried to call him (it goes straight to voicemail, and Charlie never recorded a message so I can't even use that to hear his voice). I start most of my days before the sun is up, and my eyes are streaming with water before I make it to the shower. Is there a pain more pure, more concentrated, than the pain of loss? If there is, I sure as fuck never want to experience it. I miss my friend, and that's enough suffering for me.

If I can't end Charlie's story with answers, I can at least end it with something positive. It happened to me just a few hours ago, when these storms first began to buffalo their way into town.

I was heading into the new DashMart to stock up on some Red Bulls and laundry pods when the first waves of rain and hail began to hiss down the streets in sweeping waves. I swore under my breath and began to run for the front door, already feeling my shirt growing sodden and clinging to my skin. I nearly tripped over a battered bicycle that had been blown over... actually, I can feel a bruise puffing up on my right shin from where it connected with the seat. I was grasping for the door when it was snatched out of my hand, and I collided with a kid I had never seen before.

For the briefest of moments, I could have sworn it was Charlie. I would have bet you my *dick* that it was Charlie. He was the owner of the bike that had nearly killed me, and so a bicycle helmet was strapped loosely to his head. It bounced and jostled on his shaggy curls of hair (brown, not blonde) as he ran past me like a bat out of hell.

"*Woah!*" I shouted at him, but not with anger. *"You're headed the wrong way, kid!"*

He whirled around and sprinted backwards, pausing only briefly enough to dignify me with a response. His eyes were yellow-brown and squinted against the blowing of the storm, his fingers tapping away at his phone. I could see that his camera was open, tiny beads of water already pebbling the cracked screen.

"Are you kidding?!" He shrieked back, his prepubescent voice cracking with his excitement. *"I never miss a storm, dude! You can use a video to get pics of lightning!"* With that simple justification he hurried away from me, his dirty sneakers splashing against the wet pavement and leaving slow ripples that were immediately destroyed by pea-sized hailstones. I was frozen for a minute as I watched him point his phone to the sky and snap a few pictures of the clouds, his

smile never faltering even as ice bounced off his cheeks and upturned chin.

Grow up to be like Charlie Dillon, I thought warmly. *If I can't have him, I'll take someone* like *him.*

It's true. The world desperately needs people like Pecos Charlie, people who love recklessly and allow themselves to be consumed by their passions, even if it earns the ridicule and snide laughter of the rest of the human race. People who are pure and good in the face of this god-awful world we live in. People who can find the beauty in a severe thunderstorm, the majesty in the furious winds and black eye of a tornado.

I was crying as I went in to do my shopping, but for the first time in three lonely years, I was crying because I was happy. Long live the legend of Pecos Charlie. I don't wish peace for him, and neither should you— wherever he is, I hope the weather is angry and the skies are black. I hope the wind is boisterous and violent. Destructive. I hope lightning fries the air and thunder deafens. I hope the tornadoes are ten miles wide and tear the very crust of the earth from the mantle. *God,* I hope he's somewhere like that. Then I could find some comfort in the fact that Charlie finally ended up right where he belongs: not running or hiding from the storms, but one with them. Forever.

The Box at the Front of the Room

Stopped hearts unite humanity
The working poor and royalty
Will one day stand as one and see
The wooden grin of our final doom.

For most, twilight is far away
The dark will come another day
We tell ourselves we'll never lay
In the Box at the Front of the Room.

There's nothing anyone can do
The long years take their toll on you
Each winter brings us closer to
The end, as we're all slowly consumed.

Death's embrace is cold and deep
Indifferent to the ones that weep
Who gather there to watch you sleep
In the Box at the Front of the Room.

The river flows and rapids roar
It carries us away from shore
We drift, as we are destined for
The sacred fields where etched pillars loom.

No one can say where dead ones go
Nor what we feel; nor if we know
While decades pass, and flowers grow
O'er the Box at the Front of the Room.

Abaddon

Cameron "Cam" Bradley floated in the soft glow of the *UNSI-IL Hawking*'s bridge, nervously eyeing the declining oxygen levels in what remained of the ship's fuselage. It was a simple color-coded bar graph that updated in real time, constantly monitored by the built in AI "Brain" that all United Nations Space Initiative ships carried. Green meant "habitable". Safe for human life. Yellow meant "hazardous", and of course, red meant "life unsustainable". As Cam stared at the hovering holoscreen, thumbing sweat from his eyes, the digital needle slipped into the yellow. He swallowed hard. It was *not* a false alarm or a loose sensor this time. The system was 99.8% error proof.

The Brain was blaring an emergency bulletin every five seconds or so, alerting Cam that it had detected a third crew member in the cargo hold, which was sealed off by vault-like bulkheads and currently void of all oxygen. Everything aft of the cargo hold was missing, torn away by a blitzkrieg rock barrage and slowly trailing debris and equipment as if the *Hawking* had opened an artery. The state-of-the-art computer was apparently too stupid to realize that the third crew member had been deprived of oxygen for over an hour, and that it had, in fact, used a mathematical equation to execute him.

The dead crew member was Dr. Juan Garcia, an Armstrong Base geologist who had been sent along to catalogue and analyze the rock samples the *Hawking*'s two-man astronaut team retrieved from Abaddon's surface. He had been working in the cargo hold when the accident happened, and the automatic airlock defense had triggered before he could escape through the entryway hatch. The Brain had deduced that his life was expendable, using lightning quick calculations to determine the odds of his survival. They hadn't been good. Now it seemed to be bragging, reminding Cam repeatedly that Dr. Garcia was dead.

"Acknowledge death," he said, his tone a touch colder than he had intended.

"Acknowledged," the Brain said pleasantly.

Outside the bridge's thick windows, the brilliant swaths of stars whirled in a slow maelstrom as the *Hawking* drifted. The ship was dead in the water, so to speak. Cam peered through his ghastly reflection as the crippled vessel made another slow rotation, bringing the massive swirling globe of Jupiter back into view. The Great Red Spot stared back at him like an evil eye as it tore its way across the gaseous surface, as it had been doing since the very birth of astronomy. Another glinting evil eye stared back as well, shining so brightly against the inky backdrop of space that it blotted out the constellations and moons around it.

The luminous object was an asteroid; a planet-killer, to be precise. It was the reason the *Hawking* had been sent through the light gate in the first place. It was also the reason why Cam, along with his copilot and mechanic Steve "Monty" Montgomery, was beginning the slow process of dying by suffocation now.

Abaddon (the name selected for the asteroid roughly meant "the destroyer") had been snatched out of space by Jupiter's gravitational slingshot and thrown onto a direct collision course with planet Earth. Astaroth, Abaddon's smaller sibling, had gone undetected until the last possible instant— and so had already impacted. The UNSI had been caught with their pants down, as every thinking person knew would eventually happen; their NEA monitoring programs had never been allotted the funding they desperately needed to properly protect the Earth from dangerous space objects. Now, most of the east coast of the New United States was utterly obliterated, flooded and flattened from an onslaught of colossal tsunamis (Astaroth had impacted in the Atlantic Ocean, a hundred miles or so off the coast of North Carolina) and millions of people were dead. *Millions.*

Cam had seen a handful of satellite images and civilian videos before he had been too sickened by them to watch any more, punching the feed off with a savage fist to the console that had sent a key or two drifting. He'd seen waves that were tall enough to block out the sun, the unbelievably high walls of water arching like agitated vipers and streaked with shadowy hues of sea green and navy blue. The very flesh of the Earth seemed to be peeling away as the ocean receded. He had watched immense skyscrapers topple into each other like monstrous dominos, the ultra-high-resolution cameras recording even the smallest details— such as the victims, so many victims, tumbling out of shattered windows and soaring like rag dolls into the frothy new ocean beneath them. Some never made it to the surging water. They were thrown with enough ferocity to impact the tilting columns of collapsing buildings nearby, splattering against the unforgiving brick and permasteel like flies on a windshield. Even from space, Cam could see the dark flowers of blood that blossomed from their tiny forms as their bodies ruptured and stuck.

The geeks back at Armstrong Base hadn't wasted any more time after Astaroth had depopulated the east coast. They dispatched the *Hawking* to travel to Abaddon, land on its mountainous surface, and collect as many samples of it as the cargo hold could safely carry. In their words, "We need to know if it's a slug or buckshot". Abaddon was roughly the size of the state of Montana, the pre-Civil War II size of the state, anyway— more than enough to extinguish all remaining life on Earth and block out the sun's rays for decades. Command needed to know what method was best for diverting the destroyer; a thermonuclear rocket barrage on one side of the asteroid, meant to blow it off trajectory, or the UNSI's experimental new gravity tractor, which could, theoretically, pull it off course. If Abaddon was a rubble pile asteroid, rockets would pass right through it like darts through a swarm of locusts. There just wasn't any more time to waste on experiments. Humanity needed concrete answers, and fortunately, the technology and spacefaring capabilities existed to get them. Guesses and hypotheses were relics of the past, but good old-fashioned denial was holding strong. An asteroid had killed the dinosaurs, but oh, it couldn't happen to *us*.

Abaddon had gotten an early start when it came to causing trouble. Cam and Monty had made a successful landing on the asteroid's hostile surface, despite its rapid rate of rotation and gut-squeezing axial wobble. Its sheer size made the gravity generators in their exosuit boots useless. It generated its own gravity, though the pull was weaker than on Earth's moon. The men had traversed the rocky terrain by bouncing along like rabbits, careful not to put too much oomph into each leap. A strong enough jump might send them spiraling off into the cold embrace of space, and then asteroids and mass extinction would be the least of their concerns.

They'd collected their samples using G16 mechdrills that were built into the gauntlets of their suits. They had only recently been modified from the G12, which was permanently anchored and thus difficult to repair when the internal mechanisms went haywire. G16s were detachable little wonders that siphoned the material being pulverized and stored it in tanks the astronaut crews carried on their backs. Cam and Monty had done their solemn work without incident, even taking the briefest of moments to really admire the vastness and splendor of the Milky Way, and then jetted back up to the waiting airlock. Routine sample collection. Abaddon, however, did not give her secrets easily.

Shortly after liftoff, the asteroid had suddenly spewed a blast of debris into space like a geyser, the detritus expelled by an explosive gas buildup that had ruptured the asteroid's outer layers. Hunks of rock and metal were launched toward the *Hawking* like a shotgun blast, severing the Interstellar Laboratory vessel virtually in *half.* The remaining half of the *Hawking* had been successfully sealed and isolated by the Brain (luckily, the half of the ship that housed the airlock and decon chamber) but their precious supply of oxygen was still escaping through an incalculable amount of minute bullet holes in the fuselage. Far too many to locate and patch, not in time to save them. Not even if Cam helped Monty with the repairs, as he sometimes did. Garcia was already dead. Things were looking grim.

Cam tapped the call button, a holographic icon of a satellite dish with sound waves emanating from it, instructing the Brain to prepare the *Hawking* for communications with either Earth itself or Armstrong base, whoever picked up the receiver first.

"What can I do for you, Cam?" It said in a smooth robotic tone, using the nickname he had programmed in for himself. The mechanical passiveness of the Brain's voice was infuriating.

"I need to speak to Command, pronto."

"I'm sorry, Cam," the Brain said callously. "The satellite panel has been destroyed. I have taken the liberty of activating the emergency beacon and I have received a response from Armstrong Base, emergency response bay 11A. Help will arrive in..."

It paused for a half second to calculate.

"Twenty Earth hours, forty-two Earth minutes, thirty-seven Earth seconds."

"Gee, thanks," Cam muttered, pulling himself through the hatchway of the bridge and floating towards the crew quarters.

"You're very welcome," the Brain crooned after him.

After the accident, the bridge, crew quarters, and airlock were the only rooms left unsealed by the emergency airlock— not even the restroom was accessible, and that would be a pressing issue soon enough. Everything else was already a vacuum, most of the compartments ripped open and exposed to the harshness of space if not missing entirely.

Monty had strapped himself into his bunk, lying prone against the wall as casually as he might lie on the floor. As Cam glided into the cramped room, he was bombarded with tiny, acrid-smelling globules of amber liquid. He stuck his tongue out, catching one, and shuddered. Whiskey.

"One of these days they're going to catch you smuggling that flask on board," he scolded, pushing himself over to Monty's perch against the wall.

"You're gonna be glad I brought it," Monty garbled, snatching a piece of scribbled up paper from where it fluttered above him. He brought his prized flask to his lips and glugged another swig down his throat, more globules trailing from his lips as the flask came back down and disappeared into the lapel of his jumpsuit.

"What's that?"

"Equations," he said, tossing it to Cam. "Don't need the Brain. With both of us breathing normally, that means *not* stressed out of our minds, our air runs out in, oh... four hours and change."

Cam's heart skipped a beat. No stress, indeed.

"The retrieval boat will here in *twenty*, Monty. Someone has to be alive to initiate docking, and the Brain—"

"—Can't do it without a retinal scan. Yeah, yeah." He patted the swell of the flask on his chest. "I bring my juice for a reason, you know."

He ripped the straps from around his waist with a dry rasp and hovered freely, his long hair trailing behind him like seaweed. His ponytail had long since lost any semblance of organization, the rubber band that usually held it shooting for a participation trophy at best.

"I know the *Hawking*, Cam. Like the back of my hand. I knew we were screwed before the Brain did. And we *both* know what's at stake here."

"Let's just think for a damn second. We could put our suits back on—"

"—and we'd still be just as fucked, Cam. I checked both of them already; neither suit's oxygen store is above 10%. We were breathing pretty hard on the jump back to the airlock. They might buy us a little time, but without refills, we *still* won't make it until help comes."

Cam nodded, crossing his eyes to watch a bead of fresh sweat take flight from the tip of his nose. He was supposed to be the captain of the *Hawking*. He should have known that the oxygen tanks needed replaced without needing to have his prick held for him by the copilot. They weren't *Iron Man* suits, designed for prolonged flight and combat. They were glorified space suits, meant for quick jaunts on foreign planets and not much else. In depth exploration was still reserved for the rovers, who didn't need to eat or breathe.

"Command *needs* the samples," Cam said, his voice breaking even as he fought to steady it. "They have to know how to stop Abaddon, and if they guess, and they're *wrong*...." He snatched a few pungent drops of whiskey from the thin air for himself, sucking them in through pursed lips. "Monty... how the hell do we..."

"Choose?" Monty said, smiling wearily. "I thought of that too. I think I know how. I got the idea from what happened during mission prep. Remember that bit fault my drill kept getting?"

Cam remembered, all too well. The G16 mechdrill was a vicious little tool; it operated faster than the human eye could observe. The diamond-tipped bit was not a solid cone like the ones civilian power tools used; it was comprised of four separate sections that separated like a blooming flower, opening and closing like a hungry mouth to swallow whatever sample the scientist wielding it was collecting. The drill bit was also the siphon, which eliminated excess tubing that could get an astronaut killed in tight situations. The G16 required one siphon tube only, a clear three-inch hose that fed from the back of the drill's body and up the dominant arm of the user, secured out of the way by removable button straps. The bit itself was razor sharp, and so it was protected by a cylindrical housing to avoid injury or suit puncture. Nobody wanted blood droplets drifting around in zero gravity. When the trigger of the G16 was pulled, the drill bit emerged like a groundhog peering out of his hole.

Monty had been inspecting his personal mechdrill back in the spacious hangar of Armstrong Base before loading it onto the *Hawking* and had found one of the primary airlines leaking. One small crack allowed the air pressure to fluctuate, making the drill bit random and imprecise and causing it to sometimes fire with the press of the trigger and sometimes remain in its housing. Every great invention had its flaws, and for the G16, reliance on flimsy airlines was a big one.

That pesky air, Cam thought. *Always getting in the way.*

Monty's exosuit was secured to the wall beside his bunk, his mechdrill still attached to the palm of the right glove. He detached it, yanking the siphon hose off the flailing arm of his suit with a series of sharp pops. Next, he unscrewed the four bolts that connected the drill to the suit's storage tank, allowing the suction hose to hover and flex in the dwindling air like a single spaghetti noodle in a pot of hot water. Monty held his G16 up for Cameron to inspect, as if to show him that he wasn't up to any funny business, then hooked his finger around the coils of the primary airline. He pinched it between two fingertips, folding it in half like a plastic straw, then pulled. There was a small hiss of escaping air, nothing spectacular. He pumped the trigger again and again. As expected, the bit stuttered in and out of its gun barrel housing. Random and imprecise.

Cam's blood ran cold.

"I suppose we settle it as the Russians do," Monty said, with a pained smile. "There'll be enough compressed air left in the hoses to, uh..." he winced, gnawing at the inside of his lower lip. "To do the job."

He pressed the barrel of the G16 to his sweaty temple, his wayward strands of hair embracing it like the tentacles of a hungry squid. It really did look like a handgun; with the bit retracted, the mouth of the drill was flush against his skull. He stared into Cam's eyes, and a single tear drifted away from his right eye.

"Don't," Cam said, raising a hand to stop him, to swat the drill away from his head. Monty shook his head one time, moving the mechdrill with it to ensure it never left his temple.

"Gentlemen," came the idiot voice of the Brain over the *Hawking*'s PA system. "Oxygen levels are still falling at a dangerous rate. Please take precautions until rescue arrives. A reminder: there are emergency oxygen tanks stowed in the cargo hold."

"Fuck you," Cam snarled. Monty snorted.

"You're the mission commander," Monty said, lightly tapping the pad of his pointer finger against the flat gray trigger of the mechdrill. "Maybe we shouldn't play roulette. Maybe it should just be me."

"The captain goes down with the ship," Cam fired back, a break in his voice betraying his facade of stern courage and rigid adherence to duty. "I'm supposed to keep you safe." That much, at least, was not a facade. Cam was terrified and did not want to die, was *terrified* of dying, but he was more afraid of another crew member losing his life under his command.

"We're supposed to be keeping the *Earth* safe, Cam."

Cam desperately wished for something more profound to say, some undeniable argument that would pry the drill away from Monty's head faster than his hand ever could. It came to him in the form of a memory, a photograph that Monty kept taped to the inside of his suit helmet. The photograph was of a man he'd met in the canteen of Armstrong base, a handsome rover mechanic whose shaved head and considerable arms were adorned with intricate tribal tattoos and old-school nautical stars. In the picture, the mechanic had his arms wrapped affectionately around Monty's midsection. Monty's face was frozen in laughter, not a staged smile, but legitimate bliss. His hands were clasped over those of the mechanic, whose name he couldn't recall. It had been love at first sight.

"You have a boyfriend," Cam said triumphantly. "The rover guy with the tattoos. He's probably worried sick about you, waiting for you to come home."

"He's not my boyfriend yet," Monty said in a defeated tone. "We just like each other. And if we don't get the samples back to Armstrong, he'll die too. Who gives a fuck if you're single, Cam? You have just as much right to live as I do."

Before Cam could argue, Monty's body tensed and he closed his eyes, his fingers snapping closed around the trigger. The mechdrill whirred and hissed— but the bit stayed in its housing. Monty slowly opened his eyes again, looking stunned. Surprised to be alive.

Cam clenched his teeth, extending his open palm.

"Alright," he said in a gravelly voice. "That was your turn. Now it's mine."

Monty hesitated, then handed the drill over. Even in zero grav, it somehow felt exceptionally heavy in Cam's clammy hand. He had to manually place his numb finger over the trigger, his stomach folding into doughy knots as he lifted it to his temple. He took a deep breath that felt stolen, and before his brain could plead for him to avoid destroying it, he pumped the trigger once.

Whirrr-hisss.

No pain. No darkness. He was alive.

Through the viewport Jupiter was in sight again, the Great Red Spot watching raptly. Abaddon would drift into view again soon, and Cam was glad. Seeing the glowing invader would help to steel his nerves.

"My turn," Monty said firmly. He held out his hand. Cam passed the drill to him, trailing the siphon hose behind it like an umbilical cord. "Maybe we should strap in," he said, kicking off from the viewport and gliding to the small table and chairs that served as their dining room. Each chair was equipped with a seatbelt; it was hard enough to swallow in zero grav, let alone manage it while levitating. They snapped the buckles closed and stared at each other, droplets of each man's sweat hanging between their pained, reddening faces. Monty wasted no more time, lifting the mechdrill to his temple once again.

"For Earth," Monty whispered, closing his eyes, possibly for the last time. He pulled the trigger.

Whirrr-hisss.

He sighed heavily, his shoulders slumping and his chin dropping to his chest. Long strands of his hair trailed behind his head, flailing in the weightlessness like the legs of a dying spider.

"Maybe it won't fire at all," Cam said, primal fear beginning to season his words. His pulse was burning through oxygen he knew they couldn't spare, but his heart was a runaway engine now. "Then what the fuck do we do?"

His face red and glistening, Monty brushed a rogue hair out of his face and fired the mechdrill repeatedly, staring at it with the mad concentration that only highly skilled mechanics are capable of. Finally, the razor-sharp drill bit mouth peeked from the barrel, yawned open, and snapped close again. The metallic *chink* sound it made seemed very loud in the claustrophobic box that was their quarters.

"We're not going to murder each other," Monty breathed, visible relief collapsing his indignant expression as if he had been shouldering that possibility for a while. He swiped the back of his wrist across his mouth, sending sweat droplets flying like the shooting stars outside. Monty buried his hand in his jumpsuit and brought out the flask, unscrewing the cap and tossing it into a careless drift behind him. He intended to finish the flask this time.

"Gentlemen," the Brain droned again, startling them both. Monty waved a hand at it, upending the flask. "Oxygen levels are now critically low. Please take precautions until rescue arrives. A reminder: there are emergency oxygen tanks stowed in the cargo hold."

That's not all that's stowed in the cargo hold, Cam thought darkly. *There's also about 180 pounds of fresh meat.*

Cam could feel it in his chest now. Each shuddering breath he took was no longer... satisfying. That was the only word he could think of to describe it. It was beginning to feel stuffy and close in the crew quarters, the same suffocating sensation as waking up with a thick wool blanket draped over your head. Neither man realized that they had begun to pant as they played their deadly game of chance. Simple breaths through the nostrils weren't doing the job anymore.

Cam clenched his jaw hard enough to crack the joints, then took the mechdrill for his turn. The grip was slick with Monty's sweat. He stared at it for a while, considering the tool he might use to kill himself. His eyes scanned the dull metallic shine on the drillbit housing, the boxy body of the drill itself, the pebbled plastic of the grip between his fingers. He traced the length of the dismembered airline, following it from end to end like tracing an infection up and down one of his own veins. Abaddon made an encore appearance as the *Hawking* completed another gradual rotation, and he wrapped his finger around the trigger once more. He placed the warm barrel against his temple, parting the salt and pepper hair that grew there.

"For humanity... and for your mechanic with the tattoos," he said, managing a small smile even as the saliva dried in his mouth. Monty's lips twitched in what may have been a return smile, his hands and fingers wringing each other as if locked in a battle to the death.

Cam pulled the trigger.

Whirrr-hisss.

"*Goddamn fucking piece of* SHIT!" Cam roared, cocking his arm behind his head and throwing the mechdrill as hard as his muscles would allow. It tumbled through the sparse air like a lost kite. Monty grabbed the syphon hose and plucked it down like a tuft of pollen in a spring breeze.

"We don't have time to lose our shit now, Cam," he said gravely. "Let's just get it done."

The muscles in his thin forearm were taught and shivering beneath his skin, his wrist bones jutting awkwardly as he angled the mechdrill to rest against the side of his head.

"For Ryan."

When he pulled the trigger, he felt a small, hot pinch bite into his scalp. There was no panic, nothing but a queer sense of calm and final acceptance. Somehow, it was alright that he had lost the game. Monty knew he was dead, but for the time being he was still in shock and his body hadn't realized it yet. That's all it was, just the blind, stupid shock of his bodily functions ceasing and the electricity in his brain dissipating. Perhaps it was the alcohol, doing the job he had brought it along to do, helping to ease his passage to the afterlife.

He waited. And waited. And *waited.* His heart kept on thudding, his ears kept on hearing and his teeth kept grinding together. The only sensation he felt, other than a small but persistent burning on his temple, was a hot trickle of blood tickling its way out and the long strands of his hair pulling taught. When he finally lifted the heavy manhole covers that were his eyelids, he was staring into the wide-eyed visage of the ghost that used to be Cameron Bradley.

"You're *alive*," Cam sputtered, somehow looking relieved and disappointed at the same time. Monty moved to lower the G16 and felt his hair go with it. A few follicles dangled from the barrel of the drill, white clumps of scalp still clinging to their ends like nauseating fruit.

"Son of a bitch," Monty said, stunned into a strange sleepy alertness. "It fired, but... just enough to take a chunk of me... it almost..."

He yanked one of the hairs free of the hidden drill bit with a sound like a miniature guitar string breaking and cast it away to join the other bodily secretions peppering the bright white room.

Cam didn't have anything to say. It had been close, *damn* close, but Monty was still alive. That meant it was now his turn. Monty tried to look Cam in his wide and haunted eyes as he handed the drill over, but he couldn't muster the courage. Instead, he pivoted against the tight seatbelt and gazed out into the merciless black of space, and there was Abaddon, casting its deadly luminescence back at him. He stared at the asteroid, and the asteroid stared back.

"We're going to stop you," Monty growled to himself. "We're the greatest thing this universe has ever seen, and we are going to *stop. You.*"

Whirrr-chunk.

Monty started. That hadn't been the *whirrr-hisss* of failure he had been expecting; that had been a different sound. A... *meatier* sound.

He spun in the seat to check on Cam, ignoring the angry bite of the seatbelt against the underside of his small belly, and just before he went blind he heard another sound. A much worse sound.

Glorp.

Something hot and slippery splashed into his face, setting his eyeballs on fire and filling his nose with a coppery, metallic stench. He screamed, a guttural, primal roar that he didn't think he'd ever uttered before. His first frantic explanation was that something was leaking oil, some forgotten machine or overlooked part behind the ceiling panels had finally given up the fight and ruptured. When he managed to swipe the gunk out of his eyes and stared at the glistening red stains on his palms, shocked understanding began to settle in.

The air around him was filled with reddish-gray pulp, hundreds of thousands of tiny globules that looked like pulverized lasagna noodles. There was blood, too; more blood than he had ever seen. The crew quarters had become a ghastly mockery of the universe outside, complete with blood stars and brain planets drifting this way and that at varying speeds. They combined into larger clumps of gleaming crimson jelly or simply bounced off of one another like wads of tofu in a pot of soup. Monty felt something tickling on the corner of his mouth, something semisolid and lukewarm that prevented his lips from touching completely. He raked at his mouth with the back of his hand, the skin there blessedly free of Cam's head contents, and when he looked down again, he regretted it. It had been a vein-streaked curd of brain, adorned with a little tuft of black and gray hair and a small coating of bone dust.

"*Jesus fuck!*" He screamed, clambering for the seatbelt, desperate to get away from the table. There was nowhere to go, nowhere that was free of the cloud of viscera. As he planted one foot against the edge of the table and propelled himself back, he felt cooling blood dotting the back of his neck. He refused to consider what his hair might contain; that was a horror for another time, when a shower was readily available.

Cam looked like a bizarre aquarium decoration; his corpse held in place by the seatbelt but his arms unburdened. His lifeless fingers were still draped around the handle of the mechdrill, the dismembered siphon hose clogged with brownish muck and waving at Monty like a scolding finger.

Naughty boy, he imagined it saying. *You let your commander die, naughty boy.*

Why the fuck hadn't he thought of the goddamned hose? He knew he'd had a good reason to disconnect it, to make their dark game a little easier to play, but why hadn't he considered where the brain matter would eventually end up? If the G16 had enough air pressure to fire, it had enough air pressure to force material into— and out of— the hose. He'd paid dearly for that little oversight, that much was for sure. His tacky crimson mask and the smell of Cam's drying blood was a stark reminder of how fucking stupid he could be sometimes, sober or not. The hose drifting into his face at the perfect moment, well, that had just been an act of God.

"Emergency alert," the Brain said, and Monty realized it had been repeating itself once more just as it had after the death of Dr. Garcia. "Detecting zero vital signs in..." The Brain's mechanical voice changed tone, sounding to Monty like one of those old, automated phone calls people used to get. "Cameron Bradley. Repeat, no vital signs detected from: Cameron Bradley. Recommend immediate attention. Emergency alert—"

"Acknowledge death," Monty said in a leathery voice.

"Acknowledged," the Brain said. "Oxygen levels are dangerously low but are stabilizing."

"No shit," Monty snapped to the ceiling, where he always imagined the Brain's voice originated from although he knew better. There were fresh bloodstains dotting it like fireworks, new ones blossoming on the white steel as droplets collided with it. He made himself look at Cam. Cam who had died so that he, and nine billion lives back on Earth, might not.

Cam's arms were still floating above his head like he was riding a pre-war roller coaster. His right eye had been forced most of the way out of its socket, probably from the change in pressure as the drill bit penetrated his skull. It looked impossibly huge compared to its counterpart, which had neatly and serenely closed. Monty felt like he was trapped beneath the lens of a microscope and Cam was staring at him, staring so hard that his eye was popping out of his head like that of an angry cartoon character. He willed his goosebumps away. Cam wasn't staring at anything. Cam was dead.

The Brain reminded him again that although stabilizing, oxygen levels were still dangerously low and emergency oxygen tanks could be found in the cargo hold. It was maddening; no matter how advanced humanity grew to be, computers remained unreliable pieces of shit. The *Hawking* had been equipped with a very *expensive* piece of shit, and that was where the similarities ended. Still, it was right about one thing— oxygen levels were low, and if the rescue team had any hiccups, any setbacks at all, he would be dead too. It was time to think of himself for once and focus on finishing the mission.

Gliding across the crew quarters, Monty had to fan his hands in front of him to knock bits of brain and gobbets of coagulated blood out of his way. Each time he felt the cool gel of brain matter caress his bare skin, his stomach rolled and his throat filled with burning, sour vomit. He kept his jaw clenched, his face drawing into a snarl. He would *not* add vomit to the mix. As if it wanted to chime in and be a part of the action, his bladder began to ache and throb. Fortunately, his exosuit, which he was planning to wear to prolong his oxygen, could collect and filter urine.

It was an incredibly awkward struggle. Zero gravity made the exosuit weightless, but it was still cumbersome and composed of tough material that didn't like to flex but also loved to tangle around itself. Monty spun and whirled, feeling like a turd orbiting a slow toilet as he wrestled his arms and legs into the musty confines.

Behind him Cam's slack arms still swayed and waved lazily, cheering him on, taking in all the details with one protruding eye. He was beginning to look like some sort of creature; his skin bulged awkwardly in places, his cheeks sunken but his neck and arms swelling in places. His limbs were beginning to resemble balloon animals. Cam's skin was graying, but some misshapen patches looked bruised. Deep red and purple blotches were welling up on his flesh as the blood beneath began to thicken, floating freely in the abandoned caverns of his arteries. He still held onto the mechdrill that had killed him, his fingers stiffening around the grip.

I can't wait to get the fuck out of here.

Monty was ashamed of the revulsion he felt towards the corpse of a man who had been his friend and partner mere moments before. He muttered to himself that it was normal, as common as birds in the trees to feel that way about a dead human being. Wasn't it the natural order of things, to stay as far away from death as possible? Even so, stealing one last glance at Cam as he pulled his breather helmet down and began to secure it to his collar, he was drawn to the one bulging eye. It saw everything and nothing at the same time, horrific in its glassy lifelessness. He turned his back and switched the exosuit on, mentally bracing for the inevitable barrage of alerts and alarms that would warn him that his oxygen tank needed replaced.

    Cool air began to flood his face mask, chilling the glaze of sweat and blood on his searing skin like a gentle, merciful kiss. His tired eyes shifted up and to the left, where his treasured photograph was taped.

    He didn't need to look where he was going to find the bridge. He could have navigated the *Hawking* blindfolded. He kept his eyes locked on the picture, staring at it so intently that it almost seemed to move. The tiny pixels that combined to form their smiles appeared to move and twitch, and the photograph became a silent film. He could hear Ryan's laughter, startlingly shrill despite the booming, almost hoarse voice that comprised his everyday speech. It was that laughter, echoing across the hangar bay, that had first drawn his attention to Ryan. It was impossible to consider that up until then, they hadn't even known each other existed.

    Monty eased himself into Cam's chair, and his silent film was placed on hold by a sudden stab of guilt that felt more like a heart attack. He supposed it was the act of sitting in the pilot's seat, quite literally taking the place of Cameron— who was as dead as disco because of *his* idea. *His* solution to the oxygen problem, *his* sabotage of the mechdrill to give them a fair and unbiased suicide tool.

    There you have it, right there in front of your face. It was fair. *You took your turns; hell, you almost bit the big one yourself, or have you forgotten that stinging bald spot on your temple? It was fair.* Fair.

He was momentarily deafened by the canned, mechanical whooshing sound of his breaths amplified inside the spherical helmet. He found the picture again, breathing in through his nose and out through his mouth. The metallic reek of blood was sealed in with him, but that was alright. He imagined that it wasn't blood he was smelling. It was engine oil. Oil from an F-91 *Comet* or from one of the six unreliable engines on the *UNSI-SF Leviathan,* and it was clinging to Ryan's hands and staining his clothes no matter how much washing each endured. It was a smell he had come to love, the familiarity of it. Especially when it was mixed with cologne and even a hint of sweat. The smell of a hard worker, and the smell of the man he was growing to love more and more with each second he spent away from him.

"Alert me when the rescue boat gets here," he said dreamily, catching the pithiest glimpse of the blinding spheroid that was Abaddon. The destroyer was still on its deadly course with Earth, indifferent to the attempts being made to stop it, and still shining so brightly that it hurt to look at. Monty wondered if perhaps Ryan might be out on a smoke break, looking up into the cloudy murk of the Milky Way and seeing that same fatal glow from a dingy hangar window.

"I will sound an emergency alert when rescue arrives, Monty."

Alright, he thought irritably. *Now don't talk anymore.*

He focused on the picture even as Jupiter loomed out of the darkness again and dominated the bridge windows. It was an incredible sight to behold and one that a scant few would ever see; in fact, it was reasonable to assume that he might be one of the last human beings to cross the solar system before fate wiped them all out. The picture was still the sight he preferred.

He imagined it moving again, and then his traumatized brain began to broadcast a movie in his head. He imagined parties, raucous planet-wide raves celebrating the rescue of Earth. He imagined Ryan pointing up at the sky to where they would both see Abaddon, nothing more than a speck of pulsating light, no longer moving towards Earth but drifting away to cause panic and annihilation for some other planet. He imagined getting so shitfaced drunk that he might begin to prefer women and collapsing into bed. Not a bunk he had to be strapped into but an honest-to-God *bed.*

Sleep, he thought, smirking to himself. *I don't think I'll ever sleep again.*

Monty knew his dreams would forever be marred by his mission on the *Hawking.* He would probably end many nights of shallow sleep with screams and sweaty sheets, his vision still stained with the image of Cam's swelling face and protruding eye like his face was stained with blood and brain now.

No way I'll ever sleep again after this shit.

But after leaning back in Cam's pilot chair, his booted feet crossed and propped up on the glittering control console, Monty did exactly that. His dreams were of love and Earth, not death and destruction, and Monty's dream-self was soon whispering into the prickly neck of his beloved Ryan: "If this is a dream, I don't want to wake up."

Karma: The Confession of David Lee Redfield

Dr. Compton,

Enclosed you will find the handwritten confession letter of David Lee Redfield, as per your request. Frankly we're glad to be rid of it; the case has been considered closed for more than a century now and I had marked it for disposal. I hope it helps you in that psyche study you mentioned. I've never been able to understand the mind of a serial killer myself. I suppose that's why people like you have a job. I know you can handle it but be warned. This letter will turn your hair white, especially his "Ravenous God" obsession.

I have also included a typed version, as his handwriting is little more than excited scribbles in some sections (particularly when he details his sexual exploits and murders). Speaking of the murders—we have linked Redfield to at least eight homicides here in New York City and four in Point McKellan. We cross-referenced his alleged whereabouts with relevant victim locations, focusing on victims of strangulation. The point is that we're taking his word for it, nothing is particularly solid. My personal opinion is that the man was a hopeless psychotic, and unless he had flawless memory, much of his story is probably exaggerated (I know enough about these crazies to know that they like to do that).

If you need any more information on Redfield or his known/assumed victims, don't hesitate to contact me. I'm always happy to help or locate someone who can.

Yours,
Remy Dodge
Evidence Collector

P.S. Redfield's handmade garrote is on display in our little crime museum here at the station, but if you'd like to analyze that as well, I'm sure I could pull some strings and let you borrow it for a while. Just let me know.

(ORIGINAL DOCUMENTS! DO NOT CREASE!)

(4/10/1912)

My name is David Lee Redfield, an American man of limited means from Point McKellan, Pennsylvania, and I confess to be a serial murder. I am responsible for the dead mobster on the floor beside my feet, Walter "Pale Boy" Luchino and many, many others before him. I'm writing this because I am proud of what I've done; he was a skilled and tenacious killer for hire who managed to track me here, while recovering from injury, all the way from a New York City pier. I'm writing this because I did the world a favor by ending his life, thus ushering in the karma he has so diligently sown and sending another morsel of sustenance for my Ravenous God to feast upon. I'm writing this because by the time the body is found (and unlike my other victims, he *will* be missed) I'll be long gone; relaxing in luxury while you all scramble to find me. But you won't. I'm not going back to my usual hunting grounds, and I will no longer use my real name beyond this letter. I will change my habits. You will not have a solid profile by which to hunt me. I will destroy evidence and frame others for my crimes. I will be a phantom. You will save yourselves a lot of time and sweat by framing this letter (to honor my service to you) and forgetting that I ever existed. I am, for all intents and purposes, dead to the world.

Pale Boy (so called for his strange white complexion) died by strangulation with a homemade garrote, constructed from an axe handle and some piano wire. I think you'll find it a clever contraption. I've tucked it into his right coat pocket as I've discovered that I much prefer stabbing— but more on that later. His head, which you'll find quite destroyed, was caved in with nothing more than the foot of my good leg and done just for the simple pleasure of it. It wasn't as difficult as you might think; it felt like stomping on a pumpkin that hasn't quite ripened yet. Oh, how the seeds sprayed across the floor! All the gory details in due time, however; it's best to begin at the beginning.

I am by no stretch of the imagination a good man, so don't pity my hardships; in fact, I'm a rather exact replica of the thing that served as my father. I know I am a poison person and I accept it as fact. Once I even believed a demon inhabited my body, a cruel and wicked thing that guided me along my bloody path with talons sunk into my shoulders and delicate lips that whispered horrible inspiration in my ear. I know now that I am a servant of the starved almighty, and he has forgiven me for my mistaken assumption. I hear his voice from time to time, the soothing music of his beard, and it is a beautiful song indeed. But I am not crazy. Do not *ever* think me crazy. I am the hand of karma, the tooth and claw of the Ravenous God, and you are chops on the spit.

I've never held down an honest job for very long because I don't like rules and I despise authority. I make my living as a gambler, sometimes an honest game of cards and sometimes a dishonest one— depending on how much is at stake. I've also committed more armed robberies than I can count, and I dabble in grave robbing when I know they're planting a wealthy bastard's carcass with a mess of valuables he'll never need. You'd be amazed by what people want to rot with, as if it will do them any good once the coffin lid closes and the grave diggers finish their work. I say I dabble because I don't care for the smell of decay, nor do I appreciate the unsightly mold that grows upon the flesh of the bodies.

It was my gambling habit that brought me here to Southampton in the first place. I had worked my way from Point McKellan to New York City, robbing, stealing, killing, and cheating my way up the coast and spending most of my nights in whatever warm whorehouses I stumbled across. I got the services for free, if you catch my meaning. It's easy enough to persuade a drunken whore that you'll pay after the fucking is done, and then a few stiff slaps are all it takes to convince them that they don't really *need* the money after all. Sometimes I strangled them during. The clenching of their muscles is exhilarating, the clawing of their nails pleasantly painful. Dare I recommend that you try it sometime?

Yes, my wallet was growing but not at the same pace as my nerve. The police were either too blind or too apathetic to ever notice me or my recreational activities. I've been told that I have a kind face with balmy eyes, and that I often smile without realizing it. I suppose that helps to disarm my victims, in which case I'm very grateful for it. I feel invincible; lesser men have hung or faced the firing squad for the things I've done, and I do them again and again with no consequence. It's like I was born to be a professional murderer and I am very, *very* good at what I do.

I had been in New York City only for a week or so, haunting the local slum bars and swindling men out of their meager paychecks. I happened across a dumpy little watering hole called the Bare Knuckle that even offered me a job of sorts; I helped the owner, a very fat and nearly crippled Jew by the name of Benson, clean the place up and dispose of rabble rousers. In return, I got to sleep in a cozy bar instead of out on the street or under a bridge someplace. I didn't have to spend any of my loot on room and board, and that made sleeping on a hardwood floor a little easier to tolerate. Benson never offered me a pillow or a blanket as he was always frightened of me, but nonetheless I enjoyed my first "real" job. The place never got overly filthy, save for a few spilled whiskey glasses and the occasional vomit puddle. I swelled with excitement when some drunken oaf would cause a ruckus and I'd get to drag him into the piss trough of an alley behind the Knuckle, then proceed to beat and strangle him within an inch of his life.

That was when I made the garrote I used to kill Luchino. Remember, you'll find it in his pocket. I found an old axe handle in one of the alley's trash cans, and I lifted some piano wire from a storage shed some careless cunt had neglected to lock. I attached a decent length of piano wire to the center of the axe handle, looping it through holes I made with a brick and nail. I fashioned it into a portable noose with a convenient handle, something like a wooden bow tie. All I had to do was loop that wire around a troublemaker's neck and haul him outside, slung over my shoulder like a sack of dirty laundry. Alternatively (as was the case with Luchino) I could *twist* the handle like a giant corkscrew, tightening the wire until my victim's airway was cinched shut. Claw at that wire all you want; once it digs into the flesh of your neck, you'll scratch your own skin off before you'll ever slip a finger under it. I reckon I could take someone's head completely off with it, if I was properly rested and had the motivation to do so.

My victims' heads looked like overripe plums before I let them have a breath, and by then they were too close to death to put up much of a fight. The Bare Knuckle didn't have many repeat offenders because one way or another, they didn't come back. Benson never intended for me to kill them, at least, he never ordered me to. Sometimes my urges were at the helm, and I simply took it too far. Don't pity these people, please. Sinners are born to be cast into the maw; any educated man will tell you that.

I spent a few happy months at the little establishment. One night after the Bare Knuckle had closed, I was sitting at the empty bar with a handkerchief full of ice pressed to my fist. I still bear the scar from that fight; a man's front teeth are sharper than you might think. I was flexing my stiffened hand open and closed, pressing down tight to try to stop the bleeding. I glanced up when I heard the tap-scuff of Benson approaching.

"Did he run off yet?" I asked, bringing my fist to my mouth to suck some of the blood off.

"Not yet, Lee," Benson puffed, out of breath from the exertions of supporting his bulk with a cane. He pulled out his own threadbare handkerchief and dabbed his glistening forehead with it. "I don't think he's breathing, to be frank."

Benson always called me Lee; I didn't mind. It was short and sweet. A good American nickname.

"He shouldn't have started trouble," I said, with a slight rise and fall of my shoulders. "I'll dump him in an hour or two."

"That's four, my boy," Benson replied gravely, staring down his nose at me. "Your luck is bound to run out sooner or later. And you know I don't condone these murders."

He poured some whiskey into a glass and slid it down the bar to me. No ice, just how I like it. I was training him well.

"People will learn not to act like jackasses when they come to your fine establishment," I said, smirking as I sipped my drink. My sarcasm wasn't lost on Benson. The Bare Knuckle was anything but fine, and if you were to put a pile of peanuts on the toe of your shoe, the rats would crawl right out of the holes in the walls and eat their fill with no fear.

"As much as I would hate to lose an enforcer like you, I might know of a way for you to skip town. If you're interested in a fast escape before the law comes knocking, I mean."

I downed the last of the whiskey, fighting the urge to grimace at the sting in my throat, and cast the fat little man a dark stare.

"Did you just *fire* me, Benson?"

He wilted like a cut rose, ever so carefully moving his cane to block his considerable body. It wouldn't have done him any good if I had wanted him dead. He knew full well about the garrote poking out of my back pocket and just how effective I could be with it.

"Not *firing*, Lee. I'm *helping*. I don't want to see you executed, that's all."

"That's all," I repeated in an incredulous tone of voice. "Helping me right into the gutter."

A slight fog had begun to develop around the rounded lenses of Benson's spectacles. His piggy eyes, watery and twitching with nervousness, looked like twin moons suspended in a cloudy night sky.

"Lee, don't you read the *Times*? They found one of the bodies floating in the river, and you left a deep cut around his neck from when you... you know, dragged him outside. The police will be checking establishments near the riverbanks, you *have* to see what I mean."

I hadn't read the *Times*, because I don't have much concern for matters that don't concern me. I'll admit, I was stunned. I had never considered the possibility of being caught. The Ravenous God wouldn't *allow* His avenging angel to be caught.

Benson grunted as he stooped behind the counter, rummaging around until he found the edition of the *Times* with my victim in the police reports. I read the narrow column six times, just to be sure. The description of the dead man's neck, marred with a lacerating ligature mark, sealed it for me. The New York police would indeed be hunting me, and though I was careful, I had developed a sloppy habit of leaving my garrote in plain sight.

I wadded the paper up and slammed it back onto the table, scaring Benson so badly that he jumped and broke wind.

"It's a damn shame," I growled, signaling for another glass of whiskey with two wiggles of my pointer finger. Benson obliged. "Do you believe in God, Benson?"

He swallowed hard, the fleshy pouch under his chin quivering. "You know I do, Lee."

"Mm. How about karma?"

Benson looked thoughtful for a moment, then shrugged and nodded.

"I suppose I do; what you put into the world tends to find its way back to you."

"Exactly," I said, stabbing my finger at him. I reached behind my back slowly, deliberately. Knowing it would terrify the old man. I hooked the loop of bloodstained wire and pulled it out of my pocket, chewing the tip of my tongue to keep the insistent smile from my face. Benson's eyes bugged out of his head as he looked upon it. He tried to press himself flat against the shelves of liquor behind him, a hopeless attempt at making himself small. I let the smile out as a glass decanter of brownish-gold liquor tumbled from the shelf and exploded on the floor.

"Benson, I firmly believe that I am the right hand of God. His avenger. His punisher of the wicked. And this is my fiery sword."

I slammed the stiff wire against the bar top like a whip, relishing the hissing sound it made as it rushed past my ear and the sharp crack it made as it slashed across the stained wood. Benson had begun to cry, and the fat old man wasn't even trying to hide it. I believe that *he* believed he was about to die, and I let him think so. I enjoyed the power I had over him. I could feel an erection beginning to push against the crotch of my slacks, as normally happens, though it was not as hard as it would have been had I been actively strangling Benson. Sometimes after I commit a murder, I find myself wishing I had a spare pair of underclothes. I don't much enjoy the cold stickiness that follows when my spunk begins to dry.

"W— what are you gonna do, Lee? Are you g-gonna hurt me?"

I smiled again, caressing the wooden axe handle as if it were the breast of a lover. I waited before I spoke, soaking in the electric energy of his mortal terror.

"No," I said after I'd had my fill. I thought the old sow would die of relief rather than fright. "You've been good to me, Benson. You've *enabled* me, and I believe you may be right. I've been very liberal with my work, and I wouldn't want to bring the police down on this oasis of yours."

"Like I said Lee, I want to help you."

His face said otherwise. His face said *please, for the love of Christ, get the hell out of my life.*

"Tell me your plan then."

He stooped under the counter again, and for a moment I thought he might be rummaging around for the tiny pistol I knew he kept there. Benson never bothered to clean or oil it, and so I knew he didn't realize I had filled the cylinder with empty shells the very same night I had found it. It was a painstaking job, using a pair of rusted pliers to pluck each bullet off by only the light of a candle. But it was smart. Benson wouldn't need the gun even if he had the balls to shoot someone, not as long as I was around.

Had he drawn on me that night, *he* would have been the next to bloat and bob in the river. He would have been hung by my hand rather than his own (which, I heard from a fellow traveler familiar with the bar, he did shortly after I left for England. His suicide note was little more than an apology, but he didn't specify what he was sorry for). The old man must have looped the rope around the strongest beam in the Bare Knuckle, I can tell you that much.

"I wrote it on a napkin," he huffed, pushing against the counter to stand upright again. "You never know when information might come in handy."

He unfolded it in front of me, his handwriting resembling a wad of smashed spiders rather than notes.

"You're going to have to translate."

He tapped the word "poker" (a legible letter P followed by loops and snarls of ink) impatiently, as if he were trying to teach an idiot to read.

"It's a high-stakes poker game, Lee. A secret one. One of those crime boss types was in here with a few of his goons, remember? He had the black bowler hat and the curly mustache, looked like a ghost."

I shook my head. Most likely, I had been out in the alley smothering someone and had missed the gentlemen in question.

"I don't recall seeing a ghost with a curly mustache."

Benson tapped the napkin again. He was doing a poor job of hiding how eager he was to be rid of me, and it set my blood to boiling. The urge to reach out and strike him was overpowering.

"He said they do it for fun, just a way to blow off steam and throw some money around. He said all you need to do is buy your way in, but he didn't say anything about people outside his organization joining. I figure if you can prove to them that you're not a cop, they'll let you play. I *know* how good at poker you are, Lee. You could clean them out and live like the king of England for *years*. And it doesn't happen for another two days, so you'll have time to get some money together and work on your poker face.*"*

Benson was both right and wrong. I am decent at poker, but I am a savant when it comes to *cheating* at poker. I'm a veritable magician at the card table. I suppose you could chalk it up to the Ravenous God rewarding me further, but to this day, I've only been caught once. Just once.

My usual tactic is a little maneuver I like to call "the tuck and fold". It takes a cool head to pull it off; all you do is wait for a decent hand and pluck out the card you want to keep. I like to bring my hands down under the table under the guise of keeping them hidden from the other players, but if I'm playing with a suspicious lot, I just knock my glass over. Then, when I'm safely out of view, I slip the card under my thigh or up my sleeve.

Next comes the fold, and that's the most important part. It's not unlike walking away from a murder; you have to be calm and collected, casual. No sweating or fidgeting. No shifting of the eyes. You utter a small curse and mumble something about the poor hand you've been dealt and lay your cards on the table— but you do *not* spread them out. Then the other players might count what you've laid down and realize a card is missing. If you're quick and sly, you can swindle just about anyone with that trick. Feel free to use it, dear reader.

"I have to admit, it's tempting," I said. "Dangerous but tempting."

"Well, you're a dangerous man," Benson said a little too casually, then stiffened when he realized he might have just insulted me. I took it as quite the opposite of an insult.

"That's right," I replied in the most sinister voice I could conjure. "I *am* a dangerous man."

I scooped up the napkin and tried to read the address Benson had spasmed onto it, but it was futile. I threw it back at him and laughed as it clung to the sweat-soaked fabric of his shirt.

"I can't read where this shindig is going down."

"Oh!" He cried, with delight in his voice. Old Benson really was chomping at the bit to be rid of me. His rosy cheeks swelled as he fought to hide his smile. "It's at the Silver Lion, that fancy bar with the—"

"I know where it is," I snapped, feeling the warm tingle of anticipation and conniving excitement flood into my chest. Benson was about to tell me about the sign that hung above the entrance of the Silver Lion, a monstrous metal lion's head with its mouth gaped wide in a vicious roar and its metallic fangs gleaming. That place had immediately caught my attention because the eyes of the lion were bright electric bulbs that made it look like a demonic guardian of Hell, and the inside of the mouth was an open flame torch that had to be lit by hand every evening. It was imposing and alluring at the same time, which I believe was the intent for an establishment owned by a crime lord. I won't say I was afraid; fear is something I don't normally feel. I was cautious and wary, but I was also eager to step up to the challenge. I was frothing at the mouth to collect the reward the Ravenous God would provide for me.

Benson looked relieved, but he also kept one meaty hand plastered across the swell of his gut. He looked like he was about to sick his dinner up all over the floor. He downed a glass of water, his hand shaking so badly that I could hear the tinkling sound of the ice knocking around. Then he began to puff towards the restroom.

"I need to have a movement," he said with a pained and awkward smile. "Lee, if you please... please go and check on the man in the alley." Green waves of nausea were crisscrossing his face like turbulent weather fronts colliding. "Please don't make him suffer."

I winked at him and saw his knees go weak. The man was absolutely petrified of me, and yet he had never taken any steps to stop me. What I did benefited him, kept his bar free of rabble and kept thieving hands out of his register. I wonder sometimes if he told himself that in the end, wracked with guilt but grateful for his time with me even as he tightened the noose around his throat.

When I heard the heavy thud of the restroom door closing, followed by the sharp clack of the bolt driving home, I sauntered over to the register and helped myself to a few stacks of crisp bills. I stuffed them into my pocket and began to whistle a hymn as I made my way to the Bare Knuckle's rear exit, a haunting tune that often burrowed its way into my head although I had no earthly idea where I'd learned it. It's called "Nearer my God to Thee", I believe. If you've never heard it, I pity you.

The open door cast a long and misshapen rectangle of amber light across the dirty bricks of the alley, the arms and legs of my shadow stretched and distorted into a nightmare image that crept along beside me as I walked. My whistles were shrill but precise, intermingling with my footfalls and following me down the length of the brick corridor like curious rodents. I could see the lumpy form of the man I'd dragged out there, swallowed in darkness and heaving as he snored in reflexive breaths. I approached the man, wetting my lips to start the hymn over again, and began to rifle through his pockets. His wallet was frayed and fat; it didn't hold enough to carry me to old age, but perhaps enough to get me into the poker game when combined with Benson's unwitting donation. Ah, the Ravenous God never ceases to reward His agent on Earth.

I stared into his face as I slid my fingers inside his sport coat. The color had never fully returned. Even in the darkness I could see the purple hue of his cheeks and the bluish tint of his lips. His eyes were open but unblinking. I could see the whites, speckled with broken blood vessels like seasoning salt on a frothy bowl of potato soup. It felt like minutes passed between each of his tearing breaths. He was gone, no question. His body just didn't know it yet. I placed my forehead against his, the tip of my nose scrunching against his. I whistled my hymn down into his open mouth, nearly kissing the living dead man as his body lurched to rasp in another futile gasp.

"*Nearer tooo theeeeee...*" I sang in a mock opera voice as I lifted one foot and planted it on the man's lacerated neck. I leaned into it, focusing my entire body weight on the heel of my foot. I could hear the rough scratch of the man's sweaty hair against rock as his skull was driven into the filthy paving stones. Something snapped inside the ruin of his throat with a muted crunch, vibrating the sole of my foot.

His wet snores ceased almost instantly. There was a small bubbling hiss from his mauve lips, one final agonal whisper to let me know that my job was done, and then I felt him go limp. There was a nauseating *frap* as his bowels let go. Mind you, I know why the body does such a thing and I've heard that sound numerous times before, but it never ceases to turn my stomach. I apologized to the Ravenous God for sending Him a soul in such a soiled condition. Then, with a deep breath and a brief stretch of my muscles, I looped the garrote under his slack chin and began the long and arduous process of dragging his carcass across the crooked stones and down to the river. Hauling the dead ones around feels like ice skating uphill, I assure you. It never gets any easier, and they certainly aren't any help.

I planted my shoe on the dead man's chin and kicked, sending his bulk over the ledge. His legs trailed after him, and I tittered at the way he fell. He looked like a great fat starfish; what better place for him than under the foamy murk?

He broke the surface with a resounding splash, sending jets of white-green foam into the night air like distress rockets. The sound of it startled a flock of pigeons into frenzied flight, their wings beating against one another and raining tufts of feathers like dandelion cotton. They were beautiful in their panic as they rose into the sky, skating across the icy surface of the moon before disappearing behind the darkened buildings around me. For a moment I envied the birds and their miraculous ability to take flight on a whim, to escape danger in seconds, unreachable and untamable as the other animals, prisoners of gravity, could only watch.

You are *like a bird*, I mused to myself. *You always take flight on a whim, and the lesser creatures can never get their claws into you, can they?*

No. They never have, and they never will. But that doesn't mean there haven't been close calls, close enough to make me question the Ravenous God's hand and whether it was still on my shoulder. The closest of them all was that viper pit of a poker game, the night I came the closest to death that I've ever been and the night I earned the teardrop-shaped scar on my left thigh.

* * *

I never saw old Benson again. After the shootout at the Silver Lion, my life became a runaway rail car that never slowed until very recently. The Ravenous God truly does work in ways that mortal men will never comprehend. Nevertheless, although He allowed me to be wounded, He ensured my hasty escape aboard the *Whitecap* while the bodies I left in my wake were still draining. Would you like to hear that story? Of course you would. I'll indulge you.

I spent the days leading up to that fateful game in the slummy whorehouses that I love so much. Dives that reeked of stale cigarette smoke and musty, stiffened sheets that could probably stand up on their own like perverted pieces of furniture. Somehow, that smell always feels like home to me.

I charmed my way into a new bed each night, tapping into my everlasting wellspring of charisma and guile, then nearly exhausted myself slamming homely faces into lumpy mattresses and clenching my hands around pasty, protruding hip bones. I like to make it hurt. I dug my fingertips into the wells of their pelvises hard enough to leave clusters of bruises that look like ripe grapes. I twisted many long tangles of hair into greasy knots around my fist, pulling it like reins until the skin of their necks grew so taught that it threatened to rupture, and the follicles came out in wads. My pelvis and upper thighs were constantly bruised and tender to the touch, and after the fourth or fifth "exchange" I began to walk like an old west cowboy with an awkward, bowlegged gait.

I never paid a single cent. I couldn't afford to; I needed all my cash to throw around at the poker game, and the roll of bills in my pocket still looked alarmingly small. But as I said before, there is a very simple way to persuade a whore that the privilege of being your bitch for the night is payment enough. The gruff men running the places were no obstacle either; they lacked the manhood to stand up to me or they were too intoxicated to be bothered. Some of the bottles they kept behind their counters weren't whiskey; they looked like medicine bottles to me, but they threw them back like water.

    The women would scamper to them, breasts wagging from the tatters of their lingerie and blood glistening under their noses. They'd point to where I sat drinking, babbling and blubbering, and the pimps would send them away again with the same care they might have had for a bothersome fly buzzing in their faces. I found myself longing for one of the beasts to approach me, scold me, challenge me to a fight. I have these urge, you see, these *itches*, that no amount of fucking could ever scratch. I believe they could feel my aura, the almighty energy I exude, and knew that to face me was to face the hunger of the Ravenous God Himself.

    My thigh muscles still throbbed with every step as I approached the ornate entrance to the Silver Lion. The entire place was wreathed in blue smoke, pouring out from between the ornate lion's shimmering fangs and billowing from the open double doors. There were knots of shady people dotting the front walk of the bar. Everyone seemed to be up to no good; I even saw a sickly-looking old man in a wheelchair with a revolver in his hands, barely able to lift the weapon as he held it up for another gorilla-sized thug to inspect. Even from a distance I could see the creases and valleys of his ancient face, illuminated by the cigarette clenched within his frown. Oh yes, I knew right away that I would be in considerable danger there. I couldn't resist, and I was spurred on by the gentle nudge of the Ravenous God on my back.

    Go on, soldier, I heard Him whisper from across the cosmos. *Go and be rewarded.*

    I hesitated. Would they allow me to enter with my tool? It wasn't a gun, but even so, I was quite deadly with it. To me, the garrote wasn't a weapon at all, but a child of sorts. I had crafted it, perfected it, given it noble purpose. I'm ready to part with it as I pen these words, yes, but I was not ready to lose it that night. I began to spy and plot.

Surely enough, two suited gentlemen sauntered through the open doors of the Silver Lion and extended their arms like Christ on the cross. Two monstrous arms snaked out from behind the left doorframe and began to pat them down, clumsy and heavy smacks that rocked the slender men on their feet. To my amusement, the muscled doorman even cupped the gentlemen's crotches seemingly hard enough to mash their potatoes. Very thorough. They paid him no mind. They were most likely frequent visitors and knew that this was ordinary (and truthfully, necessary).

I began to put on a show for anyone who might be observing me. I danced from foot to foot, squeezing my sore thighs together and pressing the palm of hand against my penis. I had already spied a cluster of overflowing trash cans, you see, and I needed a reason to approach them that wouldn't arouse suspicion.

I pretended to urinate, sliding my beloved garrote from my pocket and letting it clatter to the grimy brick. It felt like setting fire to a masterpiece of art; my heart ached seeing it lying there in a soiled snarl of wire and wood. It looked like nothing more than discarded trash, but that was good. I hoped it would still be there when I left the Lion, and that I wouldn't be in a hurry when I came to retrieve it.

An elephantine honk echoed across the building tops, startling me out of my determined walk to face the door oaf. It was the noisy blat of a ship's whistle, steam shrieking out from high atop a smoke funnel. It had come from the east, calibrating my mental compass. The docks were east; if it all went sour, I would simply dash to the east. Then I could buy or threaten my way onto a ship and make a clean getaway after I'd dispatched anyone foolish enough to chase me.

I nodded to myself and the whistle screamed again, as if affirming my plan. I suppressed a wry smile. I didn't *need* an escape plan. I didn't *need* a ship to run to. The Ravenous God was my escape plan, as He always had been. He would surely see me through and usher me safely to my next hunting ground. So, with His encouraging words tickling the sensitive hairs of my ear canals, I stepped in line to face the golem guarding the door.

He stared at me with the vacuous, slightly curious gaze of a feeble ape. His dim eyes flicked from my head to my shoes, slowing briefly to focus on the stains and tears in my clothing. He snorted, an animal grunt that suggested amusement. He crossed his arms, the sleeves of his plain brown shirt straining to contain the meat of his biceps.

"Arms out and spread ya legs," he growled, his voice butchered by years of cigarette smoke and hard liquor. It sounded like a thunderstorm with a cold.

"Certainly," I said with my most charming smile, and obliged. He grunted with the immense effort of leaning forward on his chair, extending his calloused hands to me. They socked into my armpits with a *whump*, hard enough to lift me from the floor. He slid his hands down my ribs, across my hips, and around to my ass. I knew what was coming next, clenching my teeth in anticipation.

"Gotta check ya jewels," he snarled, his serpentine eyes sparkling with amusement. He slammed his right hand into my crotch, forcing a hot ache up into my guts that made my knees wobble and my breath shorten. "Small stash," he added, just to add insult to injury.

How I would love to choke the life out of you, I thought menacingly. As he stopped to sweep the length of each leg, I could see the knobs of his spine poking through the layers of hairy blubber that were barely contained by his shirt. I imagined what it might feel like to draw a filet knife down the length of it, splitting the skin apart to expose the curds of fat and knots of muscle beneath it. I tried not to grin at the fantasy. I decided then and there that if the opportunity presented itself to me, the door man would be a feast for the maggots before he ever saw another sunrise.

"Ya didn't bring a piece? Smart," he rasped, giving me a jovial swat on the back. He pronounced the word "smart" as "smaht".

"I don't aim to cause trouble," I replied, careful to keep my voice steady and devoid of emotion. The simpleton wasn't hard to fool, but you understand that I had to be doubly cautious. I was unarmed and surrounded by dangerous men, and even my trusty garrote would do me no good against thirty brutes with loaded pistols.

"Alright, now show me ya wad."

I frowned down at him.

"My 'wad'?"

"Yeah, stupid. Ya wad. Ya cash. Ya dough. Any of that gettin' through?"

My blood began to burn like acid rushing through my veins. How I wanted to kill him. *No one* disrespects me like that and lives. I've killed men for far less than snide comments, and yet there I was. Groped and searched and ridiculed by a hairless, drawling baboon.

I removed my "wad" from my pocket, folding the bills around my finger to fatten it. I'm not sure what I would have done had he wanted to count it, as it wasn't nearly the fortune it appeared to be. To my astonishment, he barely glanced at it. Money was money to him, I imagine, and in his eyes, I was likely to part ways with it soon enough.

He swung one tree trunk arm towards the crowded, prattling room beyond me.

"Find an empty seat, any table, doesn't matter."

Doesn' mattah, I mocked in my head.

"There's food, but don't stuff yaself, got it? Lotta people at these games."

I nodded, smiling politely and presenting him with a small bow. He had already lost interest in me, gesturing to the bunches of men behind me for his next victim to come forward. I never lost interest in him, dear reader. He was marked.

Whether or not it was a den of thieves, the Silver Lion was a marvel of craftsmanship and magnificence that astounded me. The bar was crimson and gold themed, the flawless walls adorned with glimmering candelabras and lifelike paintings of lion prides and New York architecture. The trim beneath the high ceiling was dark mahogany, flowing vines and blooming flowers intricately carved in the hard wood from end to end. The bar itself, guarded by a gargoyle of a bartender, seemed to have no limit. There were more bottles of varying size and color than I could ever count, and ornate dishes of grapes and nuts rested on black folds of cloth at every comfortable stool. Green tablecloths had been placed over rounded tables throughout the bulk of the Lion, and though I couldn't see them for myself, I knew they were most likely constructed with wood that was worth more than all the wealth I had ever seen in my life.

    I strolled between the card tables and headed for the fireplace; a towering brick masterwork that had obviously been designed and constructed by the best masons New York had to offer. Somehow, even the fire that crackled hungrily in its wide mouth seemed to be more beautiful than the trash barrel fires I had often warmed my hands over on less fortunate nights. It lent the air a pleasant smoky aroma that mingled with the savory scents of baked ham and grilled salmon, complimented with the warm scents of cinnamon and vanilla that emanated from some whipped dessert I had never seen before. The long buffet table was positioned just to the right of the fireplace, and as I'm sure you would understand, that was my next stop.

    I took the door oaf's advice and did not eat myself sick, although the temptation to do so was hard to resist. I drew some stares as I forewent the fine china and silverware (also ornate and beautiful, mind you) and opted to grab slices of glazed ham and cubes of spicy cheese with my bare hands. If I was noticed eating with my hands like an unrefined cur, perhaps I wouldn't be suspected if any utensils went missing. I knew better than to fill myself to bursting— it's harder to move swiftly when one is burdened with a swollen gut and shrieking bladder. But my *God*, was the cuisine exquisite.

    I'm in the wrong business, I thought happily, popping the green swell of a grape into my mouth. *They can afford to share these spoils with a pauper like me.*

    There is another reason I wanted to visit the buffet table as well; surely by now, having spent this much time reading my words, you have figured my cunning plan out for yourself. What does one carve cooked meat with, I ask you?

    I pretended to study the dinner, carefully reaching out to lift and examine the various side dishes and hors d'oeuvres, all the while gazing at the glinting length of the carving knife that rested on a bed of pineapples beneath the ham. As if reaching for a sliver of roasted pineapple, I curled my fingers around the silver handle of the knife and slipped it into the waistband of my pants. No one saw me take it. It would make sitting at a card table uncomfortable, but the feel of the blade against my thigh was reassuring, nonetheless. I walked like a constipated old codger back to the card tables, adjusting the blade as I took a chair at the first empty table I came to.

I will spare you the details of the poker game as it was largely typical and uneventful, until the killing began, of course. There is one detail I must mention, however. That fateful poker game is where I met "Pale Boy" Luchino for the first time, marking the start of a cat and mouse chase that would span the Atlantic.

A cluster of shady well-to-do men soon joined me, extending cold and hardened hands to shake mine but never truly introducing themselves. I watched closely as they removed their coats; each man had a pistol or two strapped to his hip or resting in crisscrossing holsters that hung against his ribs. My eyes settled upon the deadly shine of each one. I thought a small prayer that my expression did not betray. Again, I was not afraid. But I did not want to be shot.

The old man I'd seen in the wheelchair outside was pushed up to the table, grinning a toothless smile that folded in on itself like old leather and still clutching the gun he'd been so proud of.

"Hello gentlemen," he said dryly, his lips peeling away from the infantile gums beneath. I nodded to him. "Ready to win some dough?"

"One always hopes," I said, folding my hands innocently in front of me.

"Well, good luck to ya!" The old man shrieked, then cackled as if he had just cracked the world's most hilarious joke. "But not too much."

"You as well."

That was when Luchino approached, stalking to the table with the grace and severity of a prowling shark, and I instantly knew that he had been the man Benson had overheard at the Bare Knuckle. I can only describe him as a living, breathing snow shadow. He towered over the other men in the bar, even those that weren't seated. He wore black from head to toe; even the crisp undershirt beneath his ornate paisley vest and flowing overcoat was black. He wore a tie that had a metallic shine to it, and when the firelight hit it, it shifted from black to an inky purple. His gaunt face, deathly pale, was clean shaven except for the perfectly styled curly mustache Benson had mentioned. The twirls of hair twitched as he smirked down at us, his emotionless eyes peering out from beneath the low brim of a black bowler hat. I had met the Grim Reaper.

"Christ help us," the old man howled, laying his revolver in the folds of the blanket that wrapped his legs and feebly reaching for a handshake. The shadow man bowed slightly as he took it. "Pale Boy just had to pick our table, didn't he? I'll end up betting my prick before the night is through."

Pale Boy chuckled, and I recognized it for what it was— a complete and utter fake. Murderers like me are like wolves in that we can smell our own. His demeanor, those lifeless eyes, the practiced but imperfect false charm— they were all tools I used myself. I couldn't help but wonder which of us had the higher body count, and in that moment, I admired him. Pale Boy didn't merely survive like I did; he *flourished*, and I'd wager he did his killing out in the open and all but invited the police to hassle him about it. He wielded power that I craved but knew I would most likely never wield, not even with the Ravenous God on my side. The next best option, in my opinion, was to destroy him. You could say he was my enemy from the moment I laid eyes upon his faded, bleached flour face.

"Walter, please," Pale Boy said in a silky, snaky voice untainted by the underworld dialect his associates used. "You know I'm not fond of that moniker." He removed the bowler hat, and I was stunned by what was beneath it. His chestnut hair, which had been oiled and slicked neatly back against his scalp, was splotched and streaked with patches of white. As his head pivoted from side to side, exchanging pleasantries with the other players, I noticed that his pale skin terminated just beneath the collar of his undershirt. The white patches there were ragged and misshapen, giving way to the normal pinkish hues of flesh as if someone had spilled white ink over the entirety of his head.

As if reading my thoughts, the crippled old man leaned over and whispered, "Man has a skin condition, I never seen anything like it. Had it since he was learnin' to walk, I hear." He winked and knuckled my shoulder.

"Ah," I said awkwardly. "I'll do my best not to leer at him." I could have spoken those words at a quieter volume, but the sinister and sadistic part of me delighted in the insult. Pale Boy hesitated as he was removing his overcoat from his slender shoulders, struck by my audacity. I could hear a tinny, metallic clinking from within it. I caught sight of a row of deadly blades winking in the orange firelight, throwing knives that hung in specially sewn sheathes over the left side of his ribcage.

He's right-handed, then.

Pale Boy opted to keep the overcoat on after all, calmly closing it over his chest as he took his seat.

"And you are?" He crooned, his dark eyes bright and penetrating. His voice wasn't entirely unpleasant; it was almost glossy, even soothing to listen to. It had the same effect on me that soft music always did, and I was disgusted with myself for enjoying it so. A throat had never begged to be crushed as much as his did that night. He spoke like a man who never needed to raise his voice, and the tinkling music of the blades tapping together within his coat was a fitting explanation. They spoke for him.

"Benson," I said confidently. "Lee Benson." I did not offer my hand. Instead, I pretended to adjust my chair, sliding my palm over the carving knife to ensure that it was still in place.

"Benson," he repeated, slipping an expensive-looking cigarette between his lips. One of the other goons at the table struck a match and lit it for him. Pale Boy did not blink, even as the smoke began to curl into his face. "I've not heard of you, Benson. Though I feel that I've seen you before. What is it that you do?"

"I'm a simple tradesman," I said. "I do what needs to be done for whomever *needs* it done."

"Ah," Pale Boy said disinterestedly. "I'm in a similar line of work." He puffed the cigarette, ensuring that his hot cloud of exhaled smoke found its way to my face. "I'm a banker."

This was met by chuckles and scoffs from around the table, and Pale Boy might have smiled at me then. Smiling wasn't a skill he excelled at, I'm sure.

"He'll cash your check alright," the wheelchair-bound old man said with a mischievous grin, elbowing me again as though he thought me too stupid to understand the joke. I forced myself to stutter out a few forced laughs.

"Speaking of cash," Pale Boy said, replacing the bowler and pulling the brim down over those predatory eyes, "Let's play some cards."

* * *

My tactics worked. They worked *too* well, in fact. I kept my head down and my cards close, allowing myself to lose vast sums of money before using my concealed cards to rake in the pot when it began to grow to gluttonous proportions. I pocketed the largest bills and refused to bet them again, which agitated the other men but was well within my rights. The knife protruded from one leg, a swelling roll of cash from the other.

When the men around me began twisting off rings and unsnapping watches to toss into the center of the table, I began to contemplate my exit. I had been poking the proverbial bear for long enough, and the slight motions of hiding cards and retrieving them from beneath my leg were only going to grow more suspicious. I could feel the icy stabbing of their eyes boring through me as I raked over another pile of cash and jewelry with both hands, careful not to celebrate or cast any smug expressions. It was just a simple game and I had happened to win the round, that was all. Nothing out of the ordinary.

"Christ, you boys really cleaned me out," the old man whimpered, dragging one liver-spotted hand down the front of his face and comically stretching his leathery skin. His diminished lips *plipped* back together. "I hate to do it, but I gotta bet ol' Elizabeth if I'm gonna keep at it."

He lifted his prized revolver from the nest of blankets in his lap, frowning down at the weapon as he held it in his skeletal hand for the last time. It fell onto the pile of wadded bills and coins with a jingling *clunk*. I could see the rounded heads of the bullets peering out from within the cylinder and had to clamp my teeth down on my tongue to keep from laughing at the sheer idiocy of the ancient fool. He had just placed a loaded gun within reach of every other player at the table, following a game where nearly everyone had lost sums of money that they would surely miss come morning. He bowed his head pitifully, a wayward strand of snow-white hair falling over his pouting lips.

"Yes, I believe it may be time to call it a night," I said, carefully disguising the pride that threatened to waiver my voice. I wasn't sure how much money I had taken them for, but I knew the time to collect my winnings and quit was fast approaching. There was enough money on the table in front of me to fill my nostrils with the oily stench of cloth and coins, and one more card— an ace of clubs— was stashed under my thigh.

One more round. I'll take it all, every last red cent, and spend the night in the finest whore house money can buy.

"Nobody *move*," Pale Boy snarled, freezing everyone into motionless statues. Someone swallowed hard, the sound of it audible even over the cacophony of inebriated men gambling and slurring sordid stories between belches.

"What pinched your dick?" Old man wheelchair whined, gesturing toward his discarded weapon as if to demonstrate that Pale Boy had no real reason to be upset.

"You can win your money back if you play your cards right," I added arrogantly, arching one eyebrow. I knew it was a mistake before I had uttered it, but prodding that pasty hitman was positively orgasmic for me. "One more hand, gentlemen?"

"Of course," Pale Boy said, smiling and adjusting the lapels of his coat. "We shall play another game, Mr. Benson, as soon as *you*—"

Upon the word "you", his hand whisked into his coat and back out again faster than my eye could follow. A wayward and fraying green note had been skewered to the table by a single quivering blade, the metal so sharp and refined that it sang as it vibrated. I watched it, hypnotized by the slowing swaying motions, and felt true fear for the first time in my life. Had Pale Boy wanted me dead in that instant, I would not be writing this letter of his demise now.

"*You* stand up. Empty your pockets. Remove your coat. You've been slithering your hand under that table like a whore with cunt mites."

I dropped my mouth open in exaggerated shock, staring around at the other players: the old, crippled fool who had just bet his favorite weapon in a desperate attempt to salvage some dignity. A tired-looking man with a checkered flat cap askew on his head and a gray undershirt hugging the cottage cheese of his belly and breasts, scowling at me over a cigarette that had been smoked to a smoldering nub that threatened to singe his curled lips. A snooty banker-type, his greasy hair slicked back with shiny pomade and his pretentious eyes narrowed behind wire-frame glasses that were perched on the very tip of his nose.

None of them appeared to find Pale Boy unreasonable in his accusations, and of course they were right to believe him and question me. I was a poorly dressed drifter that none of them knew from Adam, and I had wondered in off the street and emptied their pockets just as easily as the pockets of the corpses I exhumed.

I couldn't fabricate any words for them, which was apt because they didn't *want* words. They wanted something simpler— they wanted me to stand and prove to them that I wasn't a cheat. If I *wasn't* a cheat, perhaps we could have all shared a laugh and a round of stiff drinks and that would have been that. The card I was hiding, along with his partner the carving knife, insisted on a different narrative. The only narrative I had left to offer. They felt like hot coals burning against my flesh, but there was no getting rid of them. I stopped fighting the smile, letting it play across my anxious face like a minute bolt of lightning.

"Please, *please*," I said, using the most insulted tone I could muster. Pale Boy's knife, embedded impressively deep in the wood, wagged at me like a scolding finger. "I know you're all the reasonable sort, certainly not men who lose their heads so easily."

I stood slowly, gingerly inching my hand down to my pocket— not to empty it, of course, but to grab the handle of the carving knife. As my ass left the wooden chair, I tried ever so discreetly to shift my body in such a way that my hidden card might be knocked to the floor and out of sight. If it clung to the back of my thigh and hung there like an oversized maggot, even better, as long as no man saw it. Honestly, I can't say for sure what happened to that card, other than to presume that it soaked up an awful lot of blood not long after Pale Boy made me rise.

"Go on," said the man in the flat cap, his voice comically high as if he had been castrated. He said it as *"gwan"*. "If ya ain't cheatin' ya got nothin' to fret over."

"You'd better listen, boy," said the old man, but he wasn't looking at me. He was looking at his beloved gun, cast out to be gambled with like an unloved slave. "Then we'll be finished before we all go to the poor house."

The silence was deafening, a mute hurricane that twisted slowly among the men as they watched me. I brought the storm to shore before a single shocked squeak could escape the two men on either side of my liar's chair.

"*For God above!*" I roared, and my hands lashed out like vicious, hungry serpents.

There was a shredding sound as the carving knife was ripped from my pant leg, the veins standing out on the back of my left hand from the force of my grip. The tearing noise was followed by the thick popping *thunk* of the blade burying itself in Flat Cap's right lung. I felt the flat of my hand grow hot and sticky as the blood began to gush out around the handle, rapidly soaking his shirt like a dark flower unfurling glistening burgundy petals. As I went for the gun, I yanked it free, but it did not come easily; it felt like pulling a hatchet free from a tree stump. He didn't scream. He gurgled, his mouth opening and closing like that of a caught fish as bright blood bubbled from his lips. The wound sounded like water being poured from a decanter as he bled, and as Flat Cap tried to suck in air to scream his last, the puncture sucked fabric into itself like a starving mouth.

Everyone, *everything*, became a raucous blur of shock and motion. Chairs shrieked across the wooden floor and overturned with hollow clatters. Men howled. Women squealed. For a collection of degenerates that kept the company of professional killers, they were quite unprepared for the likes of me.

I saw Pale Boy's hand fly to his coat, but this time, my hand was faster. My fingers were around the butt of the revolver in an instant, my pointer finger dexterously threading the trigger guard and curling around the deadly metal lever it housed. It was indeed a hair trigger, requiring almost no effort to pull. It went off with a deafening explosion before I had even lifted it from the tabletop, belching a flash of fire that illuminated the confused face of the bespectacled man before everything below his nose became a red cavern. I distinctly saw a fragment of his jawbone and gum, gum still bearing a neat row of four yellowed teeth, skitter among the coins and bills like a startled cockroach. He truly bet it all on that last hand of cards.

I swept the gun in a wide arc, pumping my finger on the trigger, emptying the cylinder at as many warm bodies as I could see. Random figures, some clad in casual suits and more than a few in evening dresses, clutched at their limbs and bodies and collapsed against the rising tide of panic. They all became cattle panicking during a storm, trampling one another, shoving one another, flowing in a writhing river towards the door even as their expensive shoes slipped in the spreading bog of their friends' blood.

I heard Pale Boy grunt, his left shoulder jerking away from me as one of my wild bullets struck home. He stumbled and disappeared beneath the table, sending his chair tumbling. It bought me a scant head start, but before I turned to join the fleeing crowd, an urge commandeered my muscles. *The* urge. Suddenly I was pointing the revolver at the crippled old man. My face pulled into a grin I could not control, as though puppet strings were sewn into my cheeks. I was in ecstasy, and the hot copper scent of blood mixed with burnt powder in the air was somehow sexual in its terminality.

The old man who had bet the smoking gun I held had no idea what to do with his knotted hands. He wanted to grab for the smoothed wheels of his chair, to tap his pitiful stores of strength and roll himself far away from where I stood beaming at him. He also wanted to somehow defend himself, lifting his stick arms as if his glass limbs might be able to stop a bullet. His sunken mouth did not move, but he spoke to me, nonetheless. His eyes betrayed him; in the end he was not a seasoned veteran at the twilight of a career criminal's life, but a frightened animal caught in the hunter's snare. *How*, he must have been pondering, *did I end up on* this *side of the gun?*

The revolver roared and nearly leapt from my hand. I saw the frail latticework of the old man's ribs collapse inward as my final bullet punched through him. The wheelchair, wheels squeaking and whining as though in sadness, coasted sluggishly away from the table. The corpse of the old man was slumped in the seat like a sack of dirty underwear, eyes half-lidded and vacant. One of his stockinged feet clumped out from under the blanket. The white cotton began to absorb the spreading pool blood, changing from white to pink to red to black.

I believe I killed a man or woman with every shot I took, regardless of my poor aim. Sprinting to the door, I hurdled the still forms of several fallen bodies and branching oil slicks of blood like an Olympian. That was the Ravenous God, you see. *He* had guided my hand. *He* had given me the strength I needed to clasp the blood-grimed carving knife and wrench it free of Flat Cap's lung without dropping it. He kept it firmly in my hand, slick with blood as it was, as I pumped my arms and pistoned my legs. Miles ahead of me was the door, wide open and taunting me with cool sea air and the cover of night. Like a pile of fallen boulders, the door oaf who had crushed my genitals was barricading the exit. His catcher's mitt hand was wrapped around the greasy length of a shotgun, cracked open and awaiting the shells he was fumbling to pluck from a tattered box beneath his chair.

Fool, I thought. *You don't trust yourself to keep it loaded?*

A shot rang out from behind me and something buzzed past my ear. The ornate paneling above Door Oaf's head splintered apart as a bullet struck it, spewing bits of dusty wood. I had no time to look behind me, but I didn't need to; I knew who it was. Pale Boy was still alive, and his throwing blades weren't the only weapons of his trade.

"*Gonna fuckin' k—*" Door Oaf was slobbering. His gargoyle face was a twisted scowl of gritted teeth and blazing, murderous eyes. He had slid two shells home and snapped the shotgun closed.

Another shot from behind me. Another snap and puff of wood, lower this time. Zeroing in on me.

All of this took place in a matter of seconds, I must clarify. I draw it out because that is how I experienced it. So close to death, so flooded with adrenaline, that time itself froze. My eyes happened upon a towering grandfather clock, the gilded pendulum laboriously clunking back and forth behind its glass facade and counting down the final seconds of my life. The hands stood at 2:20 in the morning, an hour so early that only the most unspeakable of events could occur.

The bar had drained of patrons. I no longer had a crowd to shield me. Nothing between me and the narrowing aim of Pale Boy except for a smattering of fresh corpses. From the very side of my vision, I could perceive the small dark hump of Pale Boy, already steadying his wavering arm to take another shot. In my face, the sightless black eyes of shotgun barrels were raising to peer into my mouth.

I attacked with both weapons as more shots cracked from behind me. I swung the old man's revolver like a club, burying it in Door Oaf's gelatinous bulk. He barely felt it. As the gun came down my knife had gone up. I was sweeping the carving knife at him, and he couldn't stop it, but in that moment I knew my Ravenous God was calling me home. Even if I gutted Door Oaf, he'd still get his shot off and I would receive the last hair trim of my life.

Another muffled shot rang out from behind me, and a flaming hammer blow struck my left thigh. I felt no pain, not at first. I only felt immense pressure. My leg was suddenly full of lead balls, and I could feel the fabric of my pants growing sticky and saturated. Pale Boy had shot me, and I believe his bullet nicked an artery before skidding against my femur and tearing out the other side. The torn muscles gave out and I dropped to the floor, snarling and swearing, just as Door Oaf discharged the shotgun. A bright mushroom of white fire ignited above me, close enough to scorch my scalp and the boom so deafening that I thought my ears had ruptured. I hoped, *prayed*, that the spray of buckshot had obliterated Pale Boy. In the chaos of the moment, it looked like Door Oaf had mistakenly fired right at him. The Ravenous God was not willing to bless me so, as it turns out. One cannot give too much, you see. You can teach a man to kill, inspire and encourage him to kill, but never do the killing for him. It's just selfish to do so.

Door Oaf was slow to realize he had missed his shot. By the time the shotgun was swiveling down to finish me, I had made my move. I threw my arm upwards into the hanging softness of his gut, swinging away from my body with the serrated blade jutting from the bottom of my fist. There was very little resistance, and I felt the knife stutter across bone as I opened him from rib to rib.

It felt as though someone had upended a bucket of hot tar onto me. The world ran red as Door Oaf became a waterfall of spurting fluids. He stared down at himself in stupefied shock, watching as a shiny coil of intestine slithered from the streaming mouth in his abdomen. Absently, he tried to stuff it back into himself. It wriggled through his fingers and drooped to the floor like a string of fat, overcooked sausages. He took a dazed step backward. His hanging innards swayed, piling between his pigeon toes like greasy rope. I bent my right knee and drove my foot into his crotch, paying him the same courtesy he had given me. With interest. Door Oaf didn't react to the blow. He fell over without a sound, striking the ground hard enough to vibrate the very walls around us.

The pain came then. The pressure became a rhythmically squeezing fist, clenching and unclenching on a red-hot ball of agony. I screamed, placing my hand over the wound and touching the ragged edges of the hole. It felt like sliding my fingers into one of my many whores, though I assure you there was no pleasure in it. The rough pads of my fingers caressed raw nerves, and fuel was poured onto the searing flame in my thigh. I screamed out to the Ravenous God, *any* God, to end my pain. Instead, He ended the gunfire from behind me.

I struggled to my feet, pulling myself up with Door Oaf's overturned chair as my shoes skidded through blood and partially digested food. Pale Boy had ceased moving. His arms were wrapped around his bleached face, his back rising and falling ever so slightly. I grinned against the agony. He was still alive, but suffering. That was better.

I burst out of the front doors, gasping in chilly lungfuls of salty sea air. There was no one left outside to try to stop me. They had smartly taken their leave before the police or a bullet could catch them, and I meant to do the same.

Walking was excruciating work. My leg aches now at the memory of it, hobbling over to the trash cans and feeling hot gushes of blood pushing through my fingers with each flex of thigh muscle. My uneven footfalls echoed across the new queer emptiness and embedded within the grave post-massacre silence was the airy whine of approaching sirens. I thought again of the imposing grandfather clock, intricate gears meshing and rotating, shimmering pendulum swaying from side to side. Time was in short supply, and so were dark miracles. If I was discovered outside the Silver Lion, covered in pints of blood and brandishing my weapons, there would be no calls to freeze or raise my hands above my head. I would be shot down, and most likely by policemen in the pockets of scum like Pale Boy Luchino.

I tossed the empty revolver into the soggy contents of the trash can, crying out as I stooped to scrape up my beloved garrote. I hesitated before disposing of the knife. Visions of Door Oaf staggered through my head, his innards hanging and his abdomen laid wide open. I felt heat, *pleasant* heat, glowering in my lower stomach. I rather liked the blade. I kept it in my hand as I began the arduous journey to the docks, rasping prayers to the watching ice chip stars above that the ship I'd heard hadn't yet left port.

* * *

My head felt light and airy by the time I made it to the darkened clusters of freight and rope that marked the west entrance to the docks. Panic forced the breath from me. I saw no ships, not at first. I blinked once, twice. The third time was a forceful squint. I saw nothing but towering masses of black that blotted out the stars like icebergs. If there were lanterns burning anywhere, they were scarce enough to be invisible to me. The sirens were much closer now, wailing in harmony with me as I moaned. All I wanted was to lie down, right there on the moldering wooden planks, and drift off to sleep. I dropped to my knees, and just as my heavy eyelids began to slide closed, I saw the mythical tunnel.

You've heard of the tunnel, I'm sure. Those who walk hand in hand with the grim reaper himself tend to boast that they saw it, oh yes, they *saw* it and it was *spectacular*. It is the passageway souls must take to the other side. The beyond. The great hereafter. The white-gold kingdom of Heaven, where the one true God resides and rules over all. The passageway was opening before me, curtains of blinding light parting and unfurling like luminous wings. Through the tunnel I saw a jeweled cityscape, shimmering towers that climbed out of wisps of freezing mist and disappeared into the innocent blue of the sky.

Lee.

The voice was jarring. It hit me like a thunderclap inside my skull, sending electric shocks through my nerve endings and standing my hair on end. The bullet wound in my thigh sang sour notes, but I lifted my arms to the cityscape regardless. I could feel icy air kissing my face, and I longed to throw myself into it. To be weightless; to be like the birds.

"God," I whimpered, my lower lip fattening and quivering.

You're not done, Lee.

I opened my eyes, gawking into the tunnel even as the luminous rays forced tears that left clean streaks through the gummy mask of blood on my face. There was something in front of the city now; something that looked like a shadowed tower. Curls and tufts of mist faded and parted to reveal that the tower was not a building, but a *throne*. A monstrous golden throne that jutted far enough into the sky to eclipse the sun. A narrow set of white stairs curved up and away from where my body was dying, stairs that wriggled and writhed like plump maggots.

The stairs were not stairs at all. They were people, naked *dead* people, their skin as white as virgin snow and pulled tight on their jutting skeletons. They were each positioned on hands and knees, heavy chains of blackened metal links lashed around their necks and fastened with sturdy-looking padlocks. There were no keyholes. The locks never, *ever* came off. I was looking up at a stairway built of tortured flesh, nude corpses that were not allowed to die. They wheezed and moaned, the structure shifting and jostling as they fought to stay upright beneath unimaginable weight. One of the living stairs was sobbing uncontrollably. Another was cackling hard enough to gag himself. Somewhere, someone was insisting that "I didn't *mean* it, my *God*, it was an accident, and I didn't *mean* it…"

"Am I going to die?" I thought to the Ravenous God. My lips were crusted together. My tongue felt like a plank of wood. I was so unworthy.

No, my son. There is more infection to be excised.

Something stirred, high up on the gilded throne. I saw the shape of the Ravenous God sitting upon it, shoulders slouched and head lowered. The jagged points of an oversized crowd stood out in stark contrast against the merciless bulb of the sun. I could hear Him breathing, long and deep, and each exhale became the sea breeze that lighted upon my face and pushed the waves into the mossy rocks beneath the dock.

My Ravenous God looked like a spider from down among the damned. I saw two spindly arms unfold from His sides, bending into shadowy arrowpoints as He planted His hands on the armrests of the throne and pushed Himself upright. His silhouette was misshapen; long and lanky limbs radiating out from a bulging belly that sagged low enough to nearly brush against His ankles. A silken beard, many yards long, streamed from His head and hung suspended in the wind like a war banner. His knees lifted high above His jagged crown with each step as He began to descend the stairway of bodies, crackling and crunching spines beneath his feet. He was so, *so* beautiful.

"Show me the way," I whispered, weeping. The snapping of bone grew louder as He approached. The stairs wheezed and whimpered. Their chains rattled and clanked together like those of storybook spirits.

I will not let you die. I am here to promise you life, if you will but hold on a moment longer.

The Ravenous God stepped out of the undulating fog, and I gazed upon His features for the first time. Beneath the sharp bone crown that sat askew on His head, there were no eyes. No fleshy snout, no jutting ears on either side. Everything from the mouth up was a blank canvas of perfect, unmarked flesh. Everything below where the nose should have been was teeth.

He was smiling down upon me, crouching on the knobby back of one of the damned souls and cradling His considerable belly in his hands. I stared into the interlocking rows of razor-sharp fangs. His beard made a chiming sound, a tinny twinkling clatter of musical notes that rang out as millions of ethereal follicles tangled and brushed one another. As the music began to swell in volume, the agony in my leg began to diminish.

"I love you," I sobbed. The Ravenous God sighed through His dagger teeth, the sound of a lukewarm spring wind through trees laden with sweet, juicy fruit. It was warm with compassion, intoxicating.

I love you, son. Continue your mission.

He was reaching beneath where I knelt, far down into another plane of existence that I could not comprehend. The mists of Heaven swirled around the narrow shaft of His wrist, the taught muscles working as He searched for something. There came a shrill, warbling scream. When He withdrew his hand, He was holding what appeared to be a dismembered human arm between his pointer finger and thumb. His jaws parted like a well-oiled bear trap and an eel-like tongue slithered out from between them, enveloping the withered limb and drawing it back into the maw even as the fingers still jittered with dying nerves. The jaws snapped closed with a brittle crunch. That was the moment, right there. The moment when I learned that I was not serving the false God of the Bible, the impotent mock deity old men and women grovel to on Sundays. He was the *true* God. The *Ravenous* God.

I feed upon the souls you send me, Lee. They are so delicious. So, so delicious. Through them, the rending of their flesh and the slurping of their blood, I am eternal. Serve me well, and so shall you be.

He turned and began to climb the living stairway once more, His belly bouncing and swaying with each lift of His knees. He stopped only briefly to squat between His gangly legs, search through the mist and pluck another dangling slab of wet, red meat from some unseen victim below us. It was a torso this time, severed at the navel and spilling buckets of blood through an exposed and broken ribcage. He held the torso above His head by a long swatch of black hair, His tongue writhing and lolling as blood pattered into the pit of his mouth. I heard those powerful jaws snap closed around the torso, followed by the sharp crack and pop of disintegrating bones, but the noise was growing faint—

"—already getting late, Harrison. Ye know I like to set sail before dawn, when they're sporty."

I was ripped from my vision by the call of a weary but vigorously eager voice. I willed my heavy head to face the direction it had come from and was dumbfounded. There *was* a ship! It wasn't large enough to have been the owner of the blaring foghorn I'd heard earlier, but it looked sturdy enough to cross the ocean and return in one piece (if I allowed them to). It was small, but not *too* small, and the squat brown smokestack perched atop the ship told me that it had at least one boiler below decks. That meant it could make a long trip, and at a decent pace.

The hull of my escape ship sat low in the water, listing slightly to starboard but not enough to worry me. The once white paint was rusting and peeling away to orange, flaking from stem to stern and giving the vessel the appearance of an old birch trunk. The bridge and crew quarters were housed in a simple boxy superstructure built very near to the blunted triangle of the bow. A sun faded stripe of orange had been painted along its base. Lashed to a rickety network of railing on top of the superstructure was a faded green flag, but through my wavering vision I could only make out the words "God Save". The rest was obscured by rips and shadow, but I took it for the sign that I know it was.

The stern, where the bulk of the work was done, was a long rectangular tray clotted with fishing equipment. I could make out the slightly arched silhouettes of fishing rods, heaps of buoys and netting, and a cluster of barrels that were leaking the stink of rotten fish into the otherwise fresh air. A single row of portholes blazed along the orange base of the superstructure and just under the bow railing, the yellow orbs bobbing and nodding in the tranquil waves. *"The White Cap"* had been hand-painted in clumsy-looking cursive on the ship's prow, the letters elegant but also mildly childish in their simplicity.

"Sorry pa," came the annoyed voice of a boy. My vision was fading in and out, but with effort, I could focus on his blurry form as he bent to lift two pails. Red splashes of slimy chum splatted out onto the dock as he carelessly held them out to either side of him. I pulled my knife and began to limp toward him.

"Young man," I panted. He yelped, dropping both buckets with loud *plunks* and splashing pungent fish guts all over his baggy rubber trousers. I was on him before he could even consider running, before his vocal cords could warm up and tighten for a scream.

"*Mister—*"

"*You*," I snarled, the reek of blood coming from both of us in cloying waves. "*You* will shut your milk hole, pup."

I used the boy as a crutch, relieving the pressure on my mangled leg while pressing the congealed blade into the hairless swell of his jugular. His chest swelled and shrank in rapid succession under the vice of my left arm.

"We're just going to wait for your *pa*, yeah? Let's see what your life is worth to him, eh?"

He was a smart boy indeed. His nods were so slight that I wondered if I had imagined them, and his lips stayed sealed in a flat, tight line. Each time he struggled to support my weight, I pressed the blade into his neck a fraction further. He found strength he didn't even know he had.

"*Harrison!*" roared the man known as "Pa". I waited patiently for him to emerge from the bridge of the *White Cap*. He stormed out in a blind rage, perhaps ready to throttle young Harrison for taking too long on his chores. Pa certainly looked to be a rough and tough seaman. His spine was curved and jutting, but his arms hadn't succumbed to the savages of old age. They were stained blue gray with years of crude tattoos and crisscrossed with veins that bulged enough to cast shadows across his skin. The end of his right arm ended in a stump and his left foot was turned in, completely sideways, below the ankle. He froze at the top of the *White Cap*'s ramshackle loading ramp, and I knew he was mine. I had him by the balls, as we like to say in the good old U.S. of A.

"Let's talk," I sang pleasantly, removing the knife only long enough to beckon him over with it.

Pa held his hand and stump just above his head, dragging his decrepit foot behind him as he inched toward me. He was bald except for a horseshoe of snowy hair that connected to a scraggly, tobacco-stained beard. The hair was all uneven, as if he had groomed himself with broken glass. His eyes, sunken deep in dark pits of wrinkles and lines, were seasoned but soft. Broken.

"Sir," he said, his tongue darting out and failing to wet his lips. "Please... please don't hurt my boy. He's just a wee one, can't do nothin' for ye."

His Irish accent was diluted but still heavy enough to make him charming somehow. Like a friendly, crippled little leprechaun.

"I'm not in the business of killing children," I said with complete honesty. "I'm in the business of serving God, the *Ravenous* God. He's *hungry*. You can understand that, yes?"

He was nodding before I had even finished the question, prepared to agree to any demand I might throw at him.

"Aye, I'm a Christian, sir. Harrison is too. We're good people, sir."

"Good people," I repeated, tracing the fingers of my free hand through Harrison's curly hair. "Good *Irish* people, by the sound."

"Aye," he said again, more insistently. He was edging too close. I dragged his child away from him, yanking his head to one side so Pa could get a clear view of the carving knife at his throat.

"I propose a bargain, and you had better decide fast. Do you understand?"

Pa's eyes shifted toward the wailing sirens, and I knew he understood the situation that had fallen into his lap. He and his brat were my hostages now, simply because he had wanted an early start on fishing. Ironic, isn't it, that he was the one caught?

"I'll give ye whatever ye want. Ye can even have the *Cap*. Just don't hurt my boy."

"I can't *sail* the cunting boat," I hissed. "But *you* can. You can take me across the Atlantic."

"See reason, sir. She's a strong ship, sure, but I've not crossed the ocean—"

"I believe I have *plenty* of reason, right here, pissing himself in my arms." I was smiling drunkenly, growing delirious from the pain and blood loss. The goddamned sirens blatted out any hope I might have had of hearing the sweet windchime songs of the Ravenous God's healing beard.

Pa's mouth began to waver, his nostrils flaring as he fought tears. I did not blink. I stared holes through him, his child clasped to me and shivering like a rabbit in a snare. My pulse began to match pace with Harrison's as I prepared to kill him. Don't underestimate me, reader. I would have done it then and there if I'd had to.

"I'll take ye wherever ye want to go, sir. If you'll permit me to fish on the voyage, I can sell my catch in Southampton. I know a man, runs a wee shop."

I had never heard of nor desired to visit Southampton, wherever that was, but I knew that it was far from the reach of the crime lords of New York and the guns of the encroaching police. I had seen my vision of the Ravenous God right there where we stood, and combined with the faded creed on the ship's flag, I knew in my heart that I was right where I needed to be. Perhaps the old man was an unwitting prophet, tapped by the almighty to aid in my escape.

"Southampton it is," I said, and lowered the knife to the boy's chest. I hooked the edge under a loose shirt button and sliced it off with a delicate flick of my wrist. "I'm wounded, in case you couldn't tell. If you patch my leg and sail me out of here, no harm will come to you or your son. You have my word, the word of my God, and you will propagate glorious karma upon your souls."

Pa only nodded, lowering his hand and stump.

I stuffed my hand into my pocket and pulled out a wad of sodden loot.

"I'm not a monster," I lied, and tossed some of the bills between his mismatched feet. "I will make it worth your while."

"My boy first," he said, attempting to straighten his spine and jutting his chin out. One of his joints crackled like kindling. "Then ye can come aboard."

I hesitated, just long enough to drink in the palpable flood of his fear, and then I released Harrison. The boy sprinted to his father, collapsing into his arms hard enough to topple the old man. They fell in a sobbing tangle, the old man who had been prepared to thrash the insolent child now slathering him with kisses and caressing the boy's slender back with his stump. I allowed them to hold each other in a puddle of icy moonlight for a while before I slid the knife back into my saturated pants and began to pull myself up the ramp. I glanced back only once, and my eyes fell upon the trail of red blots I was leaving behind me. Our unwilling alliance was quite literally sealed with blood.

* * *

    Pa (real name Jacob, though he never wanted to share his surname) nor Harrison gave me any trouble as the New York City skyline faded out behind the stern and the sun, fat and orange, rose over the bow rail. I swear, I stayed true to my word. Most of the voyage kept me laid up below decks, dabbing at the fishing line stitches that bound my wounds with wads of cloth soaked in seawater. It burned fiercely, so fiercely in fact that Pa had dared to enter my dungeon and hand me a length of rope to clamp my teeth onto. When I wasn't cleaning clots of blood from the bullet holes, I was vomiting into a discarded chum bucket that came complete with a delightful little hole in the bottom of it. As it turns out, I am quite prone to sea sickness.
    The Ravenous God kept the seas relatively calm, however, and from what I could hear through the wood and steel above me, he also kept their fishing nets full. It was strange to hear the father and son muttering to each other, sometimes laughing between petty arguments or playing a wheezing accordion, while the man who had threatened their lives recuperated below their feet. They could have easily overtaken me in that state had they so chosen, but they left me alone to heal. Pa must have really needed the sums of money I had been taunting him with; either that, or he was simply grateful that I had not decapitated his son in front of him. The crippled sea captain even brought me steaming plates of grilled fish on beds of boiled brown rice, sometimes even twice a day. Sometimes with a cigarette for dessert! It rarely stayed in my stomach for long, but that didn't stop me from trying.

I know what you must be thinking, and yes, you're absolutely right. I was going to kill them anyway. In the pitch-black confines of the *White Cap*'s lower decks, rocking sickeningly from side to side, I had hours to plot their deaths. You have to understand; they had seen my *face*. They had intimate knowledge of my wounds, which could link me to the massacre in New York if a wise enough man was connecting the dots. I had also promised them money that I couldn't afford to spare. I hated to murder a child, true, but my preference did not change the situation. When I prayed to ask the Ravenous God for guidance, I received nothing in reply but the muted sloshing of the ocean against the outer hull. He, too, understood that though they did not outwardly appear to be sinners, they were a very real threat to the mission He had laid out before me. They were dead men walking, but it sounded like their last days would be happy ones.

Pa spoke to me at length for the first time on the final day of his life. He was leaning against the curved railing of the ship's bow, resting his twisted foot against a spare anchor and smoking a lumpy cigarette. Rolling cigarettes was quite the feat for a man with one hand but I had seen him do it several times, effortlessly rolling the tiny bundles of dried tobacco against his chest and never dropping a single pinch. Smoke trailed from between his furry lips as he watched the coast of England drawing nearer. From what I could see as I limped up to join him, Southampton seemed to be quite the bustling little town. Hundreds of eyes would be waiting to see us come into port. It made me uneasy.

"I've not been this far across the Atlantic since before Harry was born," he said, puffing out blue smoke and then looking down at the cigarette, watching it smolder. "Does me good to make the voyage. Though I fear we may have to row into port. I wasn't quite prepared for such a long trip."

I leaned against the rail opposite him, looping a finger under the grimy noose of piano wire jutting from my back pocket. That close to shore, it would have to be done soon. I wanted to stab him, which would be swift and satisfying, but the garrote would be much quieter. I wanted to catch Harrison off guard, you understand.

"I'm thankful," I said, doing my best to dip my words in something that sounded like gratitude. I always struggle to mimic that one. "I know I'm not a good man, but you and your son saved my life. And the fact that the two of you can crew a ship of this size alone is very impressive."

"Aye, it's hard work. Coal is getting' to be too expensive. That wee boiler is shite on the best of days. And o'course, accidents do happen."

He wiggled his stump at me.

"What happened to your hand?" I asked. "I don't think you've ever told me, Jacob."

"What do ye think? A shark. Big, ornery bull shark. He was feedin' on my catch and got a tooth or two snagged in the net. I got too close tryin' to club him out. Shark fins, *very* valuable to the right market. He chewed his way out and didn't stop when he got to flesh and bone."

"The Ravenous God was watching over you," I mused, eying his stump in amazement. He cast me a strange look. I felt something that may have been pity for him then, but as my "feelings" usually do, it disappeared almost as fast as I noticed it. I pulled the garrote free, keeping it concealed behind my stronger leg. Surely the man had done something, some vile act in his past, that would justify his murder. If he was an innocent, as you must be thinking, why would the Ravenous God allow me to take him? The boy too, disrespectful little shit that he was when chore time came around.

"Ye gotta be mindful of sharks, mister," Pa said, turning his gaze from approaching land and locking his gray eyes on mine. Seagulls venturing out from the coast began to circle and dive, squawking hungrily at the stink of fish in the air. "Some of 'em seem like they'll cruise right by ye, leave ye alone to go on livin', until they whip their snouts around and bite somethin' off."

"Truer words were never spoken," I said coldly, and took a determined step toward him. My footfall was loud and heavy on the faded wood of the deck.

"Were ye bein' followed by the man on the pier?" He suddenly asked, no doubt sensing what was coming and using his final bargaining chip to stop me. My heart stuttered in my chest.

"You saw someone following me?"

"Aye," he said stolidly, his eyes shining with the ghost of a smile. "Looked hurt, staggerin' like you were. But sure as the sunrise he was watchin' us leave, and I'd wager he got a good look at the ship. I'll tell ye all about it once we dock."

It took a matter of seconds to shrug his claim off. So what if someone had watched us leave? There had been an *awful* lot of commotion near the docks that night, after all. And would the crime lords of New York really dispatch an agent to track me to Southampton England over some fucking poker loot?

No, my brain answered, b*ut the half dozen corpses you left behind in their bar might motivate them.*

I did something then that I don't often do. I *questioned myself.* I'm ashamed to confess it here, but I suppose a confession letter is the place to do it. My faith faltered. Was I wrong? Was I *insane*? Could I possibly have gotten this far, survived this long, *without* the Ravenous God backing me? My vision of Him, perched upon His throne of wriggling agony and devouring the souls of the wicked—had that been nothing but a hallucination brought on by the pints of blood I had lost?

Southampton was drawing nearer. I could already smell soot and burning oil wafting on the air. I needed to silence the old man and his son and then hijack the *White Cap* somehow, hijack it and steer it back out to sea. I opted to swing the prow back away from shore and send it back to sea as a ghost ship. To my knowledge, it still hasn't been located. Perhaps it sank.

"We're not going to dock," I said matter-of-factly, and with superhuman speed I was on him. I felt the wire drag across his nose and chin as I dropped it around his rawhide neck, pivoting to jam my backside into his hip and yanking the protruding curve of his spine against mine. I took his full weight, which wasn't considerable, and hoisted his boots from the deck. Fragile bones snapped and popped like knuckles, the muscles of my uninjured leg flooding with fiery acid.

His dying grunts and gurgles resonated in my right ear, the scruff of his beard tickling and dotting my flesh with goosebumps. I giggled at the sensation. I began to bend my knees and bounce, using his own body weight to drive the wire deeper into his throat. His one good hand clawed weakly, the lumpy knob of his stump drumming against the side of my head. He was strong but didn't have sufficient power to hurt me. What strength he had left was fading fast.

"*M— B—,*" he attempted. "*H—*"

My boy, I deduced. *Harrison.*

"Oh, don't worry about your boy," I rasped, sweat beginning to bead on my forehead. The seagulls went on circling, screeching, watching raptly as they waited for their next meal. "I'll take care of him too."

My leg was a column of fire, and I could feel that it had sprung a leak again. I didn't let it slow me down. I continued bouncing Pa against the garrote, harder and faster than before, grunting and puffing air with each exertion. He didn't try to speak anymore. His stump didn't knock against my temple anymore. I heard one last syllable escape his lips, something like an elongated letter T, and he went as slack as a flag when the wind ceases to blow.

One down, I thought. I could feel sporadic muscles in the old man's body flexing and jumping against my sweaty back as he adjusted to being dead. I heaped his slack form over the bow railing, patted his hunchback amiably, and then tossed him over. There was a shrill splash, followed by a muted thud as the hull of the *White Cap* struck his corpse and tumbled him beneath the curved steel.

"Harrison?" I called over my shoulder to the suspiciously quiet decks behind me. There was no sound save for the sluggish chug of the aged engines, the incessant seabirds and the hiss of ocean spray. I added a flavor of concern and panic to my voice before I spoke again.

"Harrison!" I shouted. "*Your Pa fell overboard, I need your help NOW!*"

Again, there was no reply from the child, and the clock was ever counting down. I desperately needed to hunt him, finish him, point the ship back out to sea and attempt swim the rest of the way to shore before I was noticed. I did not want *any* evidence linking me to the vessel when (and if) it was found. I had slept under bridges and on park benches many times before; I would easily remain hidden until I could steal new clothes and bury the bloodstained rags I was wearing. All I had to do was find the boy and hijack the ship.

Kill the boy, hijack the ship. Kill the boy, hijack the ship.

I repeated it like a mantra.

I began to creep along the moderate forecastle of the ship, stepping carefully over lengths of oily chain and scattered tools. Nothing moved; the single row of the wheelhouse's square windows were empty and silent above me. It was if Harrison had seen the murder, given up the will to live, and abandoned ship with his father.

Little bastard.

I descended the small set of rickety stairs that led to the lower boat deck and spied an unexpected prize. It was a machete, the longish blade streaked with rust and dried gore and the cracked handle wrapped in multicolored thread to hold it in one piece. I believe it was used for fish heads, if the smell of ocean rot radiating from it was an indicator, but I had a different sort of dismemberment in mind. I wrenched it from the squat barrel it had been hacked into, pointed it in front of me, and let it lead the way like a compass needle. I felt like a pirate commandeering a vessel, and in a way, I suppose I was. My chest was tightening with stress and exhilaration. I was running out of time, but I was also enjoying myself. I was on the hunt once more!

"Harrison?" I yelled through a cupped hand. Perhaps he really had been watching as I murdered his father? He had been avoiding me throughout the journey, as was expected, but never to this extent. I abandoned my plan to convince him that his father's death had been an accident. Though I doubted I could dull his apprehension and lure him out, I decided to try anyway. He was a smart kid, but no living soul can outwit me for very long. "If you'll just come out, I promise I won't hurt you. We can talk things out. Come to an arrangement. Okay?"

I am a *terrific* liar. The echo of my words sounded calm and reassuring, the work of a veteran stage performer. The birds weren't even frightened away by my shouts; they dove and pecked at the dark mass bobbing in the wake of the ship, screeching happily. I made my way back to the stern, not daring to blink for fear that I might miss something, some tell-tale scampering or the briefest shining of sun on rubber boots.

"Come on, son," I said, softer. It was growing increasingly difficult to hide the stress and urgency in my voice. "This is pointless."

An idea struck me, and I mentally pinched myself for not thinking of it sooner. I beamed, showing all of my teeth as I poked my head around the lower edge of the ship's superstructure.

"It'll take both of us to dock the ship, Harrison. If you don't stop hiding and help me, we're going to crash right into the pier. Who knows how many people will be hurt? And your father's ship, well, I'd hate to see the *Whitecap* slip beneath the waves. Wouldn't you? Don't you hate to think of it covered in mud and fish shit?"

The boy attacked me then. I can't say for sure where he had been hiding, but I promise you his young muscles were lightning fast and iron strong. I barely had time to process the inhuman roar that tore from his throat before a bundle of dynamite went off in my head. There was a spinning sensation and then I was looking up at the wheeling seagulls, the blameless blue of the sky gazing back.

"You son of a bitch!" Harrison cried, advancing on me with a jagged length of wood raised above his head. I saw two of him, drifting around each other in drunken circles. He looked incredibly tall, his head adorned with a straw hat that was much too large to be his own and his rubber boots crusted with dried fish blood. The hat was crooked, and as he cocked the wooden plank back to strike me again his thin arms knocked it into the breeze. When his face came back into focus, it was no longer the visage of youth. It was a hollow of hurt and rage, and the wide glare and nervous twitching of his watery eyes promised me that the next blow would save my skull in.

Swing up, I thought dimly. *Swing up at him you fool.*

My rubbery fingers lay like a pile of dead snakes around the hilt of the machete. They snapped closed around it and I hacked upward at one of the blurry blobs standing over me, hoping against hope that I had chosen the correct one. I felt the blade connect with something, hesitating before continuing its smooth arc through the air. The boy cried out and my chest flooded with joy.

"You little son of a whore," I snarled at him, swaying to my feet. I still could not focus but I could see him backing away, his weapon abandoned and both hands clasped over his gut. I gingerly touched a fiery spot on my scalp and felt the tacky warmth of blood on my fingers. "I will cut your cock off and *feed* it to you."

I wanted to charge at him, make him pay for the new sickening throb in my head, but I was so weak. My limbs were so *heavy*. I could do little more than slowly advance as he backed toward the very end of the stern, though we both knew there was nowhere to go.

His head and his frail body would soon part ways, and I was glad for it. Perhaps it was the resurgence of my vision of the Ravenous God, squat-walking up His living staircase and plucking morsels from the bodies of the damned, that gave me a hunger I had never known before. I made up my mind then and there to butcher and devour the boy's corpse. Some of him, anyway; whatever I could drag to shore. I envisioned myself cutting off fat red steaks, peeling them from the bone as I used the ragged edge of the machete blade to saw through clinging tendon and sinew. I would skewer them on a longish knife or sharpened stick and then roast them over a campfire, salivating at the smell and the hissing crackle of roasting meat. Perhaps I would share it with others, as the smell of hot food tends to draw the vagrants in like flies. That would be Harrison's karma. He had managed to injure me, and for that unforgivable sin, he would in turn feed and nourish me. His journey through life would not carry him to a wedding chapel and a nursery but through the looping channels of my intestines, and his grave marker would be a tight coil of shit left between two forgotten trash cans. *Nobody* injures me, do you understand? *Nobody*. My nostrils flared, full of the imaginary scent of burnt meat, and it flooded me with strength. I began to jog at him, curling my blade arm around myself for the final strike.

The cunting child surprised me once more! Though he was bleeding from a fresh gash across the midsection, he scampered up the railing like a skittish spider and threw himself overboard.

"No!" I roared, swinging the machete impotently at the empty space where he had been. It struck the topmost rail, producing a

minute spark and clang and cleaving off chips of white paint that landed in fresh spots of boy blood like snow. Even over the thrumming of the *White Cap*'s meager engines, I could hear Harrison already swimming for shore. I don't believe he could have made it, not while injured and bleeding freely into the ocean. I hope that something else made a meal of him, as I was denied the privilege.

I snatched up the boy's oversized straw hat, crushing it into a ball between my shaking hands and tossing it into the sea after him.

"Go then!" I shouted, finally startling the gulls enough to send them flapping away, shrieking. *"Go and be with your father on the bottom! If I see you again, I'll carve your eyes out while you're still alive and piss in the holes!"*

There was no answer but frantic splashing off to starboard, already growing distant, and I ached for a gun. How easy it would have been to lean over the rail, blinking my vision back to true before squeezing off shots at the struggling boy. Surely there was a rifle somewhere on board, but I was already pressing my luck to the point that the Ravenous God himself might not have been able to help me. I couldn't afford to draw attention to myself; I had already committed murder and assault before even arriving on the streets of Southampton.

My head was foggy, and would be until the following morning, but after some deep breaths I was no longer seeing double. What a blessing that was. The tossing and turning of the ship, in conjunction with the blow to my head, was forcing hot surges of vomit into my throat. I hummed to myself, focusing on the vibrations on my lips to keep from retching as I climbed the narrow stairway to the wheelhouse on all fours.

The door swung in on creaky hinges. The wheelhouse was a pleasant enough little room, I could sense that it had been more of a home to the old man than any house ever could have been. The walls were painted a rich green that kept the atmosphere dark, but it was pleasing. Curling black and white photos were tacked up here and there with bent nails. One of them, a portrait of a homely woman with a large nose, jutting brow, and a smile that looked more pained than lovely, was the only one that had been placed in a frame. In sloppy cursive writing it read "Love, Violet". Had she been the old man's sister, or perhaps his wife?

"Ugly bitch," I said, and drove the machete into her frozen features. The glass disintegrated and the broken frame clattered to the floor beside my foot. The stuffy cabin reeked of pipe smoke, and it was fueling my bellowing headache. My leg, still bleeding and tender to any movement, answered back. The swim I was about to engage in would be the harshest struggle of my life, I knew, but it would all be worth it as I laid my head on a whore's cool pillow and drifted into a well-deserved sleep. I would sleep like the dead, safe in a new city and oceans away from the men who were hunting me. Or so I thought.

I slapped one of the wooden spokes of the ship's wheel, spinning it to starboard in a smooth blur of motion. I felt gravity shift in my pleading stomach, the blue and twinkling horizon tilting as the vessel began to lurch to port. The distant collection of boxy structures and hazy church steeples glided slowly out of sight until there was nothing ahead of the bow but open ocean. I straightened the rudder out again as best I could, using the tug of gravity as a guide, and then my final task was complete. The *White Cap* was about to become a ghost ship.

I looked for Harrison one last time before dropping down the riveted hull myself but saw nothing. I hope and pray that he drowned; his oxygen starved brain broadcasting visions of his father flailing in my garrote before the lights went out for good. Thinking of Pa's murder reminded me to secure my trusty friend of wire and wood before I attempted the swim to shore. I stuffed it deep inside my underclothes, avoiding my wounded thigh and resting it against the tightened pouch of my scrotum. My most precious belongings, all stored safely together.

There was a cracked, piss-yellow life preserver lashed to a capstan with rope that had been whitened by age and decay. I didn't even need to cut it; it pulled free in my hands like an ancient bulb of cotton. Stenciled around the faded ring was one simple word: LIFE.

How apt, I thought, grinning as I hooked it over my shoulder. That's precisely what it would help me achieve. A new life. I mumbled a quick prayer to my ravenous God, promising him more delicious souls in return for my continued survival, and threw myself into the chilly arms of the Atlantic.

* * *

    Life in Southampton has been much more difficult than I had originally projected. It's a beautiful town. The busy streets are lined with looming and ornate brick architecture painted with colorful murals and advertisements. Cable cars trundle up and down the lively streets, carrying the masses to their various tasks and worksites, but horse drawn carts are still a common sight too. The city buzzes like a giant beehive, and the people here are perfect worker bees.

    It's also a hard town. The pubs and bars have all been fairly clean and reputable thus far; no one has offered me my usual position as enforcer and my attempts at intimidation have been returned handily. I've had to search for honest work, as my poker loot will not last much longer, and that has left very little time for sex or murder. I feel like a stick of dynamite from the moment I wake up until my eyes finally drift closed.

    The first night was the hardest. It was nothing out of the ordinary for me; I've slept among the homeless countless times, and I know that brick and stones can be comfortable beds if one is exhausted enough. After my laborious swim to shore, however, I was soaked to the bone with frigid sea water and my wounds felt stiff and infected. It was mercifully dark when I pulled myself from the sea, so no one saw me collapse under the boardwalk and sink into a deep and immediate sleep. I feel very fortunate that I woke up at all.

    That first night, for the first time in years, I dreamed of my malevolent father. I dreamed that I was a small boy again, waking in the small hours of the morning with my heart thudding like a drum in my ears. My heart was racing because I was afraid. I was afraid because my pajamas and bedsheets were soaked with an invasive, lukewarm wetness— I had pissed the bed, *again*, and nothing brought on the rage of my father like a boy who could not hold his water. I sometimes think it wasn't my accidents that infuriated him.

I think the fury was always there, lurking under his false smiles and waiting for an outlet, and my frequent bedwetting was a convenient excuse to clobber me with whatever he could get his hands on. I think he hated me because I was *me*. Now that I'm grown and have become a perfect monster myself, I can see that he was right to hate me. Oh, father. How I hope your face is wriggling with maggots down there in the cold, moldy dark!

I never knew why the accidents happened. I pissed the bed until I was well into my teens, no matter what precautions I took. Once I had refused to take a sip of any liquid for twelve hours or more, desperate to keep my bladder empty regardless of my dry and sticky throat. Nothing ever worked. And no matter how silently I tried to wake my mother without disturbing the slumbering bear beside her, father always knew. And the *belt*, oh, the belt was always in his hand even before his eyes had adjusted to the candlelight.

I laid among drying tangles of seaweed, an unwilling spectator in my own head. I watched my young self frantically peel his sodden clothing off and toss it under my bed, as if there was some void under there that might make the evidence disappear. I saw myself tiptoeing, stark naked as the day I was born, down the darkened hallway to the room my parents begrudgingly shared. I heard the dull roar of my father's snores, and I could smell the sweet musk of alcohol on his exhales.

The young and nude Lee Redfield crept up to the sleeping form of my mother, gingerly shaking her shoulder. She pulled herself awake, her hair in a wild snarl of corkscrews and cowlicks, and swung her feet onto the cold floor without a word. She always knew why I was disturbing her sleep, just the way father knew when it was prime time to whip me; it was routine in our little house. Mother glanced over her shoulder, then pressed a finger to the wreck of her lips. They were purple and swollen from yet another blow my father had given her, probably for burning supper or failing to lay out his socks for him.

This nightmare was the worst I have ever had, and though it pains me to retell it, I feel that I must. Something that can generate fear in me, *real* fear, an honest to God *emotion*, is a force to be reckoned with. I will feel better once it's written down and confessed. I'm tired of carrying it with me, and I refuse to take it on my upcoming pleasure cruise. I leave it here, on these pages, forever.

As my mother escorted my dream self back to his room, quietly telling him that everything was okay, that he was just a boy and "potty accidents" happened, I began to smell her. It wasn't the smell of rosewater perfume and mild coffee breath that I associated with her, oh no. It was a smell I now know well. The smell of a bloating, rotten corpse submerged in stagnant water. My dream self was oblivious to it, but I, the alert watcher, was not.

I want to wake up, came my lucid voice. It was loud in the silence of my childhood home, but neither ghostly character took notice. *This is a bad dream and I want to wake up.* Nightmares do not let go of their prey quite so easily though, do they?

"We'll get you changed before your father wakes up," mother was whispering to my dream self, but her voice was thick and clotted. Bubbling. Her throat was full of some vile, viscous liquid. "He's had quite a lot to drink, Davey." I had all but forgotten my childhood nickname. As she knelt to look at the little boy eye to eye, I saw that her eyes had begun to dry and fade to milky cataracts. When she blinked, the lids did not close. They snagged like sandpaper on her drying eyes, giving her a chilling insectile appearance. Her head was beginning to bob and sway, much too heavy for the broken neck it sat upon.

Mother tiptoed to the washroom while my dream self hugged his small scabby knees to his chest, eyes fixated on the door and one hand cupping his small genitals. It always felt like days, waiting for father to wake up and erupt. Waiting for the whip-crack of that horrible, frayed leather belt striking the walls as he stormed down to get me.

I saw the thing that had been my mother stagger back into the room, carrying a damp washcloth and folded pajamas under her arm. She was jerking like a marionette. Her body, normally slender and rather sickly, ballooned out against her nightgown. There were dark, reddish-brown stains spreading from her armpits and cascading down the front of the pale blue material. One of her breasts, gone the color of old cabbage and swollen, hung over the elongated neck of the gown. The nipple that had once nourished me was black and deflated.

"Come here, Davey," she gurgled. Her face was marred with the final injuries my father had given her on the night he had laid hands upon her for the last time. The night I had watched him, cowering under my bed in a bunker of pissy clothes, as he clubbed her to death with one heavy work boot. He swung it by the laces like a morning star, again and again, long after she stopped clawing at him.

Her skull was now lumpy and misshapen, caved in at opposing angles. Both eyes had swollen shut, rivulets of amber liquid that looked like pus bleeding from between the blackened lids like infected tears. Her teeth were sharp and broken, gouging bloodless cuts into the slab of her tongue as she spoke. And the smell. My *god*, the smell. Piss and shit and rot, suffocating in its potency. Her jawbones crunched and ground together, her mouth falling open much too far as she repeatedly told my dream self that everything was going to be just fine.

I want to wake up, I kept screaming, but my throat was still and mute. My dream self extended his arms to hug my mother, even as knots of maggots began to boil out of her wounds and wriggle furiously in the pits of raw meat that dotted her skull.

I finally managed to wake up when my father exploded into the room, belt upraised and eyes glowing red like hot coals beneath the furrowed arrow of his brow. He wore nothing but ancient undershorts save for his feet, which were stuffed into a pair of filthy, bloody work boots. They clumped on the floor like falling boulders with each menacing step he took, his yellow skin loose and hanging like taffy.

"Quit petting him, you fucking bitch," he rumbled. His voice was the growl of a lion. He slapped the belt against his open palm like the whip of a savage slave driver. The buckle, which I dare say always hurt more than the rough black leather, boasted a deadly shine. He smiled as flies began to flutter and buzz around the room, drawn to the odor of my disintegrating mother.

My dream self snuggled into the seeping mounds of her bosom as peeling arms embraced him, his young mouth inching forward to close around her shriveled nipple. The bones of her hand crackled as she lifted the breast to meet it.

"Shhhh, Davey," she hissed. Her mutilated mouth could scarcely form the words. "It will all be over soon."

WAKE UP!

"Jesus God in Heaven," I whimpered, jolting upright in the damp sand and swiping sweat away from the searing cut on my head. "Please God, no more nightmares. I'm sorry if I displeased you, I'm so sorry if I was bad." Of course, the Ravenous God had not sent those visions into my head; it had been Harrison and the god damned length of wood he had struck me with. He had knocked the cobwebs out, as my old man liked to quip. He had opened a floodgate that allowed the red eye of Hell to peer into me, to taunt me. To show me what waited if I ever failed in my mission. Mother and father would be there, grasping for hugs and cuddles even as their flesh sloughed off their skeletons.

"God *almighty*," I repeated, and spent the rest of that long, gritty night in the sand communing with Him. When the sun rose that morning, the cleansing orange rays and the gentle sloshing of seawater chased the remnants of the horrible dream away. For a few nights, at least. I've seen Hell, reader. You had better be on the right side of the Ravenous God. What karma have you sown?

* * *

It should come as no real surprise that I've found work in a festering shipyard. Southampton is a shipping town, after all. You wouldn't believe how many ships come and go every day, laden with goods from every corner of civilization. I've come to think of this town as "little New York".

It isn't the Hell of my nightmares, but it is Hell enough to strangle the soul within me. I feel like a hungry hawk confined to a cage that does not allow me to stretch my wings. Morton Babbitt was my new boss and cell keeper, and though he always wore a friendly smirk and was generous enough to employ a disheveled and injured stranger like myself, he had a heart of frozen stone. He had the air of a man who has known nothing but labor from young years, and so mercy for the sore and tired was something to scoff at. He'd had it much worse, you understand, so there was no reason for *you* to be weary. Thanks to his view on labor and work ethic, I didn't see many days away from the yard. Not even when the blisters on my fingers and palms began to tear open and bleed. Morton also had no tolerance for lateness, and especially hated backtalk. Oh, and speaking of Babbitt, I've heard many a whispered rumor in the local pubs and coffee houses of the ongoing hunt for the man who murdered (and indeed partially consumed) the brute. Congratulations. You've found him.

"Just one," Morton had told me on my very first day, his voice firm and humorless and one dirty fingertip hovering at the tip of my nose, "*One* late start of your shift, and it'll be a new job for you, friend." He'd handed me a stiffened pair of worn work gloves and a dented metal cup to be used for "water and coffee, nothing else", and that had been the extent of his mercy. All of us yardmen knew that Morton began and ended each workday with swigs of coffee diluted with brandy, but none of us bothered to confront him about his hypocrisy. We needed money, and it was best to avoid him altogether. It may not mean much coming from me, but Morton was as cruel as they come.

"I'll work hard for you," I answered placidly, though visions of his strangled corpse were already traipsing through my shaken brain like mother had in my dream. He never smiled but grimaced, a pained flattening of his lips that looked like it took immense effort. I wanted to slice those lips from his tiny, yellowed teeth. He would wear a grin for everyone if I did, wouldn't he?

Watch yourself, I warned with twitches of my bloodshot eyes. Morton either took no notice or felt no fear of me. He didn't fear me because he didn't *know* me. Unlike Benson, that fat old coward, Morton had never seen the darkness that sulked and yearned in my soul. The garrote, tight in my back pocket, ceaselessly screamed up at me like an interrupted orgasm. I was pleased and eager when the men in expensive suits began to snoop around the shipyard, men that even a blind fool would recognize as New York City mobsters. The promise of sweet release hung in the smoky air like soft music.

I'd had nearly a month of relative (albeit grueling) peace before the crime lords of New York tracked me down. I'm admittedly unskilled when it comes to ship work, so I've been serving as what Morton calls "Johnny On The Spot". I move and organize materials, haul canvas sacks of tools and nails from man to man, pull the stubborn nails from salvageable wood and refill the cups and canteens. It is insulting, demeaning work, but it affords me this small upstairs apartment and a limited supply of groceries from time to time.

I've been struggling to maintain my double-life, but I've known from the start that this was a temporary arrangement. I'm simply not built to remain in one place like a pile of cow shit gathering fungus, and I have no desire to contribute to a society of sinners as a normal man would. My urges are volcanic. They continue to build until I can't contain them anymore, and if I'm to be smart and stay off the gallows, I *must* purge them before they reach the critical point. My point is, I felt no dread on the overcast evening that Morton pulled me from the pile of lumber I was sanding to let me know that I was hunted.

He waited until the end of shift, certainly. He wanted every drop of sweat and blood, every blister and callous that he could wring from me. When the end of shift bell tolled and the other haggard workers limped and grumbled towards the heavy wrought iron gates, Morton stayed behind. He reached out with a hand that was swaddled in bandages, touching my chest with a grave look in his frosty eyes.

"We need to chat, mate," he said, gesturing towards the small wooden shed that served as his office. The thought that dominated my mind was not concern for my job or my life. It was that for the first time in a month, I would be alone at dusk with another living person, a man with holy punishment that bagged to be delivered. I was so excited that I sprung an immediate ironclad erection, and I didn't bother to shield the wagging thing with my hands as I walked beside him. Morton was marked, and the Ravenous God was hungry. No more would he ride on the backs of the downtrodden and the desperate, growing fat with booze and wiping his hairy ass with stolen wages.

"You've seen the men hangin' around lately, have you?" He said, gesturing to a rickety chair that sat crookedly before his desk. I took a seat, the wood crying out beneath my weight. Morton peered outside, looking both ways before shutting the door and throwing the bolt behind him.

"Yes."

"The men that wear suits that cost more than the ships we repair?"

"Yes, sir."

My voice was gravelly, primal. I wanted his information only slightly more than I wanted him dead. My stomach was tied in hot, impatient knots. As he spoke, I watched the muscles and arteries of his neck flex and pulse. When I slipped the garrote out of my pocket and began to run the length of wire between my sore fingertips, I nearly ejaculated. I was panting with anticipation, and in his arrogance, he took it as nervousness.

"Well, Lee, I believe they're lookin' for *you*," he growled, his voice breaking. He stabbed the bandaged hand at me. "They say they're lookin' for a murderer who killed a lot of their friends, stole their money and crossed the Atlantic as a stowaway aboard a vessel called the *White Cap*. I've not heard of any ship of that name dockin' in Southampton, but I *have* heard of a stranger that crawled out of the ocean like a bleedin' mudskipper, came to me a broken and bloodied mess, and now does odd jobs in my shipyard like an innocent little *lamb!*"

His eyes did not leave mine as he yanked the stained bandages from his hand. He held up what looked like a swollen pork chop with five crooked sausages dangling from it. His fingers were clearly broken, blackened and missing all the fingernails save for the ring finger. Had he survived our meeting, it would never have functioned properly again. The arthritis alone would have crippled him for life, and even counting money would have driven him to suicide.

"When I told them I indeed had a new hire, one that had come to me under strange circumstances, they took a hammer to me. They didn't even bother askin' me, Lee. They started hurtin' me straight away. They told me to talk, or they would cut every finger from both my hands, all but my pinkies and my thumbs. Turn me into a fuckin' *crab*."

What a funny image that was. I mimicked his flat smile as laughter prodded, desperate to escape. I cleared my throat.

"You told them where I live?" I demanded, struggling and failing to hide my excitement.

"And what would you have me do, Lee?" He shot back, wagging his limp fingers at me. As Morton grew angrier, his thick British accent grew stronger. I could hold my snickering no longer. "Shall I keep shieldin' you until they break my legs, or cut my fuckin' throat?"

He paused, hands spread, waiting for my response. All I could do was grin at him, my body tensing and releasing and the crotch of my slacks threatening to burst.

"*And what the blue fuck are you laughin' at?* You're a creepy bastard, you know that?" He was frantic now, sweating and drawing breaths through gritted teeth. "I tried to do you a blessin' but you scare the fuck out of me, and I need you off my shipyard. Tonight. *Now*."

"You were kind to me," I said, closing my eyes and bowing my head like a child in prayer. "You took me off the streets and gave me a job when I had nothing but the rags on my back. I hear you, Morton, and I'll go in peace. But before I do, will you please let me make it up to you somehow? I *beg* you, Morton."

He barked laughter, thrusting his mutilated hand at me once more. The dead fingers flopped and knocked together.

"*How?!*" He roared. "*You've already done pretty much all the damage you can, you soppy cunt!*"

"Your hand," I said, standing to face him with my hands laced behind my back. "I can make the pain stop."

Morton looked like he had been struck across the face.

"What?" He asked, hilariously confused. He knew little else after that.

The tiny office reverberated with my laughter as I lashed out with both hooked hands, grabbing handfuls of greasy hair on either side of his head. I snatched him before he could tense a muscle, and so as I brought his face down onto the unforgiving wood of his desk, he gave no resistance. The heavy *thud* of the impact vibrated down the legs and into the floor. I felt it in the soles of my feet.

"*Guh!*" He blurted, a senseless animal sound of pure shock. I lifted him from the desk and slammed his head down again, feeling the impact jolt up my arms in delicious waves. My hair hung in my face, my tongue wagging out like that of a thirsty wolf. I was crazed. *Ravenous*. It was such a release; far better than any whore could have ever given me. I raised his head again and slammed it down with still more force, so much so that for a second or two I was in midair. The slapdash scattering of Morton's papers and pens were spotted with bright, beautiful blood. One of his teeth arced through the air and bounced off my chest like a stone thrown by a child.

I shoved him back into his chair, everything below his hairline now nothing more than a red smudge. I was *erasing him*. He was snoring, the very same wet tearing sound the sinner in the alley had made. His hands, even the mangled one, drummed against the tops of his knees in spasms.

"*Yes, Ravenous God!*" I shrieked, throwing myself over his desk and turning the office into a snow globe filled with blood-soaked papers. "*He is yours, he is yours!*" The garrote was around his neck and I was screaming laughter, pressing my full weight into the back of his chair with my strong knee. On pure irrepressible impulse, I shot my jaws forward and sank my teeth into what was left of his right cheek, snarling, forcing my teeth together until a coppery slab of meat detached. My mouth was filled with salty blood, as hot as fresh coffee. I chewed the flesh, smacking my lips like a cow chomping an oversized cud, hearing the meat pop and grind in my ears as the wire sank ever deeper. Morton did not scream. When I finally released the garrote, he slumped onto the floor in the untidy sprawl that only the dead can achieve.

The silence that followed was absolute. It was so quiet that for just a moment, I thought I could hear the melodic twinkling of the Ravenous God's beard, fluttering in the wind and helping to ease the last of my crippling urges. I smelled and tasted nothing but iron, and my stomach was comfortably full.

You'll be suspect number one, my rational self scolded. Of course, I knew they would eventually link the murder to me, especially after I failed to show up for work again and again. I was also the newest worker Babbitt had employed, still a relative stranger to most of the shipyard's haggard crew. It didn't matter; I was unafraid. It was time to move on from Southampton anyway. A single month of honest labor was too much time spent as a slave, and I had divine eyes looking down upon me. He would deliver as he always had.

    I locked the office door behind me and began the peaceful walk home, licking the salty blood from my lips and massaging the rising scar on my scalp. Sometimes, when my heart is chugging at full speed, I can feel pain radiating from that raised squiggle of tissue like waves of heat. There was nothing left for me to do but wash my body with cold water and change my undershorts— and, of course, wait for the hunters to come.

* * *

    This apartment is little more than a leaky box that guzzles money. There is only one window that looks out onto the building next door; what an exquisite view of faded bricks I have. The wavy ceiling is stained with blossoms of yellow and green water damage, and powdery black mold has begun its slow spread to the walls. Said window is missing its lower pane of glass. There is a plank of soft, peeling wood nailed across the hole. More often than not, if I go to the window to peer out, I'll find tiny bugs skittering in and out of the dry rotted wood. I bathe in a coffin-like bathtub that has no elbow room and no hot water either. My few garments are tossed into a musty dresser, and I sleep on a sunken cot that festers and grows heavy with dust mites in the corner. The door seems to be too large for the frame and was also installed crookedly on the hinges, causing the wood to scream upon each opening. It is obnoxious and, frankly, beneath a servant of the Ravenous God to sleep in such a place, but that decrepit door doubles as a burglar alarm if anyone comes for me while I'm sleeping.

    I have been laying low since Babbitt's murder, surviving on pennies and battling my incessant urges the best that I can. I knew it wouldn't be much longer until my victims came to me, which was good because it was *much* too dangerous to hunt so soon after I had killed Morton. I have been wallowing in a sort of starved limbo. When Luchino finally came for me last night, and then was arrogant or just angry enough to face me alone, he was walking into the cave of a savage animal.

I was wide awake, staring up at the spotted ceiling and listening to the cacophony of Southampton seeping in through my broken window. Like New York, sleep is optional but not required by the hardy people here. The distant clanging of ship bells and the chugging of their engines never ceases. Men shout orders and insults, heavy objects *thunk* and knock together as they are stacked or unloaded. Horses neigh and whinny and monstrous chains rattle as anchors are pulled through the streets, destined for new homes aboard ships that left their anchors resting on the bottom of the sea. It is the sound of hard labor, and I'm glad to be rid of that burden.

The sound of footsteps outside my door was fairly common in the apartment building, but never were they so willfully silent. They were always clumsy and heavy, sometimes inconsiderate in volume. Sometimes they shuffled and stomped if the owner of the feet had been drinking; I'd hear slurred words and hiccups, belches and other bodily gasses, and the broken glass jangle of keys knocking against old wood. It may sound counterintuitive to you, dear reader, but it was the silence of the approaching footfalls that alerted me. The care of each surgical step, trying to avoid any board that looked warped and therefore might squeak. The cowards had come at night, trying to catch me sleeping, and they *thought* they were being stealthy.

I could see the overlap of shadows beneath my door, blotting out the dirty orange glow of the hall light fixture. There were two men; my sense of hearing was so acute that I could hear them speaking to one another in hushed tones. They were discussing my assassination as I lay there on my cot with an ache growing in my back, fighting snickers with my hands behind my head and the garrote resting on my chest like a loyal pet. These men were *professionals*? God above, I could make a *killing* in that line of work. Pardon the pun, please.

"*I don't hear anything*," came a quiet voice, very near to the door.

"He's asleep. There's no light under the door. Now shut the fuck up and do the lock."

Small clicking and tapping sounds began to rattle under my doorknob as one of the men began to pick the lock.

"It's an old lock, what's taking so long?"

"The old ones stick, cocksucker!"

"Lower your goddamn voice."

I scanned the apartment for a place to hide and wait for my ambush. I considered waiting just inside the door, though it meant I might have to take them both at the same time. They would certainly have their guns drawn and ready to spray lead at any movement they saw. If I could garrote one, yank his body in front of mine, then perhaps I could use him as a human shield against his partner. It was a flimsy plan, but the only one I had save for jumping out the broken window and hoping I didn't snap both legs when I landed in the alley below. Hiding anywhere else in this shit pot apartment would have denied me the ability to move quickly and decisively. I knew the Ravenous God would be watching from his throne of bodies, quieting my movements and blinding their aiming eyes should they try to shoot me. I crossed the darkened room balancing on my toes, decided against the sudden impulse to duck down into my rusty bathtub, and chose to hide just inside the door after all. The men would be looking forward, not to the sides. Or so I hoped.

The lock clacked open as if it had been turned with my key.

"There," the villainous locksmith whispered. *"Ready, Pale?"*

My breath snagged in my lungs. He'd said "Pale". Could it have been a simple coincidence? Someone else with that insipid nickname, perhaps given because of his choice of beverage?

No, I thought, anxiously drumming my fingers on the axe handle and crouching, ready to pounce. *It's Pale Boy Luchino. He's come to finish me.*

An eternity passed as I waited for the door to screech open. My breathing felt much too loud, tearing in and out of me like the ocean waves against the beaches and piers down the street. I knew it was all in my head; Pale Boy and his lackey had no idea what they were dealing with. Their glorious, righteous karma was at hand.

"Wait."

They were being so very quiet, I applaud them for that, but to a trained predator like myself they might as well have been screaming. The man whispering this time was Pale Boy himself.

"*What, man? What?*"

"*Let me do it. Alone.*"

I turned my eyes up to the ceiling, imagining the roof and smog parting to reveal the dark expanse of the heavens above. I thanked my Ravenous God, clasping my hands around the garrote and raising them to his glory. I could see Him smiling down, His interlocking rows of flesh rending teeth gleaming from within His musical beard. What a merciful, generous God He is. I would only have one man to contend with. One! And it was Pale Boy Luchino! The bastard who had shot me, nearly *bled* me, and toppled the first domino of hardship in the long, merciless line that had been my life in Southampton!

"*Are you* nuts? *He stabbed Frankie Bones. He shot Violet, he shot Henry and Walter, he fucking* gutted *Billy Arms and he shot Simon the Banker. He—*"

"*He almost killed* me," Pale Boy hissed. His voice was scarcely more than hard consonants and breath, but I could still sense the rage in it. *Oh*, how he wanted me. Almost as badly as I wanted him, and when it comes to games of predator and prey, it all comes down to who wants it more. "*It's personal, Sal. I don't want help with this one. I don't* need *help with this one.* I *have the drop on* him *this time. Not the other way around. We'll tell the crew that we whacked him together, okay?*"

There was no response.

"*Go get us some whiskey,*" Pale Boy went on. "*That little place down the street with the grapes on the sign. Wait for me there. This won't take long.*"

I could almost visualize the other man, Sal, staring into Pale Boy's milky face with a dopey, concerned expression. Then, without a word of protest, I heard his clandestine footfalls tapping back down the hall. He had left his partner to die.

Thank you, Ravenous God, for this perfect murder. My finest kill, I thought.

The door jostled in its frame as Pale Boy leaned into it, trying to open it as quietly as he could. Cunning professional that he was, he noticed the slant and the scuff marks on the frame and pulled the knob in the opposite direction. There was only a tiny chirp as the door swung in instead of the scream I had grown accustomed to, and a long rectangle of light stretched across the dirty floorboards like a fiery grave. I could see the dark shape of his bowler hat, perched atop the creeping outline of his shadow, as he slithered in.

   I held my breath as he inched past me. I almost guffawed in surprised laughter; the ignorant cunt hadn't even brought a gun! His hands, clad in tight black leather gloves, were clutching his throwing knives instead of pistols. In his right hand he held a single knife in stabbing position, the silvery blade pointing at his feet and winking icily in the light from the hallway. In the left, *three* throwing knives were parked between each of his knuckles, the squat handles jutting out like blunted claws. He was dressed in his trademark black suit, though he had forgone the flowing overcoat, for ease of movement I assume. His white face was set but expressionless, the curly mustache still and steady beneath his nose. His shoulders were no longer level; the one I had plugged with a bullet sat slightly lower. He looked like a sad old seesaw. I noticed a thin black strap running through the dark hair of his temple, and as he turned his head ever so slightly, scanning the room for me as his remaining eye adjusted to the darkness, my suspicions from the Silver Lion were confirmed. Pale Boy now sported an eye patch.

   I saw the damage the rogue shotgun blast had done much later, after I had finished him. It had taken his eye and incalculable divots of flesh from his face and eye socket. Paired with his pale complexion, he resembled the pockmarked surface of the moon or perhaps, more fitting, a glass of curdled milk. His left cheek was sunken in slightly more than the right, giving him a permanent sneer, and pinkish wrinkles of fresh scar tissue branched out from beneath the eye patch like a permanent wink. He had been mangled by his own man, a man they apparently called "Billy Arms" (a nickname well-earned) who had indeed been aiming for me. His face, I realized, was no longer a hideous sight to behold but had been transformed into a wonderful work of art. Beautiful, true, but an incomplete piece. I would finish it like a true artist.

I could tell by the slow tensing of his lopsided shoulders that Pale Boy was growing suspicious. He was pointed at my empty cot, blinking and now lightly grinding his teeth together, struggling to focus with his remaining eye. Was the room empty or not? Why couldn't he hear me snoring? Was I even *home*?

I held the garrote in both hands as if powering a handcart, carefully extending my arms out to ensnare him. The clotted wire brushed the velvety brim of his hat, just hard enough to knock it from his head and clear the way for the wire. It pattered to the floor beneath his brilliantly shined dress shoes.

"Huh—" he attempted, and then the wire was around his throat. Simple as that.

"Here I am, you pig fucking son of a bitch! Looking for me, are you?! Well joy to the world, you've found me, haven't you?! Take me alone, will you?!"

I was raving, salivating, hysterical in my blood lust. Holding Pale Boy's flailing body felt like wrestling a rapacious alligator. In his blind panic he made yet another mistake— he fumbled one of the knives from his left hand. It clattered to the floor, and he then kicked it out of his own reach with one flail of his foot.

His skill with those blades was legendary and I must not deny him that; he had the sort of talent you only read about in the cheap newsstand detective novels. He didn't fight me the way my victims usually did. He didn't bother to claw at the wire; remember, he was a professional killer. He had panicked initially, yes, but he knew pulling at the garrote would do no good, and so his only hope was to disable me. Although his windpipe had been squeezed off, the wire tightening exponentially as I spun the axe handle like the wheel of a ship, he kept the presence of mind to use his knives against me.

He snapped his left arm back towards my head, moving his hand in a dexterous motion that was too fast for my eye to catch. Both throwing knives came straight at my face. It was only a last second sidestep that saved my hide. I heard the spinning blades buzz as they skirted my temple, close enough to sever a few stray hairs, and I even felt the slightest of breezes as the generated wind across my warming cheeks. They connected with something out in the hallway, and it clattered to the floor and shattered.

I had to contort my body into painful positions to avoid the knife in his right hand, which he swung behind himself in deft, brutal jabs. It was painstaking, strangling the tenacious life out of the man while also dodging his blows. The knife missed me by inches with every stab, only once making contact and shredding the fabric of my shirt across the ribs. We did our absurd dance for what felt like days, our shoes clomping together like the hooves of idiot horses as we waltzed in wide, clumsy circles. We snarled like two dogs battling for a piece of gristle.

The muscles of my arms were burning as if lava flowed through my veins, the muscles hard and aching and my fingers tingling into numbness one digit at a time. Pale Boy's knees were finally weakening. I allowed him to sag, to combine his own body weight with the force of my twisting and pulling to increase the pressure on his neck. His attempts to stab me were growing feeble, careless, desperate. I imagine he was seeing the tunnel just then, the tunnel that would lead him to the toothy maw of the Ravenous God. His white cheeks were deepening to crimson and then purple, and his tongue wagged out from beneath his silly mustache. His remaining eye, dotted with angry red splotches, rolled wildly in its socket.

"No one will stop me, do you understand?!" I roared into his ear, wanting it to hurt. I didn't care if the neighbors heard me. I think perhaps I *wanted* them to. *"Nothing will happen to me! They will never catch me! I serve the Ravenous God, and you will serve the flies!"*

I used the last supply of strength in my arms to haul Pale Boy around in a tight stumbled circle and shoved him face first into the wall. He was too far gone to try to soften the blow with his hands, and he connected hard enough to leave the tall, egg-shaped indentation you'll find beside the dresser there. His knife, which is now *my* knife, tumbled from his fingers. He gurgled from somewhere deep in his throat, his eye wide and yet wholly unseeing. I watched the consciousness fade from it, watched with a gasping grin as it became nothing more than an inanimate glass ball in a darkened hollow. His legs buckled and at last he collapsed at my feet. When I pried my fingers from the axe handle, the garrote spun like a propeller as the wire unwound itself. Much of its length was so deeply gouged into his flesh that it was no longer visible.

I hobbled over to peer out the door, searching for onlookers in the hallway. There were none to be found, which, if I'm honest, saved their lives. I would have murdered any witnesses just to extend my lusty blood high.

"Good," I said to Pale Boy's body, smiling over my trembling shoulder as I pushed the crooked door back into its frame. "I need privacy to fix your face, old boy."

Pale Boy offered nothing in response to this. I nudged him with my big toe, rolling him over onto his back. His ankles crossed as he flopped, and I think he looked astonishingly comfortable in the immediate wake of his death. Peaceful, even, if you discount the ring of blood beads circling his wrung neck. I placed the sole of my bare foot across the bridge of his nose, lifted it as high as I could manage, then paused.

"I'd better put my shoes on," I said to him genially. "You know me, I'd forget my prick if it wasn't attached." I found a cleanish pair of wool socks and stuffed my feet into them, tying my battered old shoes around them as tightly as I could manage with my exhausted fingers. As I replaced my foot over his devastated face, I saw that my pinky toe was peeking like a curious rodent from a hole in the canvas side.

"Say," I said with a grin, bending the knee again, "You wouldn't happen to be a size 11, would you?"

I grunted and slammed my foot down, and Pale Boy's face felt like stomping in thick mud dotted with buried rocks. The force of the impacts was painful. I felt it traveling through my joints like an electric current, from the ball of my foot all the way up to my hip. I held my arms out to either side like a raptor spreading its wings, steadying myself on my bad leg so that I could stomp with the stronger of the two. I could see my sweat misting from my lips, could feel ropes of saliva swinging from my gritted teeth. I brought the foot down again and again and again, the dry thuds melting into wet crunches that soon gave way to thick, gelatinous splats as the skull, or the shell of the pumpkin, if you like, came apart. Pale Boy's body rocked and hopped with each blow as though he might still be trying to escape me.

When I could bear the pain no longer and collapsed onto my cot, Pale Boy's face resembled that of a wax sculpture left much too close to the fireplace. There was nothing left above his scored neck but clots of hair, tatters of dirty flesh that resembled ribbons of charred leather, and his eye patch, caked with red and gray jelly. I could just make out the form of his mouth, smeared into a crooked oval and harboring no visible teeth. A halo of sprayed blood circled the mess like a wicked crown, perhaps one fit to adorn the head of my Ravenous God.

And now dear reader, time grows short, but I simply *must* brag about what I have laying on the dresser top beside these papers. Naturally I robbed Pale Boy after I had obliterated his head, and you wouldn't believe what the man had! A beautiful gold and silver pocket watch, hung from a chain that shines like diamonds on a string. He had come armed with a beautifully carved and silver-inlaid Derringer, so oily and clean that I wonder if he's ever bothered to use it. The small black butt of the Derringer is engraved with a fancy cursive letter L, but that L can stand for "Lee", certainly, can't it? In his back pocket I found a jeweled money clip with a wad of bills inside it, thick enough to distend its shape. In the opposite pocket, I found a pack of cigarettes that Pale Boy has reused until it is falling apart in my fingers. He has filled it with fat, hand-rolled cigarettes. And of course, folded neatly around some coins, I found the ticket.

Pale Boy's ticket home is now *my* ticket home, and true to the sort of man that he was, it is for a trip across the Atlantic on the grandest ship to ever sail the seas. She's leaving port today at noon, April the 10th of 1912, embarking on her maiden voyage from Southampton to New York. Surely, you've heard of the *R.M.S. Titanic*, yes? Who hasn't? It's all anyone in Southampton can talk about lately. She is the largest, most luxurious ship ever built by the hands of man. She is so modern, so *advanced*, that they even say God himself could not sink her. I would rather not tempt my Ravenous God on the matter, but I see no reason why he would deliver me passage on the floating palace and then deign to let anything happen to her. The ticket Pale Boy purchased is probably all that was available this close to launch, and though it *is* Third Class, I've seen the brochures and flyers in shop windows all around town. Even the lowest decks of the *Titanic* outshine the closest rivals and will certainly feel like First Class to me.

    The *Titanic* is so monstrous in size that I can see her from the roof of this building. Her riveted hull is gleaming black, her layered superstructure brilliantly white, and she is topped with four golden funnels that climb high into the sky and cast their shadows over the throngs of men bustling on her decks. I shall enjoy strolling out onto the poop deck, all the way to very end of the stern, and watching England fade away to nothing but wake and sparkling waves.

    As I said, by the time you come for me, I will be wallowing in the lap of luxury as I am carried back home in comfort and safety. Perhaps I will meet Pale Boy's wayward partner, Sal? Surely he'll be in steerage as well. Perhaps we could share a bunk, or take a leisurely stroll along the vast promenade decks together? I pray that I find him. I'm sure I will need to purge myself during the voyage as I cross the Atlantic once again, and though he did not attack me, he is marked. His karma is on its way, and with the sleek new blade I've pilfered from his fallen friend, it will be swift and bloody indeed.

    Alas, friend, we have reached the end of my tale. I have a ship to catch, and to miss the departure would mean missing my *own* karma, karma I've worked so hard to sow for myself. *Bled* to sow for myself. My reward from the Ravenous God, for doing his good work here on Earth. You don't need to thank me for my services. It has been my pleasure! Do not forget, should you choose to display my beloved garrote in a museum someplace: my name is David Lee Redfield. Catch me if you can.

Bugs

    Jamie Nielsen watched in horror as the mosquito lighted on his arm, its tiny whining body barely visible in the fading afternoon light. He cringed at the feel of it slipping between the scant hairs of his forearm, telling himself that there were only seconds before he felt the itching stab of its bite. But he didn't *dare* slap it.

    Jamie was repulsed by bugs. *All* bugs. Even cute little lady bugs and gently hovering fireflies. It was their legs; all those writhing, wriggling legs and flailing antennae. It was their black, shining, unblinking eyes. It was their slimy cheese curd eggs, laid in the tangles of your hair or deep in the well of your ear as you slept. It was their twitching, ratcheting wings. He couldn't put his finger on one specific *thing* he hated about bugs; he just hated them all, without question, and had since he had begun forming memories.

    Jamie guessed it was the diseases the bugs carried most of all. He'd spent hours on Google researching it although it terrified him, almost like a dare he reluctantly imposed on himself. Bugs carried AIDS. They carried West Nile. Zika. Chikungunya. Malaria. He refused to entertain a single thought about the botfly since learning that its larvae could burrow into your skin.

    Jamie knew all too well that a *single* mosquito was more likely to kill you than a Great White Shark. Once the mosquito was on you, you never wanted to slap it. *Never.* Then you were apt to have someone else's blood splatter onto your bare skin, and what if you had a cut? You had to act fast and brush the little monster off— but that meant you had to touch it, even with the briefest of hand swipes, and Jamie didn't want to do that either. He was paralyzed with fear, and he simply didn't have time to be.

    Jamie clawed at the lower right pocket of his muddy cargo shorts and ripped out his trusty can of bug spray. It was his talisman; he carried bug spray like pretty girls carried mace, though clearly it didn't work as well as advertised once you worked up a sweat. The mosquito hadn't bitten him yet. There was still time. He placed his pointer finger on the plastic button and pointed the nozzle at his arm.

    Slap.

Jamie blinked, trying to register what had just happened. The mosquito on his arm had been replaced by the pale and freckled hand of Gaige Hollis, his best friend in the whole world (though he often wondered *why* he was his best friend) and perpetual good-natured bully. When the hand came away, there was nothing left but a greasy black smudge across a shining blob of someone else's poisoned blood.

"*Why?!*" Jamie demanded, his prepubescent voice breaking and echoing through the towering playground equipment around them. "*Why would you slap it?!*"

Gaige smirked and wrinkled his thin beak of a nose, wiping the mess of blood and guts on his palm across the expensive Green Bay Packers jersey he always wore on the weekends. The boxy white number 8 now bore a pink stain that made Jamie want to puke.

Jamie didn't puke, but he did gag. There was no stopping it. He snatched up a wad of crabgrass and used it as a makeshift napkin, scrubbing his arm raw as Gaige threw his head back and laughed. Then he added a healthy coat of bug spray, just in case it killed germs too.

"It's probably *your* blood, numbnuts," Gaige sneered.

"It hadn't bitten me yet, you retard," Jamie snapped back, his eyes and nostrils streaming. He hated his anger. It made him feel like a baby that couldn't hand with the big kids, but his anger and disgust with insects were as uncontrollable as his gag reflex whenever one was near him.

"Why are you such a *pussy*?" Gaige volleyed.

"Why are you such a fucking *queer*?" Jamie responded.

That got them both laughing, and though he was revolted, Jamie relished the tingle of excitement that trickled through his chest and stomach every time he swore. Not only had he called Gaige a queer, which was bad enough, but he had called him a *fucking* queer. That took it to a whole new level of bad. That strapped a bomb to it and made it explode. At the ripe old age of 13, he finally understood why adults liked to cuss so much and he did it every chance he got. Never around Mom and Dad, of course, but he still fancied himself a bit of a bad boy. Bad enough to say "fuck" and "shit" and even the dreaded "cunt". But he didn't want his Xbox taken away again. Fuck that. Jamie swore in secret and minded his manners at home.

"It's just a stupid bug," Gaige said, extending his tongue and pretending to lick the guts off his palm. Jamie gagged again and shoved Gaige as hard as he could— which was not very hard at all.

"Why are you licking it? It's not a dick."

Their combined laughter tittered across the abandoned playground, and in the purple glow of approaching twilight, Jamie found the echoes just a little bit spooky. He couldn't let Gaige know that, though. He already thought he was a pussy because bugs gave him the heebie-jeebies. If he even *smelled* that Jamie might be afraid of the dark, he'd probably find a new friend.

"I *know* you're too pussy to go into the Halloran house," Gaige said ominously. "*Nobody* goes in there. I mean, I did once, but everyone else is too chicken shit."

It was Jamie's turn to mock.

"The door and all the windows are boarded up, dumb shit. You didn't go in."

"I did too," Gaige said, smiling as if he were letting Jamie in on a deliciously dirty secret. His eyebrows bobbed up and down. "There's a board missing over the living room window, and you can squeeze right in. There's no broken glass or anything. Honest."

He placed his hand over his heart like he was swearing an oath, flipping a lock of sweaty red hair from his forehead with a casual jerk of his neck.

"Are *you* too pussy to prove it?" Jamie hissed, and then felt the cold cocktail of dread and regret trickling into his guts.

I really opened a can of worms with that one, he thought morosely, unaware that he was using a metaphor his Dad always used. A *disgusting* metaphor.

"Nope," Gaige said, puffing his chest out. He slapped another mosquito off the back of his neck and peered down at the bloody goop on his palm, then presented it to Jamie with an ear-to-ear grin. Jamie felt his stomach clench, then coated himself once more with the cold, pungent bug spray. "We can go right now; we don't have to be home for another hour."

Jamie suddenly felt like he needed to drop a deuce, but there was another stirring in his abdomen that was more insistent. It was pride; foolish, childish pride. Just this once, he would not let his fear control him. Just this once, he would not back down. Then maybe Gaige would ease off him a little. The Halloran house was just a stupid fucking empty house. That was it.

Jamie jogged over to where their bikes lay, tangled together in a snarl of aluminum and brake cables. He swung his leg over and was pedaling before Gaige had even processed what was happening. No words needed to be said. Both boys knew the way, as all boys seem to know the way to their local haunted house.

* * *

Dad had told him that it wasn't supposed to rain at all over the weekend (and *that* was a real can of worms, because his tomato plants were barely hanging on by a thread) but Jamie's eyes still kept drifting up to the bruise-colored sky. The moon was full and that was good, because neither of them had flashlights and neither of their simple "emergencies only" cellphones were equipped with one. The moon was bright, but fluffy black clouds kept drifting over the silvery disc as though the sky were winking at them. Their bike tires hummed through the long pools of shadow it cast across the pavement like spectral lava. The tattered playing card Gaige had clothes pinned to his rear tire clattered like a miniature machine gun.

"He killed his wife and kids with a blowtorch, you know," Gaige called over his shoulder with a devious grin. "Old man Halloran. He took it into their rooms one by one and put the nozzle, or whatever, right in their mouths. He roasted them from the inside out."

"He chopped them up with an *axe*," Jamie yelled back, flinching at his own callousness. "Everyone knows that. If he did it with a blowtorch, he would have burnt the place down."

"It *is* burnt down," Gaige said matter-of-factly, and Jamie's heart skipped a beat as he realized that for once, his friend was absolutely right. He had seen the Halloran house only once or twice before, but he could still remember the black tentacles of soot spreading out from the empty windows and snaking across the peeling siding. He wasn't sure where he had heard the axe story; it seemed like everyone at school knew what had *really* happened to the Hallorans, and everyone was an expert. Jamie tried to imagine what it would feel like, what it would *taste* like, to have a lit blowtorch stuffed into his mouth. He had burnt his mouth on hot food before and thought that was one of the worst things he had ever felt. The thought of an open flame across his tongue, his teeth baking right in his head, made his stomach heave and roll against his ribs again. He decided he would prefer being chopped up with an axe to that kind of torture.

    Somewhere in the corridors of his young mind, where the nightmare creatures that slithered and stalked and kept him awake at night resided, he could hear the fluttering sound of the *caution* tape the police had wrapped around the gnarled bannisters of the front porch like a neon yellow spider web. It was like they strung them up and then forgot about them, case closed. He was not eager to return there, but the waving grass on either side of the street was already becoming patchy and yellow; forgotten. They were getting close to the rundown part of town, where the haunted house waited for them.

    The Halloran house always seemed to creep up on you. You tried to prepare yourself for it, and it always seemed like you had plenty of time to get ready, and then it was suddenly just there. It happened that way again tonight, and the sight of the dilapidated old house looming out of the darkness frightened Jamie so badly that he nearly flipped his bike on a fallen branch. He wanted to turn tail and run. He wanted to speed home as fast as his legs could pedal, he even wanted to do his stupid math homework and then he wanted to play *Grand Theft Auto* until Mom forced him to turn it off. He wanted to do anything but visit this old mausoleum, and he hated himself for being the one to suggest the little field trip in the first place.

    His legs did not obey him, however. He was numb as he followed Gaige up onto the porch, ducking under the faded caution tape. The slippery planks of the porch squealed in protest as they approached the open window to the right of the barricaded front door. Jamie swallowed with an audible click as he stared into the well of darkness inside it. Again, Gaige hadn't been lying.

"There's no glass," Gaige repeated, his voice oddly calm and steady. "Just throw your leg over."

Jamie did as he was told, and before he could utter any protest, he was standing in the ruined living room of the Halloran house. Everything smelled like wet leaves and mildewed laundry, and somewhere beneath was a pungent hint of old smoke and charred wood. The room was mostly empty save for an old coffee table that leaned on two legs, and what appeared to be the lumpy shape of an old sofa with a stiffened sheet draped over it. The breeze outside whistled through the boards and holes in the roof, producing a wheezing moan that made the house breathe. Jamie's teeth began to chatter.

"So... why would he use fire?" Jamie croaked, his throat completely devoid of any moisture. Gaige dug into his back pocket and removed a small object. Jamie heard the familiar *snick-snick* of a lighter. "Wouldn't it be easier to just use... like... a shotgun or something?"

Gaige said nothing, the tiny flicker of flame casting an orange glow across his eager face.

"Where'd you get *that*?" Jamie asked innocently. He was still young enough to be awed by something as exotic as a lighter, and he was jealous that Gaige actually carried one. It was such a badass thing to do, and if he ever got caught with one, Dad would probably bust his Xbox over his head.

"It was my Mom's, she has a hundred of them. Come here. I wanna show you something *really* scary. I think it's why he used fire."

Gaige took Jamie by the wrist and led him across the dead living room. Jamie did his best to block out thoughts of what might be living inside the walls; if not for the moan and sigh of the wind through the house, he probably would have been able to hear the skittering and scuttling of millions of tiny legs behind the plaster.

Stop it, Jamie. Don't be a fucking pussy.

Gaige stopped at the rear wall, lifting the lighter up to shine firelight on what Jamie had thought was just another oddly shaped soot stain.

"Look at *that* shit," Gaige whispered, and Jamie felt his hair stand on end. His bladder threatened to let go if he dropped his guard for a single moment, and he casually slipped a hand over to pinch himself off.

Above the yawning mouth of an old fireplace, someone (probably crazy old man Halloran) had painted an upside-down cross on the wall. It wasn't an ordinary cross by any stretch of the imagination. On the ends of each of the cross's four arms, Halloran had painted the head of an insect; heads complete with sharp pincers and stringy antennae. Spider-like legs had been added to the intersection of the cross, giving it the look of some sort of mutated alien bug crawling down from the ceiling. Scrawled above the insect-cross were the words "He Sent Among Them Swarms Of Flies That Devoured Them". Beneath the cross were the words "Thou Shalt Cleanse The Swarm With FIRE".

"I think it's painted in *blood*," Gaige said, reaching out to touch the lumpy surface of the cross. As the pads of his fingers contacted the dark substance his entire body became as rigid as a beam of wood. Jamie stared, slack-jawed, waiting for him to move or make a sound.

"Gaige?" he whispered tentatively. It sounded very loud in the stillness of the living room. "You okay?"

Gaige was a statue. Jamie had never seen someone stand so still, not even during a heated game of freeze tag.

"Gaige, if you're messing with me I swear I'll kick your ass."

Gaige was still frozen, but he was making a sound now. It was a thick and throaty sound, like he was trying to swallow a giant wad of snot. Jamie could see the sides of his neck pulsating, but his fingers stayed glued to the center of the upside down cross. He was pressing in on it now, hard enough to turn his fingertips white.

"*Gaige?*"

The frozen boy turned, his freckled face pale and warped with confusion. He looked like he'd never heard his own name before. His throat clicked and throbbed, his thin lips quivering.

"Gaige, are you—?"

Suddenly Gaige began to gag, violent retches that arched his spine into a scorpion tail with every heave. Jamie lunged forward on pure instinct. His friend was choking to death right in front of him; he had to do something. *Anything.* He began to slam the palm of his hand into Gaige's back again and again, trying to dislodge whatever was killing him, but the skin under his shirt felt *wrong.* It felt like there were thousands of small, hard objects under the cloth, objects that were moving and wriggling, popping like zits under his hand. The skin was *lumpy.*

"*We are many,*" Gaige bubbled in a voice that was much too deep to be his own. He pivoted upright, swaying drunkenly, and then vomited with the force of a fire hose. What issued from the boy's open mouth aged Jamie Nielsen ten years in a single second.

A yellowish foam sprayed from Gaige's head, foam that was clotted with tangles of wriggling worms and flailing centipedes. They slithered down over his chin and plopped into an ever-widening puddle between his shoes. Clouds of winged insects began to buzz out of Gaige's throat and nostrils. Flies, bees, mosquitos, wasps. They formed a staticky halo around the staggering boy, circling like miniature vultures as he continued spewing his living vomit. The vomit was congealing into glistening tentacles that were already swallowing his feet and began to consume his legs like hungry, wandering vines.

"*Gaige, what the hell is happening?!*" Jamie blubbered, backing away from the thing that had once been his friend.

Gaige tried to speak but it didn't sound like words. It sounded like thick mud boiling in a coffee pot. The boy's eyes bulged and then ruptured into glistening maggot pits, his left ear detaching and tumbling down the carpet of bugs that pulsed on his chest and shoulders. One of Gaige's arms thudded heavily to the floor, the exposed bone startlingly white and clean among the swarms of insects that moved in hurriedly to claim it. Two hairy mandibles unfurled from Gaige's gaping mouth, twitching and rubbing together with a grotesque rasping sound as they stretched his cheeks to the tearing point. The boy looked bigger somehow; bulkier. Taller. He looked like his body had become nothing more than a shell. It was a chrysalis, ripping apart so that whatever had infested him could be born.

With wet plodding sounds, the boy/insect thing began to stalk toward Jamie.

"*We are many*," it crooned, even as Gaige's bottom jaw fell off and splatted in the mass at its feet. "*Swarm with us, child, and forsake your false prophets.*"

Jamie was like a gunslinger, paralyzed and yet somehow motivated by his crippling fear at the same time. He clawed at his pocket, feeling for the reassuring bulge of bug spray.

Gaige was nothing more than a pile of crimson tatters now. In his place was a humanoid mass of legs and wings and antennae, a towering brute that looked like TV static in the shape of a giant, lumbering monster. Bloated earthworms and pus-yellow tapeworms wrapped around each other to form grasping fingers, fingers that inched closer to Jamie's pallid face. The air smelled sour.

"*Swarm, child. Swarm with us, runt.*"

"*FUCK YOU!*" Jamie screamed, drawing the bug spray like a trusty cattleman revolver and mashing the button down until the knuckles of his right hand cracked. The can hissed, filling the moldy air— and the monster's amorphous face— with noxious chemicals.

The thing shrieked loud enough to burst eardrums, but Jamie ignored the impulse to clap his hands over his ears. Instead, he did the unimaginable— he stepped *toward* the thing, keeping the button pressed even as he felt his fingertips go numb. The bug creature roared and flailed, fragmenting, losing cohesion. It tried to reform its limbs again, but Jamie would not give it a single inch. He sprayed until the can was empty, and then launched it into the quivering mound of suffering insects as hard as he could. He wanted to throw himself into the swarm, stomp and jump and grind his shoes into what was left of the creature that had killed his friend. But there was no time; the surviving bugs were already pulling themselves together again, forming the crude stalks of legs, building themselves back into a humanoid form.

It was time to go. Jamie hurdled the old furniture and singed wreckage like a pro football player, diving for the open window and shrugging off the sharp bite of the frame as it dragged across his ribs.

Behind him, the creature roared in pain and anger, loud enough to rattle dust from the crisscrossing barricades.

He was on his bike and pedaling furiously before he even realized he'd made it outside, his heart burning and aching along with his lungs and thigh muscles. His brain was in overdrive, threatening to destroy itself as he tried to process what he had just survived. It felt like a huge, infected sore inside his skull. He focused on his math homework instead, mentally forming and solving the algebraic equations that he otherwise despised.

Dead. Gaige is dead. He's not *asleep. He's* not *on vacation. He's dead. It killed him. The* bugs *killed him. He's dead. Dead. Dead. DEAD.*

He'd have to tell his parents what had happened, of course. He'd even call the cops too, if they told him he had to. He didn't know what the cops would do. How do you arrest a demon? A demon made of *bugs*? For now, he just needed to run, run far away, and focus on math. Math and maybe Kelly Cooper from History, slutty Kelly with the giant tits and short skirts. Nothing more. Nothing less. Any other thoughts would invade him and tear him to pieces just like the bugs had done to Gaige.

The wind ruffling his damp hair proved to be an effective camouflage for the tiny passengers he'd brought with him, clinging desperately to his scalp and sweat-dampened shirt until it was safe to roam free again. To burrow and root and mate. Then, they could seek out a warm and moist place to lay their eggs, and the shapeless beast might be born again.

The Avid Reader

Jeff had always liked Gus, but there was no denying the fact that he was strange. Gus was astoundingly smart and very soft spoken, but he walked with a slight limp (he had been born with one leg longer than the other) and even though he wore glasses, his green eyes tended to drift apart. An easy target for the cruelty inclined to seize upon. Jeff always tried to take his lunch break at the same time as Gus, because the rest of the guys from the warehouse usually wouldn't tease him as much if he did. But when they were separated, by scheduling or short staffing, Jeff would be forced to watch from afar as Gus spent the first half of his break feeding the birds outside with the seed he always carried in his pocket, and then when he came in to eat, the others would descend upon him like a pack of wild dogs.

They called him vicious names not only because he was deformed and cripplingly shy, but because of his book. For at least the five years Jeff had worked with Gus, he had religiously carried a huge green book everywhere he went. The binding and covers were frayed and falling apart, the pages yellowed and uneven. But Gus didn't even go to the bathroom without it. If anyone even came *near* that book, Gus's face would change into a mask of pure hatred that Jeff could only describe as murderous.

Once, at break, Jeff had asked what the book was about and extended his hand to touch it. The cover only sported one word, a word that looked like *Vengeance*, but it was impossible to read it unless you put your nose right up against the damn thing. Gus had snatched his wrist off the table with lightning speed and held it in a grip that felt like it could break bone.

"This book," he said, calmly but with a sinister shake in his voice, "is my way out. My escape from all this. The answer to *everything*. Please, Jeff. Do. *Not.* Touch it." And so, he had never tried to again. He didn't want to upset Gus, and he also didn't want to pay the hospital bill for a fractured wrist.

Unfortunately, Gus's protectiveness of the book (and the fact that he had apparently been reading the same one for a number of years) proved to be another easy target for the bullies.

"You still reading that *same* book?!" They liked to cry out at him. "How slow do you read?!"

"I don't even think he *can* read!"

"When did we start hirin' retards?!"

"I bet he reads about as fast as he walks!"

It was during a miserable overtime shift in the armpit of July when Gus died. Jeff came into the cramped break room just as the horde had surrounded the poor man, and saw Gus with his head in his hands, taking the abuse without saying a word as usual. His hands were quivering fists, tightened around wads of graying hair and yanking it out in little dandelion fluffs. And then, just as Jeff was about to set his coffee down and put a stop to it, one of them picked the book up and slammed it onto the table hard enough to rattle the plastic silverware and send paper cups rolling to the floor.

"Are you even *awake*?!" The leader of the pack bellowed. "Glen Harbison got shitcanned for sleeping on the job, you wanna get shitcanned, retard?!"

Jeff opened his mouth to speak, to maybe call them off, maybe tell them that if they didn't knock it off he would happily plant his size thirteen work boot up each one of their assholes. He hesitated a second too long, and so he wasn't fast enough to stop the carnage that followed.

Gus moved faster than any of them had ever seen him move before. He flipped open the cover of the haggard green book— and where intact pages should have been, Gus had carved a deep, gun-shaped hole. Who knew Gus, the quiet avid reader, knew his way around a firearm? As Gus pulled the .45 handgun free of the pages and pointed it at their stunned faces, he smiled for the first time in years.

Crazy Sadie

    Jonah held his Bible close, trying to keep a smile on his sunburned face despite the countless doors that had been slammed in it. It was always like this; it was one of the first things they taught you. Mormons seemed to be universally despised, and not just by the atheists either, but he and his brothers and sisters never gave up. Today would be different, however. Today he would visit a house that no one else would ever go to. He would spread the good word to the home of "Crazy" Sadie Davis.
    Of course he had heard all the local rumors about her; people said that she had once thrown a mug of scalding coffee all over a newspaper boy and scarred the flesh of his arm, sending him to the emergency room for skin grafts. They said she had drowned her infant grandsons in the bathtub while her daughter and son-in-law were out on date night, then tried to claim she had fallen asleep while somehow, *both* children drowned simultaneously. Then there was the age-old classic, that her husband Jed hadn't committed suicide by drinking antifreeze (as the police report clearly stated) but that Sadie had mixed it with his morning coffee and sat down across the breakfast table from him, munching on a homemade muffin and watching as he sipped it down. But the good Lord told him not to judge, and so he didn't. Perhaps (and most likely) she was just a lonely old lady, the victim of vicious rumors started by kids with nothing better to do.
    She lived in a cozy little house surrounded by colorful flowers and neatly painted birdhouses, and Jonah couldn't help but smile as he knocked politely on her door. He felt like he was visiting his own grandma, God bless her and keep her. *What kind of a horrible lady*, he thought, *would plant such a beautiful garden?* It took some time, but when the front door finally swung open a kindly old woman in a baggy flowered dress answered.
    "Yes?" She said, smiling and showing a perfect set of false teeth.

"Hello ma'am," Jonah said amiably, holding his Bible over his crisp black tie and bowing politely. "Would you like to hear the word of God this morning?"

The old woman's smile broadened.

"Why, of *course* I do! Why don't you come in for tea?"

Jonah was struck dumb. He had never actually been invited inside anyone's home before, and a bit of nervousness nibbled away at his midsection. He'd better make it good.

He made himself comfortable on her oversized couch, thumbing through the gospels as she tinkered around in the kitchen. The little house smelled *wonderful*. It was filled with the warm scent of baking, chocolate and vanilla and melted butter. Strangely, it made him want to take a nap. Finally, Sadie shuffled back into the living room and handed him a steaming cup of golden liquid.

"Oh, where are my *manners?*" Sadie said. "Would you like some cookies to go with your tea?"

Jonah gently took her hand, caressing the thin skin, and said "That would be wonderful, ma'am."

Sadie smiled, and it broke his Jonah's heart. Such a simple visit seemed to be everything to the old woman, and though she was happy to see him, her eyes seemed a little too soft. They were the eyes of someone who looked into the past more than they looked into the future, probably because there really wasn't much of a future to think about. It was so, so *sad*. And to think that people called this woman a murderer.

Sadie ruffled his hair and slowly made her way back to the kitchen as Jonah took his first sip. It was very hot, and very *bitter*. He would have to be careful as he drank it, so she wouldn't see his grimace as he tasted it. He took another sip. It almost tasted like medicine, but it was probably peppermint or some other herb.

Don't be rude, Jonah. You're probably the most company she's had in a long time.

All at once it felt like too much time had passed, and Jonah began to worry about Sadie. She had been gone a while and he heard no noises. What if she had fallen? What if, God forbid, she had chosen today to go be with God now that she didn't have to die alone?

"Ms. Davis?"

He stood to go and check on her, and suddenly was very dizzy. He staggered into her kitchen, calling out to her as the colors of his vision began to run and blur together. He stumbled through a rounded alcove and fell forward onto the kitchen table, where the pretty little tea kettle sat on top of a flowered oven mitt—

—and beside it sat an open bottle of pills.

Jesus please, no.

There was framed artwork hanging on the kitchen walls, and as Jonah squinted at them, he saw that they weren't works of art at all. They were pieces of tattooed human skin, cut into neat squares and dried, framed like little paintings. Some of them were skulls, some cursive letters and slogans. Most of them were flowers. He knew they were real; even through his drugged vision he could see that some of them still had hair, and one of them still had a nipple attached.

Movement behind him.

Jonah spun, making himself so dizzy that his very soul seemed to leave his body, and there was Crazy Sadie. In one wrinkled hand she held a meat tenderizer. In the other, she wielded a gleaming meat cleaver. She toddled toward him, dancing a little jig, tapping the weapons together to tap out a simple beat.

"Ready to pray now?" She asked, and her cheerful smile was suddenly much, much darker.

Friends Like These

Gary Austen knew he was dangerous, and so did his best friends. He had always liked them because they were brutally honest with him, even when it pissed him off. But now, when it came to the matter of his new girlfriend Christine, he found that he didn't want any of their fucking input. Throughout his entire life, Gary had never felt anything for *anyone* until he had made a late night (drunken) trip to Waffle House engaged in a passionate heart-to-heart with Christine, his waitress, for the first time. He had been drawn to her, drawn *into* her, immediately. Meeting Christine was a one-way trip, and he couldn't have turned his back on her even if he wanted to. Now, as he lounged with Dale and Mac on the stained couch in his basement, they were trying to convince him that he only had two options— both of which would cost him his new love.

"You're dangerous," pleaded Mac. "You know you'll hurt her too. You always hurt the people that trust you."

"We're your best friends, and look what you did to *us*," chimed in Dale. "You don't have a *soul*, Gary."

Gary clenched his fists, the veins of his wrists bulging and his nails carving half-moons into his palms.

"It's different with her, guys. I mean it," he said to their blank, indifferent faces. "I would never hurt her. *Or* her daughter."

They cackled at him as he fumed, and in that moment, he hated them more than he had ever hated anything before.

"Yeah, you've said that for years, like a broken fucking record, and you always end up hurting people again, don't you?" Mac scoffed, smirking at him.

Gary shrugged.

"I just... get these urges, guys. You know that. It's like a mosquito in my ear, it won't shut up until—"

"—Until you black out and you don't wake up until it's all over," Dale finished for him in an exhausted tone. "Yeah yeah, give us something new."

Gary really had no valid argument for them; they were both absolutely right about him. He loved Christine, and he knew it was true love because it was his very first emotion, something he had never experienced before. And yet he had known this conversation was coming from their very first kiss, and the thought of losing her made him weep after each time they had sex and she headed home for the night.

"You're right," he finally said, exasperated and defeated. "You're both right."

Gary picked up the phone, hesitated, and then dialed 9-1-1.

* * *

From the Ridgeview Times, October 31st, 2021:

RIDGEVIEW RIPPER ESCAPES DURING ARREST; TWO OFFICERS SLAIN

Local mechanic Gary D. Austen was arrested Friday night after he made a phone call confession to the R.P.D. that he was the vicious serial killer known as the Ridgeview Ripper, now suspected of murdering more than thirty Ridgeview residents. Responding officers reported that Austen was discovered in his basement, "arguing" with the badly decomposed corpses of two more as-of-yet unidentified victims. During transport to the police station, officers Howell J. Dodge and Tyler B. Ruch called for emergency backup before going radio silent. Their abandoned squad car was found in a ditch alongside county road 9, with both men unresponsive and later pronounced dead at the scene. Austen reportedly assaulted both officers with an ink pen. According to Austen's coworkers, he has been in a loving relationship with local resident Christine D. Perry, who, as of this morning, has also been reported missing along with her two-year-old daughter Makayla. The F.B.I. has issued a country-wide manhunt for Austen, offering a reward of $5,000 for information leading to his capture. Information leading to the whereabouts of Christine and Makayla Perry should be directed to the Ridgeview Police Department.

Made in the USA
Columbia, SC
14 April 2023

20fac483-de4d-419a-b8cc-ec43ad67eff7R01